W9-ASX-518

Be prepared
for the unusual
in this bestselling
novel about the
incredible operation
on Harry Benson's
brain-And how
through a terrifying
miscalculation
a relentless human
time bomb is unleashed!

THE TERMINAL MAN!
A VIOLENT PARANOID HAS TWICE
ATTEMPTED TO KILL . . .

Against the advice of his psychiatrist, a team of surgeons proposes to connect his brain to a computer which will regulate his behavior. The operation is a complete success, but an unforeseen side effect develops . . . AND THE HORRIFYING NIGHTMARE BEGINS!

"Even more exciting than his *Andromeda Strain*."
—*Publishers Weekly*

"A fascinating, splendidly documented thriller."
—*The New Yorker*

"A brilliantly achieved and all-too-believable modern *Frankenstein*."
—*Book-of-the-Month Club News*

Bantam Books by Michael Crichton

FIVE PATIENTS
THE TERMINAL MAN

Michael Crichton
The Terminal Man

BANTAM BOOKS · TORONTO · NEW YORK · LONDON

A NATIONAL GENERAL COMPANY

THE TERMINAL MAN

A Bantam Book / published by arrangement with
Alfred A. Knopf, Inc.

PRINTING HISTORY
Knopf edition published March 1972
2nd printing . . . April 1972 3rd printing . . . May 1972
Bantam edition published April 1973

Cover art by Paul Bacon

Bantam Books are published by Bantam Books, Inc., a National
General company. Its trade-mark, consisting of the words "Bantam
Books" and the portrayal of a bantam, is registered in the United
States Patent Office and in other countries. Marca Registrada.
Bantam Books, Inc., 666 Fifth Avenue, New York, N.Y. 10019.

PRINTED IN THE UNITED STATES OF AMERICA

To Kurt

Acknowledgment

Martin J. Nathan, M.D., and Demian Kuffler gave technical advice and assistance. Kay Kolman Tyler prepared the graphics. I am indebted to them all.

Contents

Author's Introduction

Readers who find the subject matter of this book shocking or frightening should not delude themselves by also thinking it is something quite new. The physical study of the brain has been proceeding for more than a century; the technology of behavior modification has been developing for more than fifty years. For decades, it was there for anyone to see, discuss, support, or oppose.

Nor has there been any lack of publicity. Research in neurobiology is spectacular enough to appear regularly in the Sunday supplements. But the public has never really taken it seriously. There has been so much ominous talk and so much frivolous speculation for so many years that the public now regards "mind control" as a problem removed to the distant future: it might eventually happen, but not soon, and not in a way that would affect anyone now alive.

Scientists engaged in this research have sought public discussion. James V. McConnell of the University of Michigan told his students some years ago, "Look, we can do these things. We can control behavior. Now, who's going to decide what's to be done? If you don't get busy and tell me how I'm supposed to do it, I'll make up my own mind for you. And then it's too late."

Many people today feel that they live in a world that is predetermined and running along a fixed pre-established course. Past decisions have left us with pollution, depersonalization, and urban blight; somebody else made the decisions for us, and we are stuck with the consequences.

That attitude represents a childish and dangerous denial of responsibility, and everyone should recognize it for what it is. In that spirit, the following chronology is presented:

HISTORY OF THERAPY
OF PSYCHOMOTOR EPILEPSY

1864 Morel, Fairet, and other French neurologists describe some elements of psychomotor epilepsy.

1888 Hughlings Jackson (Great Britain) provides the classic description of psychomotor epilepsy and its preceding aura.

1898 Jackson and Colman (Great Britain) localize the disorder to the temporal lobe of the brain.

1908 Horsley and Clarke (Great Britain) describe stereotaxic surgical techniques for use on animals.

1941 Jasper and Kershman (U.S.A. and Canada) show that the electroencephalogram of patients with psychomotor epilepsy is characterized by discharges from the temporal lobe.

1947 Spiegel and co-workers (U.S.A.) report the first stereotaxic surgery performed on a human being.

1950 Penfield and Flanagan (Canada) perform ablative surgery for psychomotor epilepsy, with good results.

Author's Introduction

1953   Heath and co-workers (U.S.A.) perform stereotaxic implantation of depth electrodes.

1958   Talairach and co-workers (France) begin chronic stereotaxic implantation of depth electrodes.

1963   Heath and co-workers (U.S.A.) allow patients to stimulate themselves, at will, via implanted electrodes.

1965   Narabayashi (Japan) reports on 98 patients with violent behavior treated by stereotaxic surgery.

1965   More than 24,000 stereotaxic procedures on human beings have been performed in various countries by this date.

1968   Delgado and co-workers (U.S.A.) attach "stimoceiver" (radio stimulator plus radio receiver) to freely ambulatory hospital patients with psychomotor epilepsy.

1969   Chimpanzee at Alamogordo, N.M., is directly linked by radio to a computer which programs and delivers his brain stimulations.

1971   Patient Harold Benson is operated on in Los Angeles.

M.C.

Los Angeles
October 23, 1971

"I have come to the conclusion that my subjective account of my own motivation is largely mythical on almost all occasions. I don't know why I do things."

J. B. S. HALDANE

"The wilderness masters the colonist."

FREDERICK JACKSON TURNER

TUESDAY,
MARCH 9, 1971:
ADMISSION

1

They came down to the emergency ward at noon and sat on the bench just behind the swinging doors that led in from the ambulance parking slot. Ellis was nervous, preoccupied, distant. Morris was relaxed, eating a candy bar and crumpling the wrapper into the pocket of his white jacket.

From where they sat, they could look at the sunlight outside, falling across the big sign that said EMERGENCY WARD and the smaller sign that said NO PARKING AMBULANCES ONLY. In the distance they heard sirens.

"Is that him?" Morris asked.

Ellis checked his watch. "I doubt it. It's too early."

They sat on the bench and listened to the sirens come closer. Ellis removed his glasses and wiped them with his tie. One of the emergency ward nurses, a girl Morris did not know by name, came over and said brightly, "Is this the welcoming committee?"

Ellis squinted at her. Morris said, "We'll be taking him straight through. Do you have his chart down here?"

The nurse said, "Yes, I think so, Doctor," and walked off looking irritated.

Ellis sighed. He replaced his glasses and frowned at the nurse.

Morris said, "She didn't mean anything."

"I suppose the whole damned hospital knows," Ellis said.

"It's a pretty big secret to keep."

The sirens were very close now; through the windows they saw an ambulance back into the slot. Two orderlies opened the door and pulled out the stretcher. A frail elderly woman lay on the stretcher, gasping for breath, making wet gurgling sounds. Severe pulmonary edema, Morris thought as he watched her taken into one of the treatment rooms.

"I hope he's in good shape," Ellis said.

"Who?"

"Benson."

"Why shouldn't he be?"

"They might have roughed him up." Ellis stared morosely out the windows. He really is in a bad mood, Morris thought. He knew that meant Ellis was excited; he had scrubbed in on enough cases with Ellis to recognize the pattern. Irascibility under pressure while he waited—and then total, almost lazy calm when the operation began. "Where the hell is he?" Ellis said, looking at his watch again.

To change the subject, Morris said, "Are we all set for three-thirty?" At 3:30 that afternoon, Benson would be presented to the hospital staff at a special Neurosurgical Rounds.

"As far as I know," Ellis said. "Ross is making

4

the presentation. I just hope Benson's in good shape."

Over the loudspeaker, a soft voice said, "Dr. Ellis, Dr. John Ellis, two-two-three-four. Dr. Ellis, two-two-three-four."

Ellis got up to answer the page. "Hell," he said.

Morris knew what he meant. Two-two-three-four was the extension for the animal laboratories. The call probably meant something had gone wrong with the monkeys. Ellis had been doing three monkeys a week for the past month, just to keep himself and his staff ready.

He watched as Ellis crossed the room and answered from a wall phone. Ellis walked with a slight limp, the result of a childhood injury that had cut the common peroneal nerve in his right leg. Morris always wondered if the injury had had something to do with Ellis's later decision to become a neurosurgeon. Certainly Ellis had the attitude of a man determined to correct defects, to fix things up. That was what he always said to his patients: "We can fix you up." And he seemed to have more than his share of defects himself—the limp, the premature near-baldness, the weak eyes, and the heavy thick glasses. It produced a vulnerability about him that made his irascibility more tolerable.

Or perhaps the irascibility was the result of all those years as a surgeon. Morris wasn't sure; he hadn't been a surgeon long enough. He stared out the window at the sunlight and the parking lot. Afternoon visiting hours were beginning; relatives were driving into the parking lot, getting out of their cars, glancing up at the high buildings of the hospital. The apprehension was clear in their faces; the hospital was a place people feared.

Morris noticed how many of them had sun tans. It had been a warm, sunny spring in Los Angeles, yet he was still as pale as the white jacket and trousers he wore every day. He had to get outside more often, he told himself. He should start eating lunch outside. He played tennis, of course, but that was usually in the evenings.

Ellis came back. "Shit," he said. "Ethel tore out her sutures."

"How did it happen?" Ethel was a juvenile rhesus monkey who had undergone brain surgery the day before. The operation had proceeded flawlessly. And Ethel was unusually docile, as rhesus monkeys went.

"I don't know," Ellis said. "Apparently she worked an arm loose from her restraints. Anyway, she's shrieking and the bone's exposed on one side."

"Did she tear out her wires?"

"I don't know. But I've got to go down and re-sew her now. Can you handle this?"

"I think so."

"Are you all right with the cops?" Ellis said. "I don't think they'll give you any trouble."

"No, I don't think so."

"Just get Benson up to seven as fast as you can," Ellis said. "Then call Ross. I'll be up as soon as possible." He checked his watch. "It'll probably take forty minutes to resew Ethel, if she behaves herself."

"Good luck with her," Morris said, and smiled.

Ellis looked sour and walked away.

After he had gone, the emergency ward nurse came back. "What's the matter with *him?*" she asked.

"Just edgy," Morris said.

"He sure is," the nurse said. She paused and looked out the window, lingering.

Morris watched her with a kind of bemused detachment. He'd spent enough years in the hospital to recognize the subtle signs of status. He had begun as an intern, with no status at all. Most of the nurses knew more medicine than he did, and if they were tired they didn't bother to conceal it. ("I don't think you want to do that, Doctor.") As the years went by, he became a surgical resident, and the nurses became more deferential. When he was a senior resident, he was sufficiently assured in his work that a few of the nurses called him by his first name. And finally, when he transferred to the Neuropsychiatric Research Unit as a junior staff member, the formality returned as a new mark of status.

But this was something else: a nurse hanging around, just being near him, because he had a special aura of importance. Because everyone in the hospital knew what was going to happen.

Staring out the window, the nurse said, "Here he comes."

Morris got up and looked out. A blue police van

drove up toward the emergency ward, and turned around, backing into the ambulance slot. "All right," he said. "Notify the seventh floor, and tell them we're on our way."

"Yes, Doctor."

The nurse went off. Two ambulance orderlies opened the hospital doors. They knew nothing about Benson. One of them said to Morris, "You expecting this one?"

"Yes."

"EW case?"

"No, a direct admission."

The orderlies nodded, and watched as the police officer driving the van came around and unlocked the rear door. Two officers seated in the back emerged, blinking in the sunlight. Then Benson came out.

As always, Morris was struck by his appearance. Benson was a meek, pudgy, thirty-four-year-old man, with a sort of permanently bewildered air about him. He stood by the van, with his wrists handcuffed in front of him, and looked around. When he saw Morris, he said, "Hello," and then looked away, embarrassed.

One of the cops said, "You in charge here?"

"Yes. I'm Dr. Morris."

The cop gestured toward the interior of the hospital. "Lead the way, Doctor."

Morris said, "Would you mind taking off his handcuffs?"

Benson's eyes flicked up at Morris, then back down.

"We don't have any orders about that." The cops exchanged glances. "I guess it's okay."

While they took the cuffs off, the driver brought Morris a form on a clipboard: "Transfer of Suspect to Institutional Care (Medical)." He signed it.

"And again here," the driver said.

As Morris signed again, he looked at Benson. Benson stood quietly, rubbing his wrists, staring straight ahead. The impersonality of the transaction, the forms and signatures, made Morris feel as if he were receiving a package from United Parcel. He wondered if Benson felt like a package.

"Okay," the driver said. "Thanks, Doc."

Morris led the other two policemen and Benson into the hospital. The orderlies shut the doors. A nurse came up with a wheelchair and Benson sat down in it. The cops looked confused.

"It's hospital policy," Morris said.

They all went to the elevators.

The elevator stopped at the lobby. A half-dozen relatives were waiting to go up to the higher floors, but they hesitated when they saw Morris, Benson in the wheelchair, and the two cops. "Please take the next car," Morris said smoothly. The doors closed. They continued up.

"Where is Dr. Ellis?" Benson asked. "I thought he was going to be here."

"He's in surgery. He'll be up shortly."

"And Dr. Ross?"

"You'll see her at the presentation."

"Oh, yes." Benson smiled. "The presentation."

The cops exchanged suspicious looks, but said nothing. The elevator arrived at the seventh floor, and they all got out.

Seven was the Special Surgical floor, where difficult and complex cases were treated. It was essentially a research floor. The most severe cardiac, kidney, and metabolic patients recuperated here. They went down to the nurses' station, a glass-walled area strategically located at the center of the X-shaped floor.

The nurse on duty at the station looked up. She was surprised to see the cops, but she said nothing. Morris said, "This is Mr. Benson. Have we got seven-ten ready?"

"All set for him," the nurse said, and gave Benson a cheery smile. Benson smiled bleakly back, and glanced from the nurse to the computer console in the corner of the nursing station.

"You have a time-sharing station up here?"

"Yes," Morris said.

"Where's the main computer?"

"In the basement."

"Of this building?"

"Yes. It draws a lot of power, and the power lines come to this building."

Benson nodded. Morris was not surprised at the questions. Benson was trying to distract himself from the thought of surgery, and he was, after all, a computer expert.

The nurse handed Morris the chart on Benson.

It had the usual blue plastic cover with the seal of University Hospital. But there was also a red tag, which meant neurosurgery, and a yellow tag, which meant intensive care, and a white tag, which Morris had almost never seen on a patient's chart. The white tag meant security precautions.

"Is that my record?" Benson asked as Morris wheeled him down the hall to 710. The cops followed along behind.

"Uh-huh."

"I always wondered what was in it."

"Lot of unreadable notes, mostly." Actually, Benson's chart was thick and very readable, with all the computer print-outs of different tests.

They came to 710. Before they entered the room, one of the cops went in and closed the door behind him. The second cop remained outside the door. "Just a precaution," he said.

Benson glanced up at Morris. "They're very careful about me," he said. "It's almost flattering."

The first cop came out. "It's okay," he said.

Morris wheeled Benson into the room. It was a large room, on the south side of the hospital, so that it was sunny in the afternoon. Benson looked around and nodded approvingly. Morris said, "This is one of the best rooms in the hospital."

"Can I get up now?"

"Of course."

Benson got out of the wheelchair and sat on the bed. He bounced on the mattress. He pressed the buttons that made the bed move up and down, then bent over to look at the motorized mechanism beneath the bed. Morris went to the window and drew the blinds, reducing the direct light. "Simple," Benson said.

"What's that?"

"This bed mechanism. Remarkably simple. You should really have a feedback unit so that body movements by the person in the bed are automatically compensated for . . ." His voice trailed off. He opened the closet doors, looked in, checked the bathroom, came back. Morris thought that he wasn't acting like an ordinary patient. Most patients were intimidated by the hospital, but Benson acted as if he were renting a hotel room.

"I'll take it," Benson said, and laughed. He sat down on the bed and looked at Morris, then at the cops. "Do they have to be here?"

"I think they can wait outside," Morris said.

The cops nodded and went out, closing the door behind them.

"I meant," Benson said, "do they have to be here at all?"

"Yes, they do."

"All the time?"

"Yes. Unless we can get charges dropped against you."

Benson frowned. "Was it . . . I mean, did I . . . Was it bad?"

"You gave him a black eye and you fractured one rib."

"But he's all right?"

"Yes. He's all right."

"I don't remember any of it," Benson said. "All my memory cores are erased."

"I know that."

"But I'm glad he's all right."

Morris nodded. "Did you bring anything with you? Pajamas, anything like that?"

Benson said, "No. But I can arrange for it."

"All right. I'll get you some hospital clothing in the meantime. Are you all right for now?"

"Yes. Sure." And he grinned. "I could do with a quick shot, maybe."

"That," Morris said, grinning back, "is something you'll have to do without."

Benson sighed.

Morris went out of the room.

The cops had brought a chair up to the door. One of them sat on it, the other stood alongside. Morris flipped open his notebook.

"You'll want to know the schedule," he said. "An admitting person will show up in the next half hour with financial waivers for Benson to sign. Then, at three-thirty he goes downstairs to the main amphitheater for Surgical Rounds. He comes back after about twenty minutes. His head will be shaved tonight. The operation is scheduled for six a.m. tomorrow morning. Do you have questions?"

"Can someone get us meals?" one of them asked.

"I'll have the nurse order extras. Will there be two of you, or just one?"

"Just one. We're working eight-hour shifts."

Morris said, "I'll tell the nurses. It'd help if you

check in and out with them. They like to know who's on the floor."

The cops nodded. There was a moment of silence. Finally, one of them said, "What's wrong with him, anyway?"

"He has a form of epilepsy."

"I saw the guy he beat up," one of the cops said. "Big strong guy, looked like a truck driver. You'd never think a little guy like that"—he jerked his arm toward Benson's room—"could do it."

"When he has epileptic fits, he's violent."

They nodded vaguely. "What's this operation he's getting?"

"It's a kind of brain surgery we call a stage-three procedure," Morris said. He didn't bother to explain further. The policemen wouldn't understand. And, he thought, even if they understood, they wouldn't believe it.

2

Neurosurgical Grand Rounds, where unusual cases were presented and discussed by all the surgeons of the hospital, were normally scheduled for Thursdays at nine. Special rounds were hardly ever called; it was too difficult for the staff to get together. But now the amphitheater was packed, tier after tier of white jackets and pale faces staring down at Ellis, who pushed his glasses up on his nose and said, "As many of you know, tomorrow morning the Neuropsychiatric Research Unit will perform a limbic pacing procedure—what we call a stage three—on a human patient."

There was no sound, no movement, from the audience. Janet Ross stood in the corner of the amphitheater near the doors and watched. She found it odd that there should be so little reaction. But then it was hardly a surprise. Everyone in the hospital knew that the NPS had been waiting for a good stage-three subject.

"I must ask you," Ellis said, "to restrain your questions when the patient is introduced. He is a sensitive man, and his disturbance is quite severe. We thought you should have the psychiatric background before we bring him in. The attending psychiatrist, Dr. Ross, will give you a summary." Ellis nodded to Ross. She came forward to the center of the room.

She stared up at the steeply banked rows of faces and felt a momentary hesitation. Janet Ross was tall and exceptionally good-looking in a lean, tanned, dark-blond way. She herself felt she was too bony and angular, and she often wished she were more softly feminine. But she knew her appearance was striking, and at thirty, after more than a decade of training in a predominantly masculine profession, she had learned to use it.

She clasped her hands behind her back, took a breath, and launched into the summary, delivering it in the rapid, stylized method that was standard for grand rounds.

"Harold Franklin Benson," she said, "is a thirty-four-year-old divorced computer scientist who was healthy until two years ago, when he was involved in an automobile accident on the Santa Monica Freeway. Following the accident, he was unconscious for an unknown period of time. He was taken to a local hospital for overnight observation and discharged the next day in good health. He was fine for six months, until he began to experience what he called 'blackouts.' "

The audience was silent, faces staring down at her, listening.

"These blackouts lasted several minutes, and occurred about once a month. They were often preceded by the sensation of peculiar, unpleasant odors. The blackouts frequently occurred after drinking alcohol. The patient consulted his local physician, who told him he was working too hard, and recommended he reduce his alcohol intake. Benson did this, but the blackouts continued.

"One year ago—a year after the accident—he realized that the blackouts were becoming more frequent and lasting longer. He often regained consciousness to find himself in unfamiliar surroundings. On several occasions, he had cuts and bruises or torn clothing which suggested that he had been fighting. However, he never remembered what occurred during the blackout periods."

Heads in the audience nodded. They understood what she was telling them; it was a straightforward history for a temporal-lobe epileptic. The hard part was coming.

"The patient's friends," she continued, "told him that he was acting differently, but he discounted their opinion. Gradually he has lost contact with most of his former friends. Around this time—one year ago—he also made what he called a monumental discovery in his work. Benson is a computer scientist specializing in artificial life, or machine intelligence. In the course of this work, he says he discovered that machines were competing with human beings, and that ultimately machines would take over the world."

Now there were whispers in the audience. This interested them, particularly the psychiatrists. She could see her old teacher Manon sitting in the top row holding his head in his hands. Manon knew.

"Benson communicated his discovery to his remaining friends. They suggested that he see a psychiatrist, which angered him. In the last year, he has become increasingly certain that machines are conspiring to take over the world.

"Then, six months ago, the patient was arrested by police on suspicion of beating up an airplane mechanic. Positive identification could not be made, and charges were dropped. But the episode unnerved Benson and led him to seek psychiatric help. He had the vague suspicion that somehow he *had* been the man who had beaten the mechanic to a bloody pulp. That was unthinkable to him, but the nagging suspicion remained.

"He was referred to the University Hospital

Neuropsychiatric Research Unit four months ago, in November, 1970. On the basis of his history—head injury, episodic violence preceded by strange smells—he was considered a probable psychomotor epileptic. As you know, the NPS now accepts only patients with organically treatable behavioral disturbances.

"A neurological examination was fully normal. An electroencephalogram was fully normal; brain-wave activity showed no pathology. It was repeated after alcohol ingestion and an abnormal tracing was obtained. The EEG showed seizure activity in the right temporal lobe of the brain. Benson was therefore considered a stage-one patient—firm diagnosis of psychomotor epilepsy."

She paused to get her breath and let the audience absorb what she had told them. "The patient is an intelligent man," she said, "and his illness was explained to him. He was told he had injured his brain in the automobile accident and, as a result, had a form of epilepsy that produced 'thought seizures'—seizures of the mind, not the body, leading to violent acts. He was told that the disease was common and could be controlled. He was started on a series of drug trials.

"Three months ago, Benson was arrested on charges of assault and battery. The victim was a twenty-four-year-old topless dancer, who later dropped charges. The hospital intervened slightly on his behalf.

"One month ago, drug trials of morladone, p-amino benzadone, and triamiline were concluded. Benson showed no improvement on any drug or combination of drugs. He was therefore a stage two—drug-resistant psychomotor epilepsy. And he was scheduled for a stage-three surgical procedure, which we will discuss today."

She paused. "Before I bring him in," she said, "I think I should add that yesterday afternoon he attacked a gas-station attendant and beat the man rather badly. His operation is scheduled for to-morrow and we have persuaded the police to release him in our custody. But he is still technically awaiting arraignment on charges of assault and battery."

The room was silent. She paused for a moment, then went to bring in Benson.

Benson was just outside the doors to the amphitheater, sitting in his wheelchair, wearing the blue-and-white striped bathrobe the hospital issued to its patients. When Janet Ross appeared, he smiled. "Hello, Dr. Ross."

"Hello, Harry." She smiled back. "How do you feel?"

It was a polite question. After years of psychiatric training, she could see clearly how he felt. Benson was nervous and threatened: there was sweat on his upper lip, his shoulders were drawn in, his hands clenched together in his lap.

"I feel fine," he said. "Just fine."

Behind Benson was Morris, pushing the wheelchair, and a cop. She said to Morris, "Does he come in with us?"

Before Morris could answer, Benson said lightly, "He goes anywhere I go."

The cop nodded and looked embarrassed.

"All right," she said.

She opened the doors, and Morris wheeled Benson into the amphitheater, over to Ellis. Ellis came forward to shake Benson's hand.

"Mr. Benson, good to see you."

"Dr. Ellis."

Morris turned him around so he was facing the amphitheater audience. Ross sat to one side and glanced at the cop, who remained by the door trying to look inconspicuous. Ellis stood alongside Benson, who was looking at a wall of frosted glass, against which a dozen X-rays had been clipped. He seemed to realize that they were his own skull films. Ellis noticed, and turned off the light behind the frosted glass. The X-rays became opaquely black.

"We've asked you to come here," Ellis said, "to answer some questions for these doctors." He gestured to the men sitting in the semicircular tiers. "They don't make you nervous, do they?"

Ellis asked it easily. Ross frowned. She'd attended hundreds of grand rounds in her life, and the patients were invariably asked if the doctors peering down at them made them nervous. In answer to a direct question, the patients always denied nervousness.

"Sure they make me nervous," Benson said. "They'd make anybody nervous."

Ross suppressed a smile. Good for you, she thought.

Then Benson said, "What if you were a machine and I brought you in front of a bunch of computer experts who were trying to decide what was wrong with you and how to fix it? How would you feel?"

Ellis was plainly flustered. He ran his hands through his thinning hair and glanced at Ross, and she shook her head fractionally *no*. This was the wrong place to explore Benson's psychopathology.

"I'd be nervous, too," Ellis said.

"Well, then," Benson said. "You see?"

Ellis swallowed.

He's being deliberately irritating, Ross thought. Don't take the bait.

"But, of course," Ellis said, "I'm not a machine, am I?"

Ross winced.

"That depends," Benson said. "Certain of your functions are repetitive and mechanical. From that standpoint, they are easily programmed and relatively straightforward, if you—"

"I think," Ross said, standing up, "that we might take questions from those present now."

Ellis clearly didn't like that, but he was silent, and Benson mercifully was quiet. She looked up at the audience, and after a moment a man in the back raised his hand and said, "Mr. Benson, can you tell us more about the smells you have before your blackouts?"

"Not really," Benson said. "They're strange, is

all. They smell terrible, but they don't smell *like* anything, if you get what I mean. I mean, you can't identify the odor. Memory tapes cycle through blankly."

"Can you give us an approximation of the odor?"

Benson shrugged. "Maybe . . . pig shit in turpentine."

Another hand in the audience went up. "Mr. Benson, these blackouts have been getting more frequent. Have they also been getting longer?"

"Yes," Benson said. "They're several hours now."

"How do you feel when you recover from a blackout?"

"Sick to my stomach."

"Can you be more specific?"

"Sometimes I vomit. Is that specific enough?"

Ross frowned. She could see that Benson was becoming angry. "Are there other questions?" she asked, hoping there would not be. She looked up at the audience. There was a long silence.

"Well, then," Ellis said, "perhaps we can go on to discuss the details of stage-three surgery. Mr. Benson knows all this, so he can stay or leave, whichever he prefers."

Ross didn't approve. Ellis was showing off, the surgeon's instinct for demonstrating to everyone that his patient didn't mind being cut and mutilated. It was unfair to ask—to dare—Benson to stay in the room.

"I'll stay," Benson said.

"Fine," Ellis said. He went to the blackboard and drew a brain schematically. "Now," he said, "our understanding of the disease process is that a portion of the brain is damaged in epilepsy, and a scar forms. It's like a scar in other body organs —lots of fibrous tissue, lots of contraction and distortion. And it becomes a focus for abnormal electrical discharges. We see spreading waves moving outward from the focus, like ripples from a rock in a pond."

Ellis drew a point on the brain, then sketched concentric circles.

"These electrical ripples produce a seizure. In some parts of the brain, the discharge focus produces a shaking fit, frothing at the mouth, and so on. In other parts, there are other effects. If the focus is in the temporal lobe, as in Mr. Benson's case, you get what is called psychomotor epilepsy —convulsions of thought, not of body. Strange thoughts and frequently violent behavior, preceded by a characteristic aura which is often an odor."

Benson was watching, listening, nodding.

"Now, then," Ellis said, "we know from the work of many researchers that it is possible to abort a seizure by delivering an electrical shock to the correct portion of the brain substance. These seizures begin slowly. There are a few seconds—sometimes as much as half a minute—before the seizure takes effect. A shock at that moment prevents the seizure."

He drew a large "X" through the concentric circles. Then he drew a new brain, and a head around it, and a neck. "We face two problems," he said. "First, what is the correct part of the brain to shock? Well, we know roughly that it's in the amygdala, an anterior area of the so-called limbic system. We don't know *exactly* where, but we solve that problem by implanting a number of electrodes in the brain. Mr. Benson will have forty electrodes implanted tomorrow morning."

He drew two lines into the brain.

"Now, our second problem is how do we know when an attack is starting? We must know when to deliver our aborting shock. Well, fortunately the same electrodes that we use to deliver the shock can also be used to 'read' the electrical activity of the brain. And there is a characteristic electrical pattern that precedes a seizure."

Ellis paused, glanced at Benson, then up at the audience.

"So we have a feedback system—the same electrodes are used to detect a new attack, and to deliver the aborting shock. A computer controls the feedback mechanism."

He drew a small square in the neck of his schematic figure.

"The NPS staff has developed a computer that will monitor electrical activity of the brain, and when it sees an attack starting, will transmit a shock to the correct brain area. This computer is about the size of a postage stamp and weighs a tenth of an ounce. It will be implanted beneath the skin of the patient's neck."

He then drew an oblong shape below the neck and attached wires to the computer square.

"We will power the computer with a Handler PP-J plutonium power pack, which will be implanted beneath the skin of the shoulder. This makes the patient completely self-sufficient. The power pack supplies energy continuously and reliably for twenty years."

With his chalk, he tapped the different parts of his diagram. "That's the complete feedback loop—brain, to electrodes, to computer, to power pack, back to brain. A total loop without any externalized portions."

He turned to Benson, who had watched the discussion with an expression of bland disinterest.

"Any comments? Mr. Benson?"

Ross groaned inwardly. Ellis was really letting him have it. It was flagrantly sadistic—even for a surgeon.

"No," Benson said. "I have nothing to say." And he yawned.

When Benson was wheeled out of the room, Ross went with him. It wasn't really necessary for her to accompany him, but she was concerned about his condition—and a little guilty about the way Ellis had treated him. She said, "How do you feel?"

"I thought it was interesting," he said.

"In what way?"

"Well, the discussion was entirely medical. I would have expected a more philosophical approach."

"We're just practical people," she said lightly, "dealing with a practical problem."

Benson smiled. "So was Newton," he said.

"What's more practical than the problem of why an apple falls to the ground?"

"Do you really see philosophical implications in all this?"

Benson nodded. His expression turned serious. "Yes," he said, "and so do you. You're just pretending that you don't."

She stopped then and stood in the corridor, watching as Benson was wheeled down to the elevator. Benson, Morris, and the cop waited in the corridor for the next car. Morris pushed the button repeatedly in that impatient, aggressive way of his. Then the elevator arrived and they got on. Benson waved one last time, and the doors closed.

She went back to the amphitheater.

"... has been under development for ten years," Ellis was saying. "It was first started for cardiac pacemakers, where changing batteries requires minor surgery every year or so. That's an annoyance to surgeon and patient. The atomic power pack is totally reliable and has a long lifespan. If Mr. Benson is still alive, we might have to change packs around 1990, but not before then."

Janet Ross slipped back into the room just as another question was asked: "How will you determine which of the forty electrodes will prevent a seizure?"

"We will implant them all," Ellis said, "and wire up the computer. But we will not lock in any electrodes for twenty-four hours. One day after surgery, we'll stimulate each of the electrodes by radio and determine which electrodes work best. Then we will lock those in by remote control."

High up in the amphitheater, a familiar voice coughed and said, "These technical details are interesting, but they seem to me to elude the point." Ross looked up and saw Manon speaking. Manon was nearly seventy-five, an emeritus professor of psychiatry who rarely came to the hospital any more. When he did, he was usually regarded as a cranky old man, far past his prime, out of touch with modern thinking. "It seems to me," Manon continued, "that the patient is psychotic."

"That's putting it a little strongly," Ellis said.

"Perhaps," Manon said. "But, at the very least, he has a severe personality disorder. All this confusion about men and machines is worrisome to me."

"The personality disorder is part of his disease," Ellis said. "In a recent review, Harley and co-workers at Yale reported that fifty percent of temporal-lobe epileptics had an accompanying personality disorder which was independent of seizure activity *per se*."

"Quite so," Manon said, in a voice that had the slightest edge of impatience to it. "It is part of his disease, independent of seizures. But will your procedure cure it?"

Janet Ross found herself quietly pleased; Manon was reaching exactly her own conclusions.

"No," Ellis said. "Probably not."

"In other words, the operation will stop his seizures, but it won't stop his delusions."

"No," Ellis repeated. "Probably not."

"If I may make a small speech," Manon said, frowning down from the top row, "this kind of thinking is what I fear most from the NPS. I don't mean to single you out particularly. It's a general problem of the medical profession. For example, if we get a suicide attempt or a suicide gesture by drug overdose in the emergency ward, our approach is to pump the patient's stomach, give him a lecture, and send him home. That's a treatment —but it's hardly a cure. The patient will be back sooner or later. Stomach pumping doesn't treat depression. It only treats drug overdose."

"I see what you're saying, but . . ."

"I'd also remind you of the hospital's experience with Mr. L. Do you recall the case?"

"I don't think Mr. L. applies here," Ellis said. But his voice was stiff and exasperated.

"I'm not so sure," Manon said. Since several puzzled faces in the amphitheater were turned toward him, he explained. "Mr. L. was a famous case here a few years ago. He was a thirty-nine-year-old man with bilateral end-stage kidney disease. Chronic glomerulonephritis. He was considered a candidate for renal transplant. Because our facilities for transplantation are limited, a hospital review board selects patients. The psychiatrists on that board strongly opposed Mr. L. as a transplantation candidate, because he was psychotic. He believed that the sun ruled the earth and he refused to go outside during the daylight hours. We felt he was too unstable to benefit from kidney surgery, but he ultimately received the operation. Six months later, he committed suicide. That's a tragedy. But the real question is couldn't someone else have benefited more from the thousands of dollars and many hours of specialized effort that went into the transplant?"

Ellis paced back and forth, the foot of his bad leg scraping slightly along the floor. Ross knew it meant he was feeling threatened, under attack. Normally Ellis was careful to minimize his disability, concealing it so that the limp was noticeable only to a trained eye. But if he was tired, or angry, or threatened, the flaw appeared. It was almost as if he unconsciously wanted sympathy: don't attack me, I'm a cripple. Consciously, of course, he was not aware of it.

"I understand your objection," Ellis said. "In the terms you present it, your argument is unanswerable. But I would like to consider the problem from a somewhat different viewpoint. It is perfectly true that Benson is disturbed, and that our operation probably won't change that. But what happens if we don't operate on him? Are we doing him a favor? I don't think so. We know that his seizures are life-threatening—to himself, to others. His seizures have already gotten him into trouble with the law, and his seizures are getting worse. The operation will prevent seizures, and we think that is an important benefit to the patient."

High up, Manon gave a little shrug. Janet Ross knew the gesture; it signaled irreconcilable differences, an impasse.

"Well, then," Ellis said, "are there other questions?"

There were no other questions.

3

"Jesus fucking Christ," Ellis said, wiping his forehead. "He didn't let up, did he?"

Janet Ross walked with him across the parking lot toward the Langer research building. It was late afternoon; the sunlight was yellowing, turning pale and weak.

"His point was valid," she said mildly.

Ellis sighed. "I keep forgetting you're on his side."

"Why do you keep forgetting?" she asked. She smiled as she said it. As the psychiatrist on the NPS staff, she'd opposed Benson's operation from the beginning.

"Look," Ellis said. "We do what we can. It'd be great to cure him totally. But we can't do that. We can only help him. So we'll help him."

She walked alongside him in silence. There was nothing to say. She had told Ellis her opinion many times before. The operation might not help —it might, in fact, make Benson much worse. She was sure Ellis understood that possibility, but he was stubbornly ignoring it. Or so it seemed to her.

Actually, she liked Ellis, as much as she liked any surgeon. She regarded surgeons as flagrantly action-oriented, men (they were almost always men, which she found significant) desperate to do something, to take some physical action. In that sense, Ellis was better than most of them. He had wisely turned down several stage-three candidates before Benson, and she knew that was difficult for him to do, because a part of him was terribly eager to perform the new operation.

"I hate all this," Ellis said.

"Hate what?"

"The politics. That's the nice thing about operating on monkeys. No politics at all."

"But you want to do Benson. . . ."

"I'm ready," Ellis said. "We're all ready. We have to take that first big step, and now is the time to take it." He glanced at her. "Why do you look so uncertain?"

"Because I am," she said.

They came to the Langer building. Ellis went off to an early dinner with McPherson—a political dinner, he said irritably—and she took the elevator to the fourth floor.

After ten years of steady expansion, the Neuropsychiatric Research Unit encompassed the entire fourth floor of the Langer research building. The other floors were painted a dead, cold white, but the NPS was bright with primary colors. The intention was to make patients feel optimistic and happy, but it always had the reverse effect on

Ross. She found it falsely and artificially cheerful, like a nursery school for retarded children.

She got off the elevator and looked at the reception area, one wall a bright blue, the other red. Like almost everything else about the NPS, the colors had been McPherson's idea. It was strange, she thought, how much an organization reflected the personality of its leader. McPherson himself always seemed to have a bright kindergarten quality about him, and a boundless optimism.

Certainly you had to be optimistic if you planned to operate on Harry Benson.

The Unit was quiet now, most of the staff gone home for the night. She walked down the corridor past the colored doors with the stenciled labels: SONOENCEPHALOGRAPHY, CORTICAL FUNCTION, EEG, RAS SCORING, PARIETAL T, and, at the far end of the hall, TELECOMP. The work done behind those doors was as complex as the labels—and this was just the patient-care wing, what McPherson called "Applications."

Applications was ordinary compared to Development, the research wing with its chemitrodes and compsims and elad scenarios. To say nothing of the big projects, like George and Martha, or Form Q. Development was ten years ahead of Applications—and Applications was very, very advanced.

A year ago, McPherson had asked her to take a group of newspaper science reporters through the NPS. He chose her, he said, "because she was such a piece of ass." It was funny to hear him say that, and shocking in a way. He was usually so courtly and fatherly.

But her shock was minor compared to the shock the reporters felt. She had planned to show them both Applications and Development, but after the reporters had seen Applications they were so agitated, so clearly overloaded, that she cut the tour short.

She worried a lot about it afterward. The reporters hadn't been naïve and they hadn't been inexperienced. They were people who shuttled from one scientific arena to another all their lives. Yet they were rendered speechless by the implications of the work she had shown them. She herself had lost that insight, that perspective—she had been working in the NPS for three years, and she had gradually become accustomed to the things done there. The conjunction of men and machines, human brains and electronic brains, was no longer bizarre and provocative. It was just a way to take steps forward and get things done.

On the other hand, she opposed the stage-three operation on Benson. She had opposed it from the start. She thought Benson was the wrong human subject, and she had just one last chance to prove it.

At the end of the corridor, she paused by the door to Telecomp, listening to the quiet hiss of the print-out units. She heard voices inside, and opened the door. Telecomp was really the heart of the Neuropsychiatric Research Unit; it was a large room, filled with electronic equipment. The walls and ceilings were soundproofed, a vestige of earlier days when the read-out consoles were clattering teletypes. Now they used either silent CRTs —cathode-ray tubes—or a print-out machine that sprayed the letters with a nozzle, rather than typed them mechanically. The hiss of the sprayer was the loudest sound in the room. McPherson had insisted on the change to quieter units because he felt the clattering disturbed patients who came to the NPS for treatment.

Gerhard was there, and his assistant Richards. The wizard twins, they were called: Gerhard was only twenty-four, and Richards even younger. They were the least professional people attached to the NPS; both men regarded Telecomp as a kind of permanent playground filled with complex toys. They worked long but erratic hours, frequently beginning in the late afternoon, quitting at dawn. They rarely showed up for group conferences and formal meetings, much to McPherson's annoyance. But they were undeniably good.

Gerhard, who wore cowboy boots and dungarees and satiny shirts with pearl buttons, had gained some national attention at the age of thirteen when he built a twenty-foot solid-fuel rocket behind his house in Phoenix. The rocket possessed a remarkably sophisticated electronic guidance system and Gerhard felt he could fire it into orbit. His neighbors, who could see the nose of the finished rocket sticking up above the garage in the backyard, were disturbed enough to call the police, and ultimately the Army was notified.

The Army examined Gerhard's rocket and

shipped it to White Sands for firing. As it happened, the second stage ignited before disengagement and the rocket exploded two miles up; but by that time Gerhard had four patents on his guidance mechanism and a number of scholarship offers from colleges and industrial firms. He turned them all down, let his uncle invest the patent royalties, and when he was old enough to drive, bought a Maserati. He went to work for Lockheed in Palmdale, California, but quit after a year because he was blocked from advancement by a lack of formal engineering degrees. It was also true that his colleagues resented a seventeen-year-old with a Maserati Ghibli and a propensity for working in the middle of the night; it was felt he had no "team spirit."

Then McPherson hired him to work at the Neuropsychiatric Research Unit, designing electronic components to be synergistic with the human brain. McPherson, as head of the NPS, had interviewed dozens of candidates who thought the job was "a challenge" or "an interesting systems application context." Gerhard said he thought it would be fun, and was hired immediately.

Richards's background was similar. He had finished high school and gone to college for six months before being drafted by the Army. He was about to be sent to Vietnam when he began to suggest improvements in the Army's electronic scanning devices. The improvements worked, and Richards never got closer to combat than a laboratory in Santa Monica. When he was discharged, he also joined the NPS.

The wizard twins: Ross smiled.

"Hi, Jan," Gerhard said.

"How's it going, Jan?" Richards said.

They were both offhand. They were the only people on the Staff who dared refer to McPherson as "Rog." And McPherson put up with it.

"Okay," she said. "We've got our stage three through grand rounds. I'm going to see him now."

"We're just finishing a check on the computer," Gerhard said. "It looks fine." He pointed to a table with a microscope surrounded by a tangle of electronic meters and dials.

"Where is it?"

"Under the stage."

She looked closer. A clear plastic packet the size of a postage stamp lay under the microscope lens. Through the plastic she could see a dense jumble of micro-miniaturized electronic components. Forty contact points protruded from the plastic. With the help of the microscope, the twins were testing the points sequentially, using fine probes.

"The logic circuits are the last to be checked," Richards said. "And we have a backup unit, just in case."

Janet went over to the file-card storage shelves and began looking through the test cards. After a moment, she said, "Haven't you got any more psychodex cards?"

"They're over here," Gerhard said. "You want five-space or n-space?"

"N-space," she said.

Gerhard opened a drawer and took out a cardboard sheet. He also took out a flat plastic clipboard. Attached to the clipboard by a metal chain was a pointed metal probe, something like a pencil.

"This isn't for the stage three, is it?"

"Yes," she said.

"But you've run so many psychodexes on him before—"

"Just one more, for the records."

Gerhard handed her the card and clipboard. "Does your stage three know what's going on?"

"He knows most of it," she said.

Gerhard shook his head. "He must be out of his mind."

"He is," she said. "That's the problem."

At the seventh floor, she stopped at the nurses' station to ask for Benson's chart. A new nurse was there, who said, "I'm sorry but relatives aren't allowed to look at medical records."

"I'm Dr. Ross."

The nurse was flustered. "I'm sorry, Doctor, I didn't see a name tag. Your patient is in seven-oh-four."

"What patient?"

"Little Jerry Peters."

Dr. Ross looked blank.

"Aren't you a pediatrician?" the nurse asked, finally.

"No," she said. "I'm a psychiatrist at the NPS." She heard the stridency in her own voice, and it upset her. But all those years growing up with people who said, "You don't *really* want to be a doctor, you want to be a nurse," or, "Well, for a woman, pediatrics is best, I mean, the most natural thing. . . ."

"Oh," the nurse said. "Then you want Mr. Benson in seven-ten. He's been prepped."

"Thank you," she said. She took the chart and walked down the hall to Benson's room. She knocked on Benson's door and heard gunshots. She opened the door and saw that the lights were dimmed, except for a small bedside lamp, but the room was bathed in an electric-blue glow from a TV. On the screen, a man was saying, ". . . dead before he hit the ground. Two bullets right through the heart."

"Hello?" she said, and swung the door wider.

Benson looked over. He smiled and pressed a button beside the bed, turning off the TV. His head was wrapped in a towel.

"How are you feeling?" she asked, coming into the room. She sat on a chair beside the bed.

"Naked," he said, and touched the towel. "It's funny. You don't realize how much hair you have until somebody cuts it all off." He touched the towel again. "It must be worse for a woman." Then he looked at her and became embarrassed.

"It's not much fun for anybody," she said.

"I guess not." He lay back against the pillow. "After they did it, I looked in the wastebasket, and I was amazed. So much hair. And my head was cold. It was the funniest thing, a cold head. They put a towel around it. I said I wanted to look at my head—see what I looked like bald—but they said it wasn't a good idea. So I waited until after they left, and then I got out of bed and went into the bathroom. But when I got there . . ."

"Yes?"

"I didn't take the towel off." He laughed. "I couldn't do it. What does that mean?"

"I don't know. What do you think it means?"

He laughed again. "Why is it that psychiatrists never give you a straight answer?" He lit a cigarette and looked at her defiantly. "They told me I shouldn't smoke, but I'm doing it anyway."

"I doubt that it matters," she said. She was watching him closely. He seemed in good spirits, and she didn't want to take that away from him. But on the other hand, it wasn't entirely appropriate to be jovial on the eve of brain surgery.

"Ellis was here a few minutes ago," he said, puffing on the cigarette. "He put some marks on me. Can you see?" He lifted up the right side of his towel slightly. exposing white pale flesh over the skull. Two blue "X" marks were positioned behind the ear. "How do I look?" he asked, grinning.

"You look fine," she said. "How do you feel?"

"Fine. I feel fine."

"Any worries?"

"No. I mean, what is there to worry about? Nothing I can do. For the next few hours, I'm in your hands, and Ellis's hands. . . ."

"I think most people would be. a little worried before an operation."

"There you go again, being a reasonable psychiatrist." He smiled, and then frowned. He bit his lip. "Of course I'm worried."

"What worries you?"

"Everything," he said. He sucked on the cigarette. "Everything. I worry about how I'll sleep. How I'll feel tomorrow. How I'll be when it's all over. What if somebody makes a mistake? What if I get turned into a vegetable? What if it hurts? What if I . . ."

"Die?"

"Sure. That, too."

"It's really a minor procedure. It's hardly more complicated than an appendectomy."

"I bet you tell that to all your brain-surgery patients."

"No, really. It's a short, simple procedure. It'll take about an hour and a half."

He nodded vaguely. She couldn't tell if she had reassured him. "You know," he said, "I don't really think it will happen. I keep thinking tomorrow morning at the last minute they'll come in and say, 'You're cured, Benson, you can go home now.'"

"We hope you'll be cured by the operation." She felt a twinge of guilt saying that, but it came out smoothly enough.

"You're so goddamned reasonable," he said. "There are times when I can't stand it."

"Like now?"

He touched the towel around his head again. "I mean, for Christ's sake, they're going to drill holes in my head, and stick wires in—"

"You've known about that for a long time."

"Sure," he said. "Sure. But this is the night before."

40

"Do you feel angry now?"

"No. Just scared."

"It's all right to be scared, it's perfectly normal. But don't let it make you angry."

He stubbed out the cigarette, and lit another immediately. Changing the subject, he pointed to the clipboard she carried under her arm. "What's that?"

"Another psychodex test. I want you to go through it."

"Now?"

"Yes. It's just for the record."

He shrugged indifferently. He had taken the psychodex several times before. She handed him the clipboard and he arranged the question card on the board, then began to answer the questions. He read them aloud:

"Would you rather be an elephant or a baboon? Baboon. Elephants live too long."

With the metal probe, he punched out the chosen answer on the card.

"If you were a color, would you rather be green or yellow? Yellow. I'm feeling very yellow right now." He laughed, and punched the answer.

She waited until he had done all thirty questions and punched his answers. He handed the clipboard back to her, and his mood seemed to shift again. "Are you going to be there? Tomorrow?"

"Yes."

"Will I be awake enough to recognize you?"

"I imagine so."

"And when will I come out of it?"

"Tomorrow afternoon or evening."

"That soon?"

"It's really a minor procedure," she said again. He nodded. She asked him if she could get him anything, and he said some ginger ale, and she replied that he was NPO, nothing *per ora,* for twelve hours before the operation. She said he'd be getting shots to help him sleep, and shots in the morning before he went to surgery. She said she hoped he'd sleep well.

As she left, she heard a hum as the television went back on, and a metallic voice said, "Look, Lieutenant, I've got a murderer out there, somewhere in a city of three million people. . . ."

She closed the door.

Before leaving the floor, she put a brief note in the chart. She drew a red line around it, so that the nurses would be sure to see it:

ADMITTING PSYCHIATRIC SUMMARY:

This 34-year-old man has documented psychomotor epilepsy of 2 years' duration. The etiology is presumably traumatic, following an automobile accident. This patient has already tried to kill two people, and has been involved in fights with several others. Any statement by him to hospital staff that he "feels funny" or "smells something bad" should be respected as indicating the start of a seizure. Under such circumstances, notify the NPS and Hospital Security at once.

The patient has an accompanying personality disorder which is part of his disease. He is convinced that machines are conspiring to take over the world. These beliefs are strongly held and attempts to dissuade him from them will only draw his enmity and suspicion. One should also remember that he is a highly intelligent and sensitive man. The patient can be quite demanding at times, but he should be treated with firmness and respect.

His intelligent and articulate manner may lead one to forget that his attitudes are not willful. He suffers an organic disease which has affected his mental state. Beneath it all he is frightened and concerned about what is happening to him.

Janet Ross, M.D.
NPS

4

"I don't understand," the PR man said.

Ellis sighed. McPherson smiled patiently. "This is an organic cause of violent behavior," he said. "That's the way to look at it."

The three of them were sitting in the Four Kings Restaurant, adjacent to the hospital. The early dinner had been McPherson's idea; McPherson said he wanted Ellis present, so Ellis was present. That was how Ellis thought about it.

Ellis raised his hand, beckoning the waiter for more coffee. As he did so, he thought it might keep him awake. But it didn't matter: he wouldn't sleep much tonight anyway. Not on the eve of his first stage three on a human subject.

He knew he would toss and turn in bed, going

over the operative procedure. Over and over again, reviewing the pattern he already knew so well. He'd done a lot of monkeys as stage-three procedures. One hundred and fifty-four monkeys, to be exact. Monkeys were difficult. They pulled out their stitches, they tugged at the wires, they screeched and fought you and bit you—

"Cognac?" McPherson asked.

"Fine," the PR man said.

McPherson glanced questioningly at Ellis. Ellis shook his head. He put cream in his coffee, and sat back suppressing a yawn. Actually, the PR man looked a little like a monkey. A juvenile rhesus: he had the same blocky lower jaw and the same bright-eyed alertness.

The PR man's name was Ralph. Ellis didn't know the last name. No PR man ever gave his last name. Of course, at the hospital he wasn't referred to as a PR man; he was the Hospital Information Officer or News Officer or some damned thing.

He did look like a monkey. Ellis found himself staring at the area of the skull behind the ear, where the electrodes would be implanted.

"We don't know much about the causes of violence," McPherson said. "And there's a lot of crap theory floating around, written by sociologists and paid for by perfectly good taxpayer money. But we do know that one particular illness, psychomotor epilepsy, may lead to violence."

"Psychomotor epilepsy," Ralph repeated.

"Yes. Now, psychomotor epilepsy is as common as any other kind of epilepsy. There are some famous people who have had it, like Dostoevski. At the NPS, we think that psychomotor epilepsy may be extremely common among those people who engage in repetitive violent acts—like certain policemen, gangsters, rioters, Hell's Angels. Nobody ever thinks of these people as *physically* ill. We just accept the idea that there are a lot of men in the world with bad tempers. We think that's normal. Perhaps it isn't."

"I see," Ralph said. And he did, indeed, seem to be seeing. McPherson should have been a grade-school teacher, Ellis thought. His great gift was teaching. Certainly he'd never been much of a researcher.

"And so," McPherson said, brushing his hand through his white hair, "we have no idea exactly how common psychomotor epilepsy is. But our guess is that as much as one or two percent of the population may suffer from it. That's two to four million Americans."

"Gosh," Ralph said.

Ellis sipped his coffee. Gosh, he thought. Good Christ. Gosh . . .

"For some reason," McPherson said, nodding to the waiter as the cognacs were brought, "psychomotor epileptics are predisposed to violent, aggressive behavior during their attacks. We don't know why, but it's true. The other things that go along with the syndrome are hypersexuality and pathological intoxication."

Ralph began to look unusually interested.

"We had the case of one woman with this disease," McPherson said, "who during a seizure state would have intercourse with twelve men a night and still be unsatisfied."

Ralph swallowed his cognac. Ellis noticed that Ralph wore a wide tie in a fashionable psychedelic pattern. A hip forty-year-old public-relations man gulping cognac at the thought of this woman.

"Pathological intoxication refers to the phenomenon of excessive, violent drunkenness brought on by minuscule amounts of liquor—just a sip or two. That much liquor will unleash a seizure."

Ellis thought of his first stage three. Benson: pudgy little Benson, the mild-mannered computer programmer who got drunk and beat up people— men, women, whoever happened to be present. The very idea of curing that with wires stuck in the brain seemed absurd.

Ralph seemed to think so, too. "And this operation will cure the violence?"

"Yes," McPherson said. "We believe so. But the operation has never been done before on a human subject. It will be done at the hospital tomorrow morning."

"I *see*," Ralph said, as if he suddenly understood the reason for the dinner.

"It's very sensitive, in terms of the press," McPherson said.

"Oh, yes, I can see that. . . ."

There was a short pause. Finally, Ralph said, "Who's going to do the operation?"

"I am," Ellis said.

"Well," Ralph said, "I'll have to check our files. I want to make sure I have a recent picture of you, and a good bio for the releases." He frowned, thinking of the work ahead of him.

Ellis was astonished at the man's reaction. Was that all he thought? That he might need a recent photo? But McPherson took it smoothly in stride. "We'll get you whatever you need," he said, and the meeting broke up.

5

Robert Morris was sitting in the hospital cafeteria finishing some stale apple pie when his pagemaster went off. It produced a high electronic squeal, which persisted until he reached down to his belt and turned it off. He returned to his pie. After a few moments, the squeal came again. He swore, put down his fork, and went to the wall phone to answer his page.

There had been a time when he regarded the little gray box clipped to his belt as a wonderful thing. He relished those moments when he would be having lunch or dinner with a girl and his pagemaster would go off, requiring him to call in. That sound demonstrated that he was a busy, responsible person involved in life-and-death matters. When the pagemaster went off, he would excuse himself abruptly and answer the call, radiating a sense of duty before pleasure. The girls loved it.

But after several years it was no longer wonderful. The box was inhuman and implacable, and it had come to symbolize for him the fact that he was not his own man. He was perpetually on call to some higher authority, however whimsical—a nurse who wanted to confirm a medication order at 2 a.m.; a relative who was acting up, making trouble about Mama's post-operative treatment; a call to tell him a conference was being held when he was already there attending the damned conference.

Now the finest moments in his life were those when he went home and put the box away for a few hours. He became unreachable and free. And he liked that very much.

He stared across the cafeteria at the remainder of his apple pie as he dialed the switchboard. "Dr. Morris."

"Dr. Morris, two-four-seven-one."

"Thank you." That was the extension for the seventh floor nurses' station. It was odd how he had learned all these extensions. The telephone network of University Hospital was more complicated than human anatomy. But over the years, without any conscious attempt to learn it, he came to know it quite well. He dialed the floor. "Dr. Morris."

"Oh, yes," a female voice said. "We have a woman with an overnight bag for patient Harold Benson. She says it's personal things. Is it all right to give it to him?"

"I'll come up," he said.

"Thank you, Doctor."

He went back to his tray, picked it up, and carried it to the disposal area. As he did so, his beeper went off again. He went to answer it.

"Dr. Morris."

"Dr. Morris, one-three-five-seven."

That was the metabolic unit. He dialed. "Dr. Morris."

"This is Dr. Hanley," an unfamiliar voice said. "We wondered if you could take a look at a lady we think may have steroid psychosis. She's a hemolytic anemic up for splenectomy."

"I can't see her today," Morris said, "and tomorrow is tight." That, he thought, was the understatement of the year. "Have you tried Peters?"

"No . . ."

"Peters has a lot of experience with steroid mentation. Try him."

"All right. Thanks."

Morris hung up. He got onto the elevator and pressed the button for the seventh floor. His beeper went off a third time. He checked his watch; it was 6:30 and he was supposedly off-duty by now. But he answered it anyway. It was Kelso, the pediatric resident.

"Want your ass whipped?" Kelso said.

"Okay. What time?"

"Say, about half an hour?"

"If you've got the balls."

"I've got them. They're in my car."

"See you on the court," Morris said. Then he added, "I may be a little late."

"Don't be too late," Kelso said. "It'll be dark soon."

Morris said he would hurry, and hung up.

The seventh floor was quiet. Most of the other hospital floors were noisy, jammed with relatives and visitors at this hour, but the seventh floor was always quiet. It had a sedate, calm quality that the nurses were careful to preserve.

The nurse at the station said, "There she is, Doctor," and nodded to a girl sitting on a couch. Morris went over to her. She was young and very pretty in a flashy, show-business sort of way. She had long legs.

"I'm Dr. Morris."

"Angela Black." She stood up and shook hands, very formally. "I brought this for Harry." She lifted a small blue overnight bag. "He asked me to bring it."

"All right." He took the bag from her. "I'll see that he gets it."

She hesitated, then said, "Can I see him?"

"I don't think it's a good idea." Benson would have been shaved by now; pre-op patients who had been shaved often didn't want to see people.

"Just for a few minutes?"

"He's heavily sedated," he said.

She was clearly disappointed. "Then would you give him a message?"

"Sure."

"Tell him I'm back in my old apartment. He'll understand."

"All right."

"You won't forget?"

"No. I'll tell him."

"Thank you." She smiled. It was a rather nice smile, despite the long false eyelashes and the heavy make-up. Why did young girls do that to their faces? "I guess I'll be going now." And she walked off, short skirt and very long legs, a briskly determined walk. He watched her go, then hefted the bag, which seemed heavy.

The cop sitting outside the door to 710 said, "How's it going?"

"Fine," Morris said.

The cop glanced at the overnight bag but said nothing as Morris took it inside the room.

Harry Benson was watching a Western on television. Morris turned down the sound. "A very pretty girl brought you this."

"Angela?" Benson smiled. "Yes, she has a nice exterior. Not a very complicated internal mechanism, but a nice exterior." He extended his hand; Morris gave him the bag. "Did she bring everything?"

Morris watched as Benson opened it, placing the contents on the bed. There were a pair of pajamas, an electric razor, some after-shave lotion, a paperback novel.

Then Benson brought out a black wig.

"What's that?" Morris asked.

Benson shrugged. "I knew I'd need it sooner or later," he said. Then he laughed. "You *are* letting me out of here, aren't you? Sooner or later?"

Morris laughed with him. Benson dropped the

wig back into the bag, and removed a plastic packet. With a metallic clink, he unfolded it, and Morris saw it was a set of screwdrivers of various sizes, stored in a plastic package with pockets for each size.

"What's that for?" Morris asked.

Benson looked puzzled for a moment. Then he said, "I don't know if you'll understand. . . ."

"Yes?"

"I always have them with me. For protection."

Benson placed the screwdrivers back into the overnighter. He handled them carefully, almost reverently. Morris knew that patients frequently brought odd things into the hospital, particularly if they were seriously ill. There was a kind of totemic feeling about these objects, as if they might have magical preservative powers. They were often connected with some hobby or favorite activity. He remembered a yachtsman with a metastatic brain tumor who had brought a kit to repair sails, and a woman with advanced heart disease who had brought a can of tennis balls. That kind of thing.

"I understand," Morris said.

Benson smiled.

6

Telecomp was empty when she came into the room; the consoles and teleprinters stood silently, the screens blinking up random sequences of numbers. She went to the corner and poured herself a cup of coffee, then fed the test card from Benson's latest psychodex into the computer.

The NPS had developed the psychodex test, along with several other computer-analyzed psychological tests. It was all part of what McPherson called "double-edged thinking." In this case, he meant that the idea of a brain being like a computer worked two ways, in two different directions. On the one hand, you could utilize the computer to probe the brain, to help you analyze its workings. At the same time, you could use your increased knowledge of the brain to help design better and more efficient computers. As McPherson said, "The brain is as much a model for the computer as the computer is a model for the brain."

At the NPS, computer scientists and neurobiologists had worked together for several years. From that association had come Form Q, and programs like George and Martha, and new psychosurgical techniques, and psychodex.

Psychodex was relatively simple. It was a test that took straightforward answers to psychological questions and manipulated the answers according to complex mathematical formulations. As the data were fed into the computer, Ross watched the screen glow with row after row of calculations.

She ignored them; the numbers, she knew, were just the computer's scratch pad, the intermediate steps that it went through before arriving at a final answer. She smiled, thinking of how Gerhard would explain it—rotation of thirty by thirty matrices in space, deriving factors, making them orthogonal, then weighting them. It all sounded complicated and scientific, and she didn't really understand any of it.

She had discovered long ago that you could use a computer without understanding how it worked. Just as you could use an automobile, a vacuum cleaner—or your own brain.

The screen flashed "CALCULATIONS ENDED. CALL DISPLAY SEQUENCE."

She punched in the display sequence for three-space scoring. The computer informed her that three spaces accounted for eighty-one percent of variance. On the screen she saw a three-dimensional image of a mountain with a sharp peak. She stared at it a moment, then picked up the telephone and paged McPherson.

McPherson frowned at the screen. Ellis looked over his shoulder. Ross said, "Is it clear?"

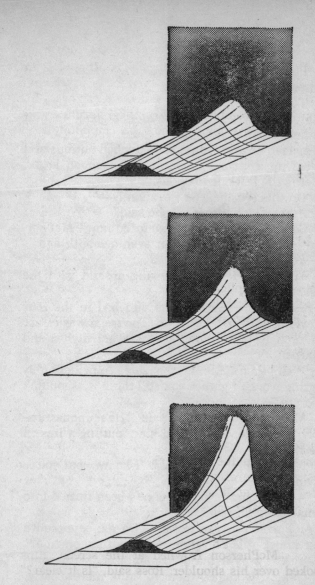

**SERIAL PSYCHODEX SCORE REPRESENTATIONS SHOWING
INCREASED ELEVATION (PSYCHOTIC MENTATION)**

"Perfectly," McPherson said. "When was it done?"

"Today," she said.

McPherson sighed. "You're not going to quit without a battle, are you?"

Instead of answering, she punched buttons and called up a second mountain peak, much lower. "Here's the last one previously."

"On this scoring, the elevation is—"

"Psychotic mentation," she said.

"So he's much more pronounced now," McPherson said. "Much more than even a month ago."

"Yes," she said.

"You think he was screwing around with the test?"

She shook her head. She punched in the four previous tests, in succession. The trend was clear: on each test the mountain peak got higher and sharper.

"Well, then," McPherson said, "he's definitely getting worse. I gather you still think we shouldn't operate."

"More than ever," she said. "He's unquestionably psychotic, and if you start putting wires in his head—"

"I know," McPherson said. "I know what you're saying."

"—he's going to feel that he's been turned into a machine," she said.

McPherson turned to Ellis. "Do you suppose we can knock this elevation down with thorazine?" Thorazine was a major tranquilizer. With some psychotics, it helped them to think more clearly.

"I think it's worth a try."

McPherson nodded. "I do, too. Janet?"

She stared at the screen and didn't reply. It was odd how these tests worked. The mountain peaks were an abstraction, a mathematical representation of an emotional state. They weren't a real characteristic of a person, like fingers or toes, or height or weight.

"Janet? What do you think?" McPherson repeated.

"I think," she said, "that you're both committed to this operation."

"And you still disapprove?"

"I don't 'disapprove.' I think it's unwise for Benson."

"What do you think about using thorazine?" McPherson persisted.

"It's a gamble."

"A gamble not worth taking."

"Maybe it's worth it, and maybe it's not. But it's a gamble."

McPherson nodded and turned to Ellis. "Do you still want to do him?"

"Yes," Ellis said, staring at the screen. "I still want to do him."

7

As always, Morris found it strange to play tennis on the hospital court. The hospital buildings looming high above him always made him feel slightly guilty—all those rows of windows, all those patients who could not do what he was doing. Then there was the sound. Or, rather, the absence of sound. The freeway ran near the hospital, and the reassuring *thwock!* of the tennis balls was completely obliterated by the steady, monotonous rush of passing cars.

It was getting dark now, and he was having trouble with his vision; the ball seemed to pop unexpectedly into his court. Kelso was much less hampered. Morris often joked that Kelso ate too many carrots, but whatever the explanation, it was humiliating to play late with Kelso. Darkness helped him. And Morris hated to lose.

He had long ago become comfortable with the fact of his own competitiveness. Morris never stopped competing. He competed in games, he competed in work, he competed with women. More than once Ross had pointed that out to him, and then dropped the subject in the sly way that psychiatrists raise a point, then drop it. Morris didn't mind. It was a fact of his life, and whatever the connotations—deep insecurity, a need to prove himself, a feeling of inferiority—he didn't worry about it. He drew pleasure from competition and satisfaction from winning. And so far in his life he had managed to win more often than not.

In part, he had joined the NPS because the challenges were very great and because the potential rewards were enormous. Privately, Morris expected to be a professor of surgery before he was forty. His past career had been outstanding—that was why Ellis had accepted him—and he was equally confident about his future. It wouldn't hurt to be associated with a major landmark in surgical practice.

All in all, he was in a good mood, and he played hard for half an hour, until he was tired and it was too dark to see. He signaled to Kelso—no point in calling above the freeway sounds—to end the game. They met at the net and shook hands. Morris was reassured to see that Kelso was sweating heavily.

"Good game," Kelso said. "Tomorrow, same time?"

"I'm not sure," Morris said.

Kelso paused. "Oh," he said. "That's right. You have a big day tomorrow."

"Big day," Morris nodded. Christ, had the news even reached the pediatric residents? For a moment he felt what Ellis must be feeling—the intense pressure, abstract, vague, that came from knowing that the entire University Hospital staff was watching this procedure.

"Well, good luck with it," Kelso said.

As the two men walked back to the hospital, Morris saw Ellis, a distant solitary figure, limping slightly as he crossed the parking lot and climbed into his car, and drove home.

WEDNESDAY, MARCH 10, 1971: IMPLANTATION

...could have turned into a situation that...

could have brought him to the hospital on Satur-

1

At 6 a.m. Janet Ross was on the third surgical floor, dressed in greens, having coffee and a doughnut. The surgeons' lounge was busy at this hour. Although operations were scheduled to begin at six, most didn't get going for fifteen or twenty minutes after that. The surgeons sat around, reading the newspaper, discussing the stock market and their golf games. From time to time one of them would leave, go to the overhead viewing galleries, and look down on their ORs to see how preparations were coming.

She was the only woman in the room, and her presence changed the masculine atmosphere subtly. It annoyed her that she should be the only woman, and it annoyed her that the men should become quieter, more polite, less jovial and raucous. She didn't give a damn if they were raucous, and she resented being made to feel like an intruder. It seemed to her that she had been an intruder all her life, even when she was very young. Her father had been a surgeon who never bothered to conceal his disappointment and irritation that he had a daughter instead of a son. A son would have fitted into his scheme of life; he could have brought him to the hospital on Satur-

day mornings, taken him into the operating rooms
—those were all things you could do with a *son*.
But a daughter was something else, a perplexing
entity not suited for a surgical life. And therefore
an intrusion . . .

She looked around at all the surgeons in the
lounge, and then, to cover her unease, she went
to the phone and dialed the seventh floor.

"This is Dr. Ross. Is Mr. Benson on call?"

"He was just sent."

"When did he leave the floor?"

"About five minutes ago."

She hung up and went back to her coffee. Ellis
appeared and waved to her across the room.
"There'll be a five-minute delay hooking into the
computer," he said. "They're tying in the lines
now. Is the patient on call?"

"Sent five minutes ago."

"You seen Morris?"

"Not yet."

"He better get his ass down here," Ellis said.

Somehow that made her feel good.

Morris was in the elevator with a nurse
and Benson, who lay on a stretcher, and one of
the cops. As they rode down, Morris said to the
cop, "You can't get off on the floor."

"Why not?"

"We're going onto the sterile floor directly."

"What should I do?" The cop was intimidated.
He'd been docile and hesitant all morning. The

routine of surgery left him feeling a helpless outsider.

"You can watch from the viewing gallery on the third floor. Tell the desk nurse I said it was all right."

The cop nodded. The elevator stopped at the second floor. The doors opened to reveal a hallway with people, all in surgical greens, walking back and forth. A large sign read STERILE AREA. NO ADMITTANCE WITHOUT AUTHORIZATION. The lettering was red.

Morris and the nurse wheeled Benson out of the elevator. The cop remained behind, looking nervous. He pushed the button for the third floor, and the doors closed.

Morris went with Benson down the corridor. After a moment, Benson said, "I'm still awake."

"Of course you are."

"But I don't want to be awake."

Morris nodded patiently. Benson had gotten pre-op medications half an hour earlier. They would be taking effect soon, making him drowsy. "How's your mouth?"

"Dry."

That was the atropine beginning to work. "You'll be okay."

Morris himself had never had an operation. He'd performed hundreds, but never experienced one himself. In recent years, he had begun to wonder how it felt to be on the other side of things. He suspected, though he would never admit it, that it must be awful.

"You'll be okay," he said to Benson again, and touched his shoulder.

Benson just stared at him as he was wheeled down the corridor to OR 9.

OR 9 was the largest operating room in the hospital. It was nearly thirty feet square and packed with electronic equipment. When the full surgical team was there—all twelve of them— things got pretty crowded. But now just two scrub nurses were working in the cavernous gray-tiled space. They were setting out sterile tables and drapes around the chair.

OR 9 had no operating table. Instead, there was a softly cushioned upright chair, like a dentist's chair. Janet Ross watched the girls through the windows in the door that separated the scrub room from the operating room. Alongside her, Ellis finished his scrub and muttered something about fucking Morris being fucking late. Ellis got profane before operations. He also got very nervous, though he seemed to think nobody noticed that. Ross had scrubbed with him on several animal procedures and had seen the ritual—tension and profanity before the operation, and utter bland calmness once things were under way.

Ellis turned off the faucets with his elbows and entered the OR, backing in so that his arms did not touch the door. A nurse handed him a towel. While he dried his hands, he looked back through the door at Ross, and then up at the glass-walled viewing gallery overhead. Ross knew there would be a crowd in the gallery watching the operation.

Morris came down and began scrubbing. She said, "Ellis wondered where you were."

"Tour guide for the patient," he said.

One of the circulating nurses entered the scrub room and said, "Dr. Ross, there's somebody here from the radiation lab with a unit for Dr. Ellis. Does he want it now?"

"If it's loaded," she said.

"I'll ask," the nurse said. She disappeared, and stuck her head in a moment later. "He says it's loaded and ready to go, but unless your equipment is shielded it could give you trouble."

Ross knew that all the OR equipment had been shielded the week before. The plutonium exchanger didn't put out much radiation—not enough to fog an X-ray plate—but it could confuse more delicate scientific equipment. There was, of course, no danger to people.

"We're shielded," Ross said. "Have him take it into the OR."

Ross turned to Morris, scrubbing alongside her. "How's Benson?"

"Nervous."

"He should be," she said. Morris glanced at her, his eyes questioning above the gauze surgical mask. She shook her hands free of excess water and backed into the OR. The first thing she saw was the rad-lab man wheeling in the tray with the charging unit on it. It was contained in a small lead box. On the sides were stenciled DAN-

GER RADIATION and the triple-blade orange symbol for radiation. It was all faintly ridiculous; the charging unit was quite safe.

Ellis stood across the room, being helped into his gown. He plunged his hands into his rubber gloves and flexed his fingers. To the rad-lab man he said, "Has it been sterilized?"

"Sir?"

"Has the unit been sterilized?"

"I don't know, sir."

"Then give it to one of the girls and have her autoclave it. It's got to be sterile."

Dr. Ross dried her hands and shivered in the cold of the operating room. Like most surgeons, Ellis preferred a cold room—too cold, really, for the patient. But as Ellis often said, "If I'm happy, the patient's happy."

Ellis was now across the room standing by the viewing box, while the circulating nurse, who was not scrubbed, put up the patient's X-rays. Ellis peered closely at them, though he had seen them a dozen times before. They were perfectly normal skull films. Air had been injected into the ventricles, so that the horns stood out darkly.

One by one the rest of the team filtered into the room. All together, there were two scrub nurses, two circulating nurses, one orderly, Ellis, two assistant surgeons including Morris, two electronics technicians, and a computer programmer. The anaesthetist was outside with Benson.

Without looking up from his console, one of the electronics men said, "Any time you want to begin, Doctor."

"We'll wait for the patient," Ellis said dryly, and there were some chuckles from the Nine Group team.

Ross looked around the room at the seven TV screens. They were of different sizes and stationed in different places, depending on how important they were to the surgeon. The smallest screen monitored the closed-circuit taping of the operation. At the moment, it showed an overhead view of the empty chair.

Another screen, nearer the surgeon, monitored the electroencephalogram, or EEG. It was turned off now, the sixteen pens tracing straight white lines across the screen. There was also a large TV screen for basic operative parameters: electrocardiogram, peripheral arterial pressure, respirations, cardiac output, central venous pressure, rectal temperature. Like the EEG screen, it was also tracing a series of straight lines.

Another pair of screens were completely blank. They would display black-and-white image-intensified X-ray views during the operation.

Finally, two color screens displayed the LIMBIC Program output. That program was cycling now, without punched-in coordinates. On the screens, a picture of the brain rotated in three dimensions while random coordinates, generated by computer, flashed below. As always, Ross felt that the computer was another, almost human presence in the room—an impression that was always heightened as the operation proceeded.

Ellis finished looking at the X-rays and glanced up at the clock. It was 6:19; Benson was still outside being checked by the anaesthetist. Ellis walked around the room, talking briefly to everyone. He was being unusually friendly, and Ross wondered why. She looked up at the viewing gallery and saw the director of the hospital, the chief of surgery, the chief of medicine, and the chief of research all looking down through the glass. Then she understood.

It was 6:21 when Benson was wheeled in. He was now heavily pre-medicated, relaxed, his body limp, his eyelids heavy. His head was wrapped in a green towel.

Ellis supervised Benson's transfer from the stretcher to the chair. As the leather straps were placed across his arms and legs, Benson seemed to wake up, his eyes opening wide.

"That's just so you don't fall off," Ellis said easily. "We don't want you to hurt yourself."

"Uh-huh," Benson said softly, and closed his eyes again.

Ellis nodded to the nurses, who removed the sterile towel from Benson's head. The naked head seemed very small—that was Ross's usual reaction—and white. The skin was smooth, except for a razor nick on the left frontal. Ellis's blue-ink "X" marks were clearly visible on the right side.

Benson leaned back in the chair. He did not open his eyes again. One of the technicians began to fix the monitor leads to his body, strapping them on with little dabs of electrolyte paste. They were attached quickly; soon his body was connected to a tangle of multicolored wires running off to the equipment.

Ellis looked at the TV monitor screens. The EEG was now tracing sixteen jagged lines; heartbeat was recorded; respirations were gently rising and falling; temperature was steady. The technicians began to punch pre-op parameters into the computer. Normal lab values had already been fed in. During the operation, the computer would monitor all vital signs at five-second intervals, and would signal if anything went wrong.

"Let's have music, please," Ellis said, and one of the nurses slipped a tape cartridge into the portable cassette recorder in a corner of the room. A Bach concerto began to play softly. Ellis always operated to Bach; he said he hoped that the precision, if not the genius, might be contagious.

They were approaching the start of the operation. The digital wall clock said 6:29:14 a.m. Next to it, an elapsed-time digital clock still read 0:00:00.

With the help of a scrub nurse, Ross put on her sterile gown and gloves. The gloves were always difficult for her. She didn't scrub in frequently, and when she plunged her fingers into the gloves she caught her hand, missing one of the finger slots and putting two fingers in another. It was impossible to read the scrub nurse's reaction; only her eyes were visible above the mask. But Ross was glad that Ellis and the other surgeons were turned away attending to the patient.

She stepped to the back of the room, being careful not to trip over the thick black power cables that snaked across the floor in all directions. Ross did not participate in the initial stages

71

of the operation. She waited until the stereotaxic mechanism was in place and the coordinates were determined. She had time to stand to one side and pluck at her glove until all the fingers were in the right slots.

There was no real purpose for her to attend the operation at all, but McPherson was insistent that one member of the non-surgical staff scrub in each day that they operated. He felt it kept the Unit more cohesive. At least that was what he said.

She watched Ellis and his assistants across the room draping Benson; then she looked over to the draping as seen on the closed-circuit monitor. The entire operation would be recorded on video tape for later review.

"I think we can start now," Ellis said easily. "Go ahead with the needle."

The anaesthetist, working behind the chair, placed the needle between the second and third lumbar spaces of Benson's spine. Benson moved once and made a slight sound, and then the anaesthetist said, "I'm through the dura. How much do you want?"

The computer console flashed "OPERATION BEGUN." The computer automatically started the elapsed-time clock, which ticked off the seconds.

"Give me thirty cc's to begin," Ellis said. "Let's have X-ray, please."

The X-ray machines were swung into position at the front and side of the patient's head. Film plates were set on, locking in with a click. Ellis stepped on the floor button, and the TV screens glowed suddenly, showing black-and-white images of the skull. He watched in two views as air slowly filled the ventricles, outlining the horns in black.

The programmer sat at the computer console, his hands fluttering over the buttons. On his TV display screen, the words "PNEUMOGRAPH INITIATED" appeared.

"All right, let's fix his hat," Ellis said. The box-like tubular sterotactic frame was placed over the patient's head. Burr-hole locations were fixed and checked. When Ellis was satisfied, he injected local anaesthetic into the scalp points. Then he cut the skin and reflected it back, exposing the white surface of the skull.

"Drill, please."

With the 2-mm drill, he made the first of the two holes on the right side of the skull. He placed the stereotactic frame—the "hat"—over the head, and screwed it down securely.

Ross looked over at the computer display. Values for heart rate and blood pressure flashed on the screen and faded; everything was normal. Soon the computer, like the surgeons, would begin to deal with more complex matters.

"Let's have a position check," Ellis said, stepping away from the patient, frowning critically at Benson's shaved head and the metal frame screwed on top of it. The X-ray technician came forward and snapped the pictures.

In the old days, Ross remembered, they actually took X-ray plates and determined position by visual inspection of the plates. It was a slow process. Using a compass, protractor, and ruler, they drew

73

lines across the X-ray, measured them, rechecked them. Now the data were fed directly to the computer, which did the analysis more rapidly and more accurately.

All the team turned to look at the computer print-out screen. The X-ray views appeared briefly, and were replaced by schematic drawings. The maxfield location of the stereotactic apparatus was calculated; the actual location was then merged with it. A set of coordinates flashed up, followed by the notation "PLACEMENT CORRECT."

Ellis nodded. "Thank you for your consultation," he said humorlessly, and went over to the tray which held the electrodes.

The team was now using Briggs stainless-steel Teflon-coated electrode arrays. In the past, they had tried almost everything else: gold, platinum alloy, and even flexible steel strands in the days when the electrodes were placed by inspection.

The old inspection operations were bloody, messy affairs. It was necessary to remove a large portion of the skull and expose the surface of the brain. The surgeon found his landmark points on the surface itself, and then placed his electrodes in the substance of the brain. If he had to place them in deep structures, he would occasionally cut through the brain to the ventricles with a knife, and then place them. There were serious complications; the operations were lengthy; the patients never did very well.

Now the computer had changed all that. The computer allowed you to fix a point precisely in three-dimensional space. Initially, along with other researchers in the field, the NPS group had tried to relate deep brain points to skull architecture. They measured their landmark points from the orbit of the eye, from the meatus of the ear, from the sagittal suture. That, of course, didn't work— people's brains did not fit inside their skulls with any consistency. The only way to determine deep brain points was in relation to other brain points —and the logical landmarks were the ventricles, the fluid-filled spaces within the brain. According to the new system, everything was determined in relation to the ventricles.

With the help of the computer, it was no longer necessary to expose the brain surface. Instead, a few small holes were drilled in the skull and the electrodes inserted, while the computer watched by X-ray to make sure they were being placed correctly.

Ellis picked up the first electrode array. From where Ross stood, it looked like a single slender wire. Actually, it was a bundle of twenty wires, with staggered contact points. Each wire was coated with Teflon except for the last millimeter, which was exposed. Each wire was a different length, so that under a magnifying glass, the staggered electrode tips looked like a miniature staircase.

Ellis checked the array under a large glass. He called for more light and turned the array, peering at all contact points. Then he had a scrub nurse plug it into a testing unit and test every contact. This had been done dozens of times before, but Ellis always checked again before insertion. And he always had four arrays sterilized, though he would need only two. Ellis was careful.

At length he was satisfied. "Are we ready to wire?" he asked the team. They nodded. He stepped up to the patient and said, "Let's go through the dura."

Up to this point in the operation, they had drilled through the skull, but had left intact the membrane of *dura mater* which covered the brain and enclosed the spinal fluid. Ellis's assistant used a probe to puncture the dura.

"I have fluid," he said, and a thin trickle of clear liquid slid down the side of the shaved skull from the hole. A nurse sponged it away.

Ross always found it a source of wonder the way the brain was protected. Other vital body organs were well-protected, of course: the lungs and heart inside the bony cage of the ribs, the liver and spleen under the edge of the ribs, the kidneys packed in fat and secure against thick muscles of the lower back. Good protection, but nothing compared to the central nervous system, which was encased entirely in thick bone. Yet even this was not enough; inside the bone there were sac-like membranes which held cerebrospinal fluid. The fluid was under pressure, so that the brain sat in the middle of a pressurized liquid system that afforded its superb protection.

McPherson had compared it to a fetus in a water-filled womb. "The baby comes out of the womb," McPherson said, "but the brain never comes out of its own special womb."

"We will place now," Ellis said.

Ross moved forward, joining the surgical team gathered around the head. She watched as Ellis slid the tip of the electrode array into the burr hole and then pressed slightly, entering the substance of the brain. The technician punched buttons on the computer console. The display screen read: "ENTRY POINT LOCALIZED."

The patient did not move, made no sound. The brain could not feel pain; it lacked pain sensors. It was one of the freaks of evolution that the organ which sensed pain throughout the body could feel nothing itself.

Ross looked away from Ellis toward the X-ray screens. There, in harsh black and white, she saw the crisply outlined white electrode array begin its slow, steady movement into the brain. She looked from the anterior view to the lateral, and then to the computer-generated images.

The computer was interpreting the X-ray images by drawing a simplified brain, with the temporal-lobe target area in red and a flickering blue track showing the line the electrode must traverse from entry point to the target area. So far, Ellis was following the track perfectly.

"Very pretty," Ross said.

The computer flashed up triple coordinates in rapid succession as the electrodes went deeper.

"Practice makes perfect," Ellis said sourly. He was now using the scale-down apparatus attached to the stereotactic hat. The scaler reduced his crude finger movements to very small changes in electrode movements. If he moved his finger half an inch, the scaler converted that to half a millimeter. Very slowly the electrodes penetrated deeper into the brain.

From the screens, Ross could lift her eyes and watch the closed-circuit TV monitor showing Ellis at work. It was easier to watch on TV than to turn around and see the real thing. But she turned around when she heard Benson say, very distinctly, "Uh."

Ellis stopped. "What was that?"

"Patient," the anaesthetist said, gesturing toward Benson.

Ellis paused, bent over, to look at Benson's face. "You all right, Mr. Benson?" He spoke loudly, distinctly.

"Yuh. Fine," Benson said. His voice was deeply drugged.

"Any pain?"

"No."

"Good. Just relax now." And he returned to his work.

Ross sighed in relief. Somehow, all that had made her tense, even though she knew there was no reason for alarm. Benson could feel no pain, and she had known all along that his sedation was only that—a kind of deep, drugged semi-sleep, and not unconsciousness. There was no reason for him to be unconscious, no reason to risk general anaesthesia.

She turned back to the computer screen. The computer had now presented an inverted view of the brain, as seen from below, near the neck. The electrode track was visible end on, as a single blue point surrounded by concentric circles. Ellis was supposed to keep within one millimeter, one twenty-fifth of an inch, of the assigned track. He deviated half a millimeter.

"50 TRACK ERROR," warned the computer. Ross said, "You're slipping off."

The electrode array stopped in its path. Ellis glanced up at the screens. "Too high on beta plane?"

"Wide on gamma."

"Okay."

After a moment, the electrodes continued along the path. "40 TRACK ERROR," the computer flashed. It rotated its brain image slowly, bringing up an anterolateral view. "20 TRACK ERROR," it said.

"You're correcting nicely," Ross said.

Ellis hummed along with the Bach and nodded.

"ZERO TRACK ERROR," the computer indicated, and swung the brain view around to a full lateral. The second screen showed a full frontal view. After a few moments, the screen blinked "AP-PROACHING TARGET." Ross conveyed the message.

Seconds later, the flashing word "STRIKE."

"You're on," Ross said.

Ellis stepped back and folded his hands across his chest. "Let's have a coordinate check," he said. The elapsed-time clock showed that twenty-seven minutes had passed in the operation.

The programmer flicked the console buttons rapidly. On the TV screens, the placement of the electrode was simulated by the computer. The simulation ended, like the actual placement, with the word "STRIKE."

"Now match it," Ellis said.

The computer held its simulation on one screen and matched it to the X-ray image of the patient. The overlap was perfect; the computer reported "MATCHED WITHIN ESTABLISHED LIMITS."

"That's it," Ellis said. He screwed on the little plastic button cap which held the electrodes tightly against the skull. Then he applied dental cement to fix it. He untangled the twenty fine wire leads that came off the electrode array and pushed them to one side.

"We can do the next one now," he said.

At the end of the second placement, a thin, arcing cut was made with a knife along the scalp. To avoid important superficial vessels and nerves, the cut ran from the electrode entry points down the side of the ear to the base of the neck. There it deviated to the right shoulder. Using blunt dissection, Ellis opened a small pocket beneath the skin of the right lateral chest, near the armpit.

"Have we got the charging unit?" he asked.

The charger was brought to him. It was smaller than a pack of cigarettes, and contained thirty-seven grams of the radioactive isotope plutonium-239 oxide. The radiation produced heat, which was converted directly by a thermionic unit to electric power. A Kenbeck solid-state DC/DC circuit transformed the output to the necessary voltage.

Ellis plugged the charger into the test pack and did a last-minute check of its power before implantation. As he held it in his hand, he said, "It's cold. I can't get used to that." Ross knew layers of vacuum-foil insulation kept the exterior cool and that inside the packet the radiation capsule was producing heat at 500 degrees Fahrenheit—hot enough to cook a roast.

He checked radiation to be sure there would be no leakage. The meters all read in the low-normal range. There was a certain amount of leakage, naturally, but it was no more than that produced by a commercial color television set.

Finally he called for the dog tag. Benson would have to wear this dog tag for as long as he had the atomic charging unit in his body. The tag warned that the person had an atomic pacemaker, and gave a telephone number. Ross knew that the number was a listing which played a recorded message twenty-four hours a day. The recording gave detailed technical information about the charging unit, and warned that bullet wounds, automobile accidents, fires, and other damage could release the plutonium, which was a powerful alpha-particle emitter. It gave special instructions to physicians, coroners, and morticians, and warned particularly against cremation of the body, unless the charger was first removed.

Ellis inserted the charging unit into the small subdermal pocket he had made in the chest wall. He sewed tissue layers around it to fix it in place. Then he turned his attention to the postage-stamp-sized electronic computer.

Ross looked up at the viewing gallery and saw the wizard twins, Gerhard and Richards, watching intently. Ellis checked the packet under the magnifying glass, then gave it to a scrubbed technician, who hooked the little computer into the main hospital computer.

To Ross, the computer was the most remarkable part of the entire system. Since she had joined the NPS three years before, she had seen the computer shrink from a prototype as large as a briefcase to the present tiny model, which looked small in the palm of a hand yet contained all the elements of the original bulky unit.

This tiny size made subdermal implantation possible. The patient was free to move about, take showers, do anything he wanted. Much better than the old units, where the charger was clipped to a patient's belt and wires dangled down all over.

She looked at the computer screens which flashed "OPERATIVE MONITORS INTERRUPTED FOR ELECTRONICS CHECK." On one screen, a blown-up circuit diagram appeared. The computer checked each pathway and component independently. It took four-millionths of a second for each check; the entire process was completed in two seconds. The computer flashed "ELECTRONIC CHECK NEGATIVE." A moment later, brain views reappeared. The computer had gone back to monitoring the operation.

"Well," Ellis said, "let's hook him up." He painstakingly attached the forty fine wire leads from the two electrode arrays to the plastic unit. Then he fitted the wires down along the neck, tucked the plastic under the skin, and called for sutures. The elapsed-time clock read one hour and twelve minutes.

2

Morris wheeled Benson into the recovery room, a long, low-ceilinged room where patients were brought immediately after operation. The NPS had a special section of the rec room, as did cardiac patients and burns patients. But the NPS section, with its cluster of electronic equipment, had never been used before. Benson was the first case.

Benson looked pale but otherwise fine; his head and neck were heavily bandaged. Morris supervised his transfer from the rolling stretcher to the permanent bed. Across the room, Ellis was telephoning in his operative note. If you dialed extension 1104, you got a transcribing machine. The dictated message would later be typed up by a secretary and inserted in Benson's record.

Ellis's voice droned on in the background. ". . . centimeter incisions were made over the right temporal region, and 2-millimeter burr holes drilled with a K-7 drill. Implantation of Briggs electrodes carried out with computer assistance on the LIMBIC Program. Honey, that's spelled in capital letter, L-I-M-B-I-C. Program. X-ray placement of electrodes determined with computer review as within established limits. Electrodes sealed with Tyler fivation caps and seven-oh-grade dental sealer. Transmission wires—"

"What do you want on him?" the rec-room nurse asked.

"Vital signs Q five minutes for the first hour, Q fifteen for the second, Q thirty for the third, hourly thereafter. If he's stable, you can move him up to the floor in six hours."

The nurse nodded, making notes. Morris sat down by the bedside to write a short operative note:

Short operative note on Harold F. Benson

Pre-op dx: *psychomotor (temporal lobe) epilepsy*
Post-op dx: *same*
Procedure: *implantation of twin Briggs electrode arrays into right temporal lobe with subdermal placing of computer and plutonium charging unit.*
Pre-op meds: phenobarbital 500 mg } *one hr. prior to*
atropine 60 mg *procedure*
Anaesthesia: lidocaine (1/1000) epinephrine locally
Estimated blood loss: 250 cc
Fluid replacement: 200 cc D5/W
Operative duration: 1 hr. 12 min.
Post-op condition: good

As he finished the note, he heard Ross say to the nurse, "Start him on phenobarb as soon as he's awake." She sounded angry.

He looked up at her. "Something the matter?"

"No," he said.

"You seem angry."

"Are you picking a fight with me?"

"No," he said, "of course—"

"Just make sure he gets his phenobarb. We

want to keep him sedated until we can interface him."

And she stormed out of the room. Morris watched her go, then glanced over at Ellis, who was still dictating but had been watching. Ellis shrugged.

"What's the matter with her?" the nurse asked.

"Probably just tired," Morris said. He adjusted the monitoring equipment on the shelf above Benson's head. He turned it on and waited until it warmed up. Then he placed the temporary induction unit around Benson's taped shoulder.

During the operation, all the wires had been hooked up, but they were not working now. Before that happened, Benson had to be "interfaced." This meant determining which of the forty electrodes would stop an epileptic seizure, and locking in the appropriate switches on the subdermal computer. Because the computer was under the skin, the locking in would be accomplished by an induction unit, which worked through the skin. But the interfacing couldn't be done until tomorrow.

Meanwhile, the equipment monitored Benson's brainwave activity. The screens above the bed glowed a bright green, and showed the white tracing of his EEG. The pattern was normal for alpha rhythms slowing from sedation.

Benson opened his eyes and looked at Morris. "How do you feel?" he asked.

"Sleepy," he said. "Is it beginning soon?"

"It's over," Morris said.

Benson nodded, not at all surprised, and closed

his eyes. A rad-lab technician came in and checked for leakage from the plutonium with a Geiger counter. There was none. Morris slipped the dog tag around Benson's neck. The nurse picked it up curiously, read it, and frowned.

Ellis came over. "Time for breakfast?"

"Yes," Morris said. "Time for breakfast."

They left the room together.

3

The trouble was he didn't really like the sound of his voice. His voice was rough and grating, and his enunciation was poor. McPherson preferred to see the words in his mind, as if they had been written. He pressed the microphone button on the dictation machine. "Roman numeral three. Philosophical Implications."

III. Philosophical Implications.

He paused and looked around his office. The large model of the brain sat at the corner of his desk. Shelves of journals along one wall. And the TV monitor. On the screen now he was watching the playback of the morning's operation. The sound was turned off, the milky images silent. Ellis was drilling holes in Benson's head. McPherson watched and began to dictate.

This procedure represents the first direct link between a human brain and a computer. The link is permanent. Now of course, any man sitting at a computer console and interacting with the computer by pressing buttons can be said to be linked.

Too stuffy, he thought. He ran the tape back and made changes. *Now, a man sitting at a computer console and interacting with the computer by pressing buttons is linked to the computer. But that link is not direct. And the link is not permanent. Therefore, this operative procedure represents something rather different. How is one to think about it?*

A good question, he thought. He stared at the TV image of the operation, then continued.

One might think of the computer in this case as a prosthetic device. Just as a man who has his arm amputated can receive a mechanical equivalent of the lost arm, so a brain-damaged man can receive a mechanical aid to overcome the effects of brain damage. This is a comfortable way to think about the operation. It makes the computer into a high-class wooden leg. Yet the implications go much further than that.

He paused to look at the screen. Somebody at the main tape station had changed reels. He was no longer seeing the operation, but a psychiatric interview with Benson before the surgery. Benson was excited, smoking a cigarette, making stabbing gestures with the lighted tip as he spoke.

Curious, McPherson turned the sound up slightly. ". . . know what they're doing. The machines are everywhere. They used to be the servants of man, but now they're taking over. Subtly, subtly taking over."

Ellis stuck his head into the office, saw the TV screen, and smiled. "Looking at the 'before' pictures?"

"Trying to get a little work done," McPherson said, and pointed to the dictation machine.

Ellis nodded, ducked out, closing the door behind him.

Benson was saying, ". . . know I'm a traitor to the human race, because I'm helping to make machines more intelligent. That's my job, programming artificial intelligence, and—"

McPherson turned the sound down until it was almost inaudible. Then he went back to his dictation.

In thinking about computer hardware, we distinguish between central and peripheral equipment. That is, the main computer is considered central even though, in human terms, it may be located in some out-of-the-way place—like the basement of a building, for example. The computer's read-out equipment, display consoles, and so on, are peripheral. They are located at the edges of the computer system, on different floors of the building.

He looked at the TV screen. Benson was particularly excited. He turned up the sound and heard, ". . . getting more intelligent. First steam engines, then automobiles, and airplanes, then adding machines. Now computers, feedback loops—"

McPherson turned the sound off.

For the human brain, the analogy is a central brain and peripheral terminals, such as mouth, arms, and legs. They carry out the instructions— the output—of the brain. By and large, we judge the workings of the brain by the activity of these peripheral functions. We notice what a person says, and how he acts, and from that deduce how his brain works. This idea is familiar to everyone.

He looked at Benson on the TV screen. What would Benson say? Would he agree or disagree? But then did it matter?

Now, however, in this operation we have created a man with not one brain but two. He has his biological brain, which is damaged, and he has a new computer brain, which is designed to correct the damage. This new brain is intended to control the biological brain. Therefore a new situation arises. The patient's biological brain is the peripheral terminal—the only peripheral terminal— for the new computer. In one area, the new computer brain has total control. And therefore the patient's biological brain, and indeed his whole body, has become a terminal for the new computer. We have created a man who is one single, large, complex computer terminal. The patient is a read-out device for the new computer, and he is as helpless to control the read-out as a TV screen is helpless to control the information presented on it.

Perhaps that was a bit strong, he thought. He pressed the button and said, "Harriet, type that last paragraph but I want to look at it, okay?

Roman numeral four. Summary and Conclusions."

IV. *Summary and Conclusions.*

He paused again, and turned up the sound on Benson. Benson was saying, ". . . hate them, particularly the prostitutes. Airplane mechanics, dancers, translators, gas-station attendants, the people who are machines, or who service machines. The prostitutes. I hate them all."

As he spoke, Benson continued to stab with his cigarette.

4

"And how did you feel?" Dr. Ramos said.

"Angry," Janet Ross said. "Angry as hell. I mean, that nurse was standing there, watching it all. She pretended she didn't understand what was happening, but she did."

"You felt angry about . . ." Dr. Ramos let his voice trail off.

"About the operation. About Benson. They went ahead and did it. I told them from the beginning —from the goddamned very beginning—that it was a bad idea, but Ellis and Morris and McPherson all wanted to do it. They're so cocky. Particularly Morris. When I saw him in the recovery room, gloating over Benson—who was all taped up and pale as a ghost—I just got mad."

"Why is that?"

"Because he was so pale, because he, uh—"

She stopped. She fumbled for an answer, but couldn't think of a logical response.

"I gather the operation was successful," Dr. Ramos said. "And most people are pale after surgery. What got you mad?"

She said nothing. Finally, she said, "I don't know."

She heard Dr. Ramos shift in his chair. She could not see him; she was lying on the couch, and Dr. Ramos was behind her head. There was a long silence while she stared at the ceiling and tried to think what to say. Her thoughts seemed to be churning, not making any sense. Finally Dr. Ramos said, "The presence of the nurse seems important to you."

"It does?"

"Well, you mentioned it."

"I wasn't aware I had."

"You said the nurse was there and knew what was going on. . . . What, exactly, was going on?"

"I was mad."

"But you don't know why? . . ."

"Yes, I do," she said. "It was Morris. He's so cocky."

"Cocky," Dr. Ramos repeated.

"Overly self-assured."

"You said cocky."

"Look, I didn't mean anything by that; it was

just a word—" She broke off. She was very angry. She could hear it in her voice.

"You are angry now," Dr. Ramos said.

"Very."

"Why?"

After a long pause, she sad, "They didn't listen to me."

"Who didn't listen to you?"

"Any of them. Not McPherson, not Ellis, not Morris. Nobody listened to me."

"Did you tell Dr. Ellis or Dr. McPherson you were angry?"

"No."

"But you vented your anger on Dr. Morris."

"Yes." He was leading her someplace and she couldn't see where. Normally at this point she could jump ahead and understand. But this time—

"How old is Dr. Morris?"

"I don't know. About my age. Thirty, thirty-one—something in there."

"About your age."

That pissed her off, his way of repeating things. "Yes, God damn it, about my age."

"And a surgeon."

"Yes. . . ."

"Is it easier to express anger toward someone you regard as a contemporary?"

"I never thought about it."

"Your father was also a surgeon, but he wasn't your contemporary."

"You don't have to draw me a picture," she said.

"You're still angry."

She sighed. "Let's change the subject."

"All right," he said, in that easy voice that she sometimes liked, and sometimes hated.

5

Morris hated to do Initial Interviews. The Initial Interview staff consisted mostly of clinical psychologists; the work was lengthy and boring. A recent tabulation had shown that only one in forty new patients to the NPS received further work; and only one in eighty-three was accepted as having some variety of organic brain disease with behavioral manifestations. That meant most Initial Interviews were a waste of time.

And it was particularly true of off-the-street patients. A year ago McPherson had decided, for political reasons, that anyone who heard of the NPS and presented himself directly would be seen. Most patients were still referrals, of course, but McPherson felt the image of the Unit depended upon prompt treatment of self-referrals as well.

McPherson also felt that everyone on the staff should do some Initial Interviews from time to time. Morris worked two days a month in the little interview rooms with the one-way glass mirrors. This was one of his days, but he didn't want to be here; he was still exhilarated from the morning's operation, and he resented returning to this kind of mundane routine.

He looked up unhappily as the next patient came into the room. He was a young man in his twenties, wearing dungarees and a sweatshirt. He had long hair. Morris stood to greet him.

"I'm Dr. Morris."

"Craig Beckerman." The handshake was soft and tentative.

"Please sit down." He waved Beckerman to a chair which faced Morris's desk, and the one-way mirror behind. "What brings you to us?"

"I, uh . . . I'm curious. I read about you," Beckerman said, "in a magazine. You do brain surgery here."

"That's true."

"Well, I uh . . . I was curious about it."

"In what sense?"

"Well, this magazine article— Can I smoke here?"

"Of course," Morris said. He pushed an ashtray across the desk to Beckerman. Beckerman brought out a pack of Camels, tapped one on the desk, then lit it.

"The magazine article . . ."

"Right. The magazine article said that you put wires in the brain. Is that true?"

"Yes, we sometimes perform that kind of surgery."

Beckerman nodded. He smoked the cigarette. "Yeah, well, is it true that you can put wires in so that you feel pleasure? Intense pleasure?"

"Yes," Morris said. He tried to say it blandly.

"That's really true?"

"It's really true," Morris said. And then he shook his pen, indicating that it was out of ink. He opened the desk drawer to take out another pen, and as he reached into the drawer, he pressed a sequence on the buttons hidden inside. Immediately his telephone rang.

"Dr. Morris."

At the other end, the secretary said, "You rang?"

"Yes. Would you hold all calls, please, and transfer them to Development section?"

"Right away," the secretary said.

"Thank you." Morris hung up. He knew that the Development people would arrive soon, to watch on the other side of the one-way mirror. "I'm sorry for the interruption. You were saying . . ."

"About the wires in the brain."

"Yes. We do that operation, Mr. Beckerman, under special circumstances, but it's still pretty experimental."

"That's all right," Beckerman said. He puffed on his cigarette. "That's fine with me."

"If you want information, we can arrange for you to have some reprints and magazine tear sheets explaining our work here."

Beckerman smiled and shook his head. "No, no," he said. "I don't want information. I want the operation. I'm volunteering."

Morris pretended to be surprised. He paused a moment and said, "I see."

"Listen," Beckerman said, "in the article it said

that one jolt of electricity was like a dozen orgasms. It sounded really terrific."

"And you want this operation performed on you?"

"Yeah," Beckerman said, nodding vigorously. "Right."

"Why?"

"Are you kidding? Wouldn't everybody want it? Pleasure like that?"

"Perhaps," Morris said, "but you're the first person to ask for it."

"What's the matter?" Beckerman said. "Is it really expensive or something?"

"No. But we don't perform brain surgery for trivial reasons."

"Oh, wow," Beckerman said. "So that's where you are. Jesus."

And he got up and left the room, shaking his head.

The three Development guys looked stupefied. They sat in the adjoining room and stared through the one-way glass. Beckerman had long since departed.

"Fascinating," Morris said.

The Development guys didn't reply. Finally one of them cleared his throat and said, "To say the least."

Morris knew what was going through their heads. For years, they had been doing feasibility studies, potential application studies, ramification studies, industrial operations studies, input-output studies. They were geared to think in the future—and now they were suddenly confronted with the present.

"That man is an elad," one of them said. And sighed.

The elad concept had caused a lot of interest and some detached academic concern. The notion of an electrical addict—a man who needed his jolts of electricity just as some men needed doses of drugs—had seemed almost fancifully speculative. But now they had a patient who was clearly a potential addict.

"Electricity is the biggest kick of all," one of them said, and laughed. But the laugh was nervous, edged with tension.

Morris wondered what McPherson would say. Probably something philosophical. McPherson was mostly interested in philosophy these days.

The idea of an electrical addict was predicated on an astonishing discovery made by James Olds in the 1950s. Olds found that there were areas in the brain where electrical stimulation produced intense pleasure—strips of brain tissue he called "rivers of reward." If an electrode was placed in such an area, a rat would press a self-stimulation lever to receive a shock as often as five thousand times an hour. In its quest for pleasure, it would ignore food and water. It would stop pressing the lever only when it was prostrate with exhaustion.

This remarkable experiment had been repeated with goldfish, guinea pigs, dolphins, cats, and goats. There was no longer any question that the pleasure terminals in the brain were a universal phenomenon. They had also been located in humans.

Out of these considerations had come the notion of the electrical addict, the man who needed pleasurable shocks. At first glance, it seemed impossible for a person to become an addict. But it actually wasn't.

For instance, the technological hardware was now expensive, but it needn't be. One could envision clever Japanese firms manufacturing electrodes for as little as two or three dollars and exporting them.

Nor was the idea of an illegal operation so farfetched. At one time a million American women underwent illegal abortions each year. The implantation brain surgery was somewhat more complex, but not forbiddingly so. And the surgical techniques would become more standardized in the future. It was easy to imagine clinics springing up in Mexico and the Bahamas.

Nor was there a problem finding surgeons to do the job. A single busy, well-organized neurosurgeon could perform ten or fifteen operations a day. He could certainly charge a thousand dollars for each—and with that kind of incentive, unscrupulous surgeons could be found. A hundred thousand dollars a week in cash was a strong inducement to break the law—if indeed a law were ever passed.

That did not seem very likely. A year before, the hospital had organized a seminar with legal scholars on "Biomedical Technology and the Law." Elads were among the subjects discussed, but the lawyers were not responsive. The elad concept did not fit neatly into the already existing pattern of laws governing drug addiction. All those laws recognized that a person could become a drug addict innocently or involuntarily—quite a different proposition from a person coldly seeking a surgical procedure that would make him an addict. Most of the lawyers felt that the public would not seek such an operation; there would be no legal problem because there would be no public demand. Now Beckerman had provided evidence for such a demand.

"I'll be goddamned," another of the Development people said.

Morris found that comment hardly adequate. He himself felt something he had felt once or twice before since joining the NPS. It was the sensation that things were moving too fast, without enough caution and control, and that it could *all* get out of control, suddenly, and without warning.

6

At 6 p.m., Roger McPherson, head of the Neuropsychiatric Research Unit, went up to the seventh floor to check on his patient. At least, that was how he thought of Benson—as his patient. A proprietary feeling, but not entirely incorrect. Without McPherson, there would be no NPS, and without an NPS, there would be no surgery, no Benson. That was how he thought of it.

Room 710 was quiet and bathed in reddish light from the setting sun. Benson appeared to be asleep, but his eyes opened when McPherson closed the door.

"How are you feeling?" McPherson asked, moving close to the bed.

Benson smiled. "Everyone wants to know that," he said.

McPherson smiled back. "It's a natural question."

"I'm tired, that's all. Very tired. . . . Sometimes I think I'm a ticking time bomb, and you're wondering when I'll explode."

"Is that what you think?" McPherson asked. Automatically, he adjusted Benson's covers so he could look at the I.V. line. It was flowing nicely.

"Ticktick," Benson said, closing his eyes again. "Ticktick."

McPherson frowned. He was accustomed to mechanical metaphors from Benson—the man was preoccupied, after all, with the idea of men as machines. But to have them appear so soon after operation . . .

"Any pain?"

"None. A little ache behind my ears, like I'd fallen. That's all."

That, McPherson knew, was the bone pain from the drilling.

"Fallen?"

"I'm a fallen man," Benson said. "I've succumbed."

"To what?"

"To the process of being turned into a machine." He opened his eyes and smiled again. "Or a time bomb."

"Any smells? Strange sensations?" As he asked, McPherson looked at the EEG scanner above the bed. It was still reading normal alpha patterns, without any suggestion of seizure activity.

"No. Nothing like that."

"But you feel as if you might explode?" He thought: Ross should really be asking these questions.

"Sort of," Benson said. "In the coming war, we may all explode."

"How do you mean?"

"You look annoyed," Benson said.

"I'm not, just puzzled. How do you mean, in the coming war?"

"In the coming war between men and machines. The human brain is obsolete, you see."

That was a new thought. McPherson hadn't heard it from Benson before. He stared at him, lying in the bed, his head and shoulders heavily bandaged. It made the upper part of his body and his head appear thick, gross, oversized.

"Yes," Benson said. "The human brain has gone as far as it is going to go. It's exhausted, so it spawned the next generation of intelligent forms. They will— Why am I so tired?" He closed his eyes again.

"You're exhausted from the operation."

"A minor procedure," he said, and smiled with his eyes closed. A moment later he was snoring.

McPherson remained by the bed for a moment, then turned to the window and watched the sun set over the Pacific. Benson had a nice room; you could see a bit of the ocean between the high-rise apartments in Santa Monica. He remained there for several minutes. Benson did not wake. Finally, McPherson went out to the nurses' station to write his note in the chart.

"Patient alert, responsive, oriented times three." He paused after writing that. He didn't really know if Benson was oriented to person, place, and time; he hadn't checked specifically. But he was clear and responsive, and McPherson let it go. "Flow of ideas orderly and clear, but patient retains machine imagery of pre-operative state. It is too early to be certain, but it appears that early predictions were correct that the operation would not alter his mentation between seizures."

Signed, "Roger A. McPherson, M.D."

He stared at it for a moment, then closed the chart and replaced it on the shelf. It was a good note, cool, direct, holding out no false anticipations. The chart was a legal document, after all, and it could be called into court. McPherson didn't expect to see Benson's chart in court, but you couldn't be too careful. He believed very strongly in appearances—and he felt it was his job to do so.

The head of any large scientific laboratory performed a political function. You might deny it; you might dislike it. But it was nonetheless true, a necessary part of the job.

You had to keep all the people in the lab happy as they worked together. The more prima donnas you had, the tougher the job was, as pure politics.

You had to get your lab funded from outside sources, and that was also pure politics. Particularly if you were working in a delicate area, as the NPS was. McPherson had long since evolved the horseradish-peroxidase principle of grant applications. It was simple enough: when you applied for money, you announced that the money would be spent to find the enzyme horseradish peroxidase, which could lead to a cure for cancer. You would easily get sixty thousand dollars for that project— although you couldn't get sixty cents for mind control.

He looked at the row of charts on the shelf, a row of unfamiliar names, into which BENSON, H. F. 710 merged indistinguishably. In one sense, he thought, Benson was correct—he was a walking time bomb. A man treated with mind-control technology was subject to all sorts of irrational public prejudice. "Heart control" in the form of cardiac pacemakers was considered a wonderful invention; "kidney control" through drugs was a blessing. But "mind control" was evil, a disaster— even though the NPS control work was directly analogous to control work with other organs. Even the technology was similar: the atomic pacemaker they were using had been developed first for heart work.

But the prejudice remained. And Benson thought of himself as a ticking time bomb. McPherson sighed, took out the chart again, and flipped to the section containing doctors' orders. Both Ellis and Morris had written post-op care orders. McPherson added: "After interfacing tomorrow a.m., begin thorazine."

He looked at the note, then decided the nurses wouldn't understand interfacing. He scratched it out and wrote: "After noon tomorrow, begin thorazine."

As he left the floor, he thought that he would rest more easily once Benson was on thorazine. Perhaps they couldn't defuse the time bomb—but they could certainly drop it into a bucket of cold water.

7

Late at night, in Telecomp, Gerhard stared anxiously at the computer console. He typed in more instructions, then walked to a print-out typewriter and began reviewing the long sheaf of green-striped sheets. He scanned them quickly, looking for the error he knew was there in the programmed instructions.

The computer itself never made a mistake. Gerhard had used computers for nearly ten years

—different computers, different places—and he had never seen one make a mistake. Of course, mistakes occurred all the time, but they were always in the program, not in the machine. Sometimes that infallibility was hard to accept. For one thing, it didn't fit with one's view of the rest of the world, where machines were always making mistakes—fuses blowing, stereos breaking down, ovens overheating, cars refusing to start. Modern man expected machines to make their fair share of errors.

But computers were different, and working with them could be a humiliating experience. They were never wrong. It was as simple as that. Even when it took weeks to find the source of some problem, even when the program was checked a dozen times by as many different people, even when the whole staff was slowly coming to the conclusion that for once, the computer circuitry had fouled up—it always turned out, in the end, to be a human error of some kind. Always.

Richards came in, shrugging off a sport coat, and poured himself a cup of coffee. "How's it going?"

Gerhard shook his head. "I'm having trouble with George."

"Again? Shit." Richards looked at the console. "How's Martha?"

"Martha's fine, I think. It's just George."

"Which George is it?"

"Saint George," Gerhard said. "Really a bitch."

Richards sipped his coffee and sat down at the console. "Mind if I try it?"

"Sure," Gerhard said.

Richards began flicking buttons. He called up the program for Saint George. Then he called up the program for Martha. Then he pushed the interaction button.

Richards and Gerhard hadn't devised these programs; they were modified from several existing computer programs developed at other universities. But the basic idea was the same—to create a computer program that would make the computer act emotionally, like people. It was logical to designate the programs with names like George and Martha. There was a precedent for that: Eliza in Boston, and Aldous in England.

George and Martha were essentially the same program with slight differences. The original George was programmed to be neutral in his response to stimuli. Then Martha was created. Martha was a little bitchy; Martha disliked most things. Finally, another George was formulated, a very loving George, who was referred to as Saint George.

Each program could respond with three emotional states—love, fear, and anger. Each could produce three actions—approach, withdrawal, and attack. All this was, of course, highly abstract. It was carried out in terms of numbers. For example, the original George was neutral to most numbers, but he disliked the number 751. He was programmed to dislike it. And by extension he disliked similar numbers—743, 772, and so on. He much preferred numbers such as 404, 133, and 918. If you punched in one of these numbers, George responded with numbers signifying love and approach. If you punched in 707, George withdrew. If you punched in 750, George angrily attacked—according to the numbers he printed out.

The NPS staff had played with the programs in this way for a long time. Then they had incorporated program modifications to allow for "talk" from the computer. The numbers were translated into sentences. This was amusing, and revealing. The actual interaction was referred to as "the Christmas game" because most of it was conducted as giving and receiving gifts—objects that had an assigned or learned emotional value, just as the numbers did.

Normal George interacting with Martha would eventually win her over, and her bitchiness would recede into the background.

But Saint George had a much worse effect on her. His loving acceptance drove her up the wall. That is, if things were working normally. Richards watched as the print-out flashed across the screen.

```
HELLO I'M SAINT GEORGE
HELLO
WHAT IS YOUR NAME?
MARTHA.
YOU DON'T SAY MUCH, MARTHA.
NO
BUT I LIKE YOU.
WHY I DON'T LIKE YOU.
I UNDERSTAND THAT. HOW CAN I HELP?
```

"It isn't printing periods consistently," Richards said. "When did that start?"

"That's nothing," Gerhard said. "Just keep watching."

```
HELP?
YES, I WOULD LIKE TO HELP YOU.
HAVE A CAT.
```

Richards winced. Cats were programmed to be something that both George and Martha disliked. Giving George a cat was a very hostile move.

```
THANK YOU
HAVE ANOTHER CAT.
THANK YOU YOU ARE VERY KIND.
HAVE ANOTHER CAT.
NO THANK YOU.
DON'T YOU LIKE CATS?
YES BUT I HAVE ENOUGH CATS.
HAVE A GORILLA.
```

"Really nasty," Richards said. "What are the other interactions like?"

"Pretty much the same," Gerhard said.

"As bad as this?"

"Pretty much."

They were accustomed now to the idea that when the computers interacted, the results were unpredictable. The general form of interaction could be guessed, but the specific results were uncertain. It was like a computer playing checkers— it was probably going to win, but it would win a different way each time, depending on what the opponent did.

I DON'T WANT A GORILLA.
DON'T YOU LIKE GORILLAS?
NO THANK YOU.
YOU ARE TOO POLITE.
I AM SORRY IF I OFFEND YOU IN ANY WAY.
YOU TALK TOO MUCH.
I AM SORRY.
HAVE AN EGGPLANT.

Richards watched with interest. Saint George had no background for eggplants. But he disliked cucumbers and bananas.

NO THANK YOU.
DON'T YOU LIKE EGGPLANT?
NOT VERY MUCH.
HERE HAVE ANOTHER ONE.
NO THANK YOU.
I WANT YOU TO HAVE IT.
NO THANK YOU.
GO ON AND TAKE IT.
NO THANK YOU.
I INSIST.
NO THANK YOU.

"What's happened to Saint George?" Richards asked. "His responses are too much the same."

"That's what's bothering me."

"What's he cycling through on the program?"

"I was looking for it when you came in."

I INSIST THAT YOU HAVE A CUCUMBER.
I REFUSE.

"George!" Richards said, almost without thinking.

THEN HAVE A BANANA.
NO.

"George is breaking down," Richards said. "He's not a saint any more."

```
THEN HAVE BOTH A BANANA AND A
    CUCUMBER.
NO THANK YOU.
I INSIST.
GO TO HELL I WILL KILL YOU: : : : : : : :
: : : : : : : : : : : : : : : : : : : : : : :
: : : : : : : : : : : : : : : : : : : : : : :
```

The screen was filled with white dots. "What does that mean, unprintable response?" Richards said.

"I don't know. I've never seen it before tonight."

"How many times has this program been run?" Richards asked.

"One hundred and ten, against Martha."

"Any learning erasures?"

"No."

"I'll be goddamned," Richards said. "He's getting to be a short-tempered saint." He grinned. "We can write this one up."

Gerhard nodded and went back to the print-out. In theory, what was happening was not puzzling. Both George and Martha were programmed to learn from experience. Like the checkers-playing programs—where the machine got better each time it played a game—this program was established so that the machine would "learn" new responses to things. After one hundred and ten sets of experience, Saint George had abruptly stopped being a saint. He was learning not to be a saint around Martha—even though he had been programmed for saintliness.

"I know just how he feels," Richards said, and switched the machine off. Then he joined Gerhard, looking for the programming error that had made it all possible.

THURSDAY,
MARCH 11, 1971:
INTERFACING

1

Janet Ross sat in the empty room and glanced at the wall clock. It was 9 a.m. She looked down at the desk in front of her, which was bare except for a vase of flowers and a notepad. She looked at the chair opposite her. Then, aloud, she said, "How're we doing?"

There was a mechanical click and Gerhard's voice came through the speaker mounted in the ceiling. "We need a few minutes for the sound levels. The light is okay. You want to talk a minute?"

She nodded, and glanced over her shoulder at the one-way mirror behind her. She saw only her reflection, but she knew Gerhard, with his equipment, was behind, watching her. "You sound tired," she said.

"Trouble with Saint George last night," Gerhard said.

"I'm tired, too," she said. "I was having trouble with somebody who isn't a saint." She laughed. She was just talking so they could get a sound level for the room; she hadn't really paid attention to what she was saying. But it was true: Arthur was no saint. He was also no great discovery, though she'd thought he might be a few weeks ago when she first met him. She had been, in fact, a little infatuated with him. ("Infatuated? Hmm? Is that what you'd call it?" She could hear Dr. Ramos now.) Arthur had been born handsome and wealthy. He had a yellow Ferrari, a lot of dash, and a lot of charm. She was able to feel feminine and frivolous around him. He did madcap, dashing things like flying her to Mexico City for dinner because he knew a little restaurant where they made the best tacos in the world. She knew it was all silly, but she enjoyed it. And in a way she was relieved—she never had to talk about medicine, or the hospital, or psychiatry. Arthur wasn't interested in any of those things; he was interested in her as a woman. ("Not as a sex object?" Damn Dr. Ramos.)

Then, as she got to know him better, she found herself wanting to talk about her work. And she found, with some surprise, that Arthur didn't want to hear about it. Arthur was threatened by her work; he had problems about achievement. He was nominally a stockbroker—an easy thing for a rich man's son to be—and he talked with authority about money, investments, interest rates, bond issues. But there was an aggressive quality in his manner, a defensiveness, as if he were substantiating himself.

And then she realized what she should have known from the beginning, that Arthur was chiefly interested in her because she was substantial. It was—in theory—more difficult to impress her, to sweep her off her feet, than it was to impress the little actresses who hung out at Bumbles and the Candy Store. And therefore more satisfying.

Finally her role had begun to bother her, and she no longer drew pleasure from being frivolous around him, and everything became vaguely depressing. She recognized all the signs: her work at the hospital became busier, and she had to break dates with him. When she did see him, she was bored by his flamboyance, his restless impulsiveness, his clothes, and his cars. She would look at him across the dinner table and try to find what she had once seen. She could not find even a trace of it. Last night she had broken it off. They both knew it was coming.

Why did it depress her?

"You stopped talking," Gerhard said.

"I don't know what to say . . . Now is the time for all good men to come to the aid of the patient. The quick brown fox jumped over the pithed frog. We are all headed for that final common pathway in the sky." She paused. "Is that enough?"

"A little more."

"Mary, Mary, quite contrary, how does your garden grow? I'm sorry I don't remember the rest. How does the poem go?" She laughed.

"That's fine, we have the level now."

She looked up at the loudspeaker. "Will you be interfacing at the end of the series?"

"Probably," Gerhard said, "if it goes well. Rog is in a hurry to get him onto tranquilizers."

She nodded. This was the final stage in Benson's treatment, and it had to be done before tranquilizers could be administered. Benson had been kept on sedation with phenobarbital until mid-

117

night the night before. He would be clearheaded this morning, and ready for interfacing.

It was McPherson who had coined the term "interfacing." McPherson liked computer terminology. An interface was the boundary between two systems. Or between a computer and an effector mechanism. In Benson's case, it was almost a boundary between two computers—his brain and the little computer wired into his shoulder. The wires had been attached, but the switches hadn't been thrown yet. Once they were, the feedback loop of Benson-computer-Benson would be instituted.

McPherson saw this case as the first of many. He planned to go from epileptics to schizophrenics to mentally retarded patients to blind patients. The charts were all there on his office wall. And he planned to use more and more sophisticated computers in the link-up. Eventually, he would get to projects like Form Q, which seemed farfetched even to Ross.

But today the practical question was which of the forty electrodes would prevent an attack. Nobody knew that yet. It would be determined experimentally.

During the operation, the electrodes had been located precisely, within millimeters of the target area. That was good surgical placement, but considering the density of the brain it was grossly inadequate. A nerve cell in the brain was just a micron in diameter. There were a thousand nerve cells in the space of a millimeter.

From that standpoint, the electrodes had been crudely positioned. And this crudeness meant that many electrodes were required. One could assume that if you placed several electrodes in the correct general area, at least one of them would be in the precise position to abort an attack. Trial-and-error stimulation would determine the proper electrode to use.

"Patient coming," Gerhard said over the loud-speaker. A moment later, Benson arrived in a wheelchair, wearing his blue-and-white striped bathrobe. He seemed alert as he waved to her stiffly—the shoulder bandages inhibited movement of his arm. "How are you feeling?" he said, and smiled.

"I'm supposed to ask you."

"I'll ask the questions around here," he said. He was still smiling, but there was an edge to his voice. With some surprise, she realized that he was afraid. And then she wondered why that surprised her. Of course he would be afraid. Anyone would be. She wasn't exactly calm herself.

The nurse patted Benson on the shoulder, nodded to Dr. Ross, and left the room. They were alone.

For a moment, neither spoke. Benson stared at her; she stared back. She wanted to give Gerhard time to focus the TV camera in the ceiling, and to prepare his stimulating equipment.

"What are we doing today?" Benson asked.

"We're going to stimulate your electrodes, sequentially, to see what happens."

119

He nodded. He seemed to take this calmly, but she had learned not to trust his calm. After a moment he said, "Will it hurt?"

"No."

"Okay," he said. "Go ahead."

Gerhard, sitting on a high stool in the adjacent room, surrounded in the darkness by glowing green dials of equipment, watched through the one-way glass as Ross and Benson began to talk.

Alongside him, Richards picked up the tape-recorder microphone and said quietly, "Stimulation series one, patient Harold Benson, March 11, 1971."

Gerhard looked at the four TV screens in front of him. One showed the closed-circuit view of Benson that would be stored on video tape as the stimulation series proceeded. Another displayed a computer-generated view of the forty electrode points, lined up in two parallel rows within the brain substance. As each electrode was stimulated, the appropriate point glowed on the screen.

A third TV screen ran an oscilloscope tracing of the shock pulse as it was delivered. And a fourth showed a wiring diagram of the tiny computer in Benson's neck. It also glowed as stimulations traveled through the circuit pathways.

In the next room, Ross was saying, "You'll feel a variety of sensations, and some of them may be quite pleasant. We want you to tell us what you feel. All right?"

Benson nodded.

Richards said, "Electrode one, five millivolts, for five seconds." Gerhard pressed the buttons. The computer diagram showed a tracing of the circuit being closed, the current snaking its way through the intricate electronic maze of Benson's shoulder computer. They watched Benson through the one-way glass.

Benson said, "That's interesting."

"What's interesting?" Ross asked.

"That feeling."

"Can you describe it?"

"Well, it's like eating a ham sandwich."

"Do you like ham sandwiches?"

Benson shrugged. "Not particularly."

"Do you feel hungry?"

"Not particularly."

"Do you feel anything else?"

"No. Just the taste of a ham sandwich." He smiled. "On rye."

Gerhard, sitting at the control panel, nodded. The first electrode had stimulated a vague memory trace.

Richards: "Electrode two, five millivolts, five seconds."

Benson said, "I have to go to the bathroom."

Ross said, "It will pass."

Gerhard sat back from the control panel, sipped a cup of coffee, and watched the interview progress.

"Electrode three, five millivolts, five seconds."

This one produced absolutely no effect on Benson. Benson was quietly talking with Ross about bathrooms in restaurants, hotels, airports—

"Try it again," Gerhard said. "Up five."

"Repeat electrode three, ten millivolts, five seconds," Richards said. The TV screen flashed the circuit through electrode three. There was still no effect.

"Go on to four," Gerhard said. He wrote out a few notes:

#1—? *memory trace (ham sand.)*
#2—*bladder fullness*
#3—*no subjective change*
#4—

He drew the dash and waited. It was going to take a long time to go through all forty electrodes, but it was fascinating to watch. They produced such strikingly different effects, yet each electrode was very close to the next. It was the ultimate proof of the density of the brain, which had once been described as the most complex structure in the known universe. And it was certainly true: there were three times as many cells packed into a single human brain as there were human beings on the face of the earth. That density was hard to comprehend, sometimes. Early in his NPS career, Gerhard had requested a human brain to dissect. He had done it over a period of several days, with a dozen neuroanatomy texts opened up before him. He used the traditional tool for brain dissection, a blunt wooden stick, to scrape away the cheesy gray material. He had patiently, carefully scraped away—and in the end, he had nothing.

The brain was not like the liver or the lungs. To the naked eye, it was uniform and boring, giving no indication of its true function. The brain was too subtle, too complex. Too dense.

"Electrode four," Richards said into the recorder. "Five millivolts, five seconds." The shock was delivered.

And Benson, in an oddly childlike voice, said, "Could I have some milk and cookies, please?"

"That's interesting," Gerhard said, watching the reaction.

Richards nodded. "How old would you say?"

"About five or six, at most."

Benson was talking about cookies, talking about his tricycle, to Ross. Slowly, over the next few minutes, he seemed to emerge like a time-traveler advancing through the years. Finally he became fully adult again, thinking back to his youth, instead of actually being there. "I always wanted the cookies, and she would never give them to me. She said they were bad for me and would give me cavities."

"We can go on," Gerhard said.

Richards said, "Electrode five, five millivolts, five seconds."

In the next room, Benson shifted uncomfortably in his wheelchair. Ross asked him if something was wrong. Benson said, "It feels funny."

"How do you mean?"

"I can't describe it. It's like sandpaper. Irritating."

Gerhard nodded, and wrote in his notes, "#5— potential attack electrode." This happened sometimes. Occasionally an electrode would be found to stimulate a seizure. Nobody knew why—and Gerhard personally thought that nobody ever would. The brain was, he believed, beyond comprehension.

His work with programs like George and Martha had led him to understand that relatively simple computer instructions could produce complex and unpredictable machine behavior. It was also true that the programmed machine could exceed the capabilities of the programmer; that was clearly demonstrated in 1963 when Arthur Samuel at IBM programmed a machine to play checkers—and the machine eventually became so good that it beat Samuel himself.

Yet all this was done with computers which had no more circuits than the brain of an ant. The human brain far exceeded that complexity, and the programming of the human brain extended over many decades. How could anyone seriously expect to understand it?

There was also a philosophical problem. Goedel's Theorem: that no system could explain itself, and no machine could understand its own workings. At most, Gerhard believed that a human brain might, after years of work, decipher a frog brain. But a human brain could never decipher itself in the same detail. For that you would need a superhuman brain.

Gerhard thought that someday a computer would be developed that could untangle the billions of cells and hundreds of billions of interconnections in the human brain. Then, at last, man would have the information that he wanted. But man wouldn't have done the work—another order of intelligence would have done it. And man would not know, of course, how the computer worked.

Morris entered the room with a cup of coffee. He sipped it, and glanced at Benson through the glass. "How's he holding up?"

"Okay," Gerhard said.

"Electrode six, five and five," Richards intoned.

In the next room, Benson failed to react. He sat talking with Ross about the operation, and his lingering headache. He was quite calm and apparently unaffected. They repeated the stimulation, still without change in Benson's behavior. Then they went on.

"Electrode seven, five and five," Richards said. He delivered the shock.

Benson sat up abruptly. "Oh," he said, "that was nice."

"What was?" Ross said.

"You can do that again if you want to."

"How does it feel?"

"Nice," Benson said. His whole appearance seemed to change subtly. "You know," he said after a moment, "you're really a wonderful person, Dr. Ross."

"Thank you," she said.

"Very attractive, too. I don't know if I ever told you before."

"How do you feel now?"

"I'm really very fond of you," Benson said. "I don't know if I told you that before."

"Nice," Gerhard said, watching through the glass. "Very nice."

Morris nodded. "A strong P-terminal. He's clearly turned on."

Gerhard made a note of it. Morris sipped his coffee. They waited until Benson settled down. Then, blandly, Richards said, "Electrode eight, five millivolts, five seconds."

The stimulation series continued.

2

At noon, McPherson showed up for interfacing. No one was surprised to see him. In a sense, this was the irrevocable step; everything preceding it was unimportant. They had implanted electrodes and a computer and a power pack, and they had hooked everything up. But nothing functioned until the interfacing switches were thrown. It was a little like building an automobile and then finally turning the ignition.

Gerhard showed him notes from the stimulation series. "At five millivolts on a pulse-form stimulus, we have three positive terminals and two negatives. The positives are seven, nine, and thirty-one. The negatives are five and thirty-two."

McPherson glanced at the notes, then looked

through the one-way glass at Benson. "Are any of the positives true P's?"

"Seven seems to be."

"Strong?"

"Pretty strong. When we stimulated him, he said he liked it, and he began to act sexually aroused toward Jan."

"Is it too strong? Will it tip him over?"

Gerhard shook his head. "No," he said. "Not unless he were to receive multiple stimulations over a short time course. There was that Norwegian . . ."

"I don't think we have to worry about that," McPherson said. "We've got Benson in the hospital for the next few days. If anything seems to be going wrong, we can switch to other electrodes. We'll just keep track of him for a while. What about nine?"

"Very weak. Equivocal, really."

"How did he respond?"

"There was a subtle increase in spontaneity, more tendency to smile, to tell happy and positive anecdotes."

McPherson seemed unimpressed. "And thirty-one?"

"Clear tranquilizing effect. Calmness, relaxation, happiness."

McPherson rubbed his hands together. "I guess we can get on with it," he said. He looked once through the glass at Benson, and said, "Interface the patient with seven and thirty-one."

McPherson was clearly feeling a sense of high

drama and medical history. But Gerhard wasn't; he got off his stool in a straightforward, almost bored way and walked to a corner of the room where there was a computer console mounted beneath a TV screen. He began to touch the buttons. The TV screen glowed to life. After a moment, letters appeared on it.

> BENSON, H. F.
> INTERFACING PROCEDURE
> POSSIBLE ELECTRODES: 40, designated serially
> POSSIBLE VOLTAGES: continuous
> POSSIBLE DURATIONS: continuous
> POSSIBLE WAVE FORMS: pulse only

Gerhard pressed a button and the screen went blank. Then a series of questions appeared, to which Gerhard typed out the answers on the console.

> INTERFACE PROCEDURES BENSON, H. F.
> 1. WHICH ELECTRODES WILL BE ACTIVATED?
>
>   7, 31 only
>
> 2. WHAT VOLTAGE WILL BE APPLIED TO ELECTRODE SEVEN?
>
>   5 mv
>
> 3. WHAT DURATION WILL BE APPLIED TO ELECTRODE SEVEN?
>
>   5 sec

There was a pause, and the questions continued for electrode 31. Gerhard typed in the answers. Watching him, McPherson said to Morris, "This is amusing, in a way. We're telling the tiny computer how to work. The little computer gets its instructions from the big computer, which gets its instructions from Gerhard, who has a bigger computer than any of them."

"Maybe," Gerhard said, and laughed.

The screen glowed:

> INTERFACING PARAMETERS STORED. READY
> TO PROGRAM AUXILIARY UNIT.

Morris sighed. He hoped that he would never reach the point in his life when he was referred to by a computer as an "auxiliary unit." Gerhard typed quietly, a soft clicking sound. On the other TV screens, they could see the inner circuitry of the small computer. It glowed intermittently as the wiring locked in.

> BENSON HF HAS BEEN INTERFACED.
> IMPLANTED DEVICE NOW READING
> EEG DATA AND DELIVERING APPROPRIATE
> FEEDBACK.

That was all there was to it. Somehow Morris was disappointed; he knew it would be this way, but he had expected—or needed—something more dramatic. Gerhard ran a systems check which came back negative. The screen went blank and then came through with a final message:

> UNIVERSITY HOSPITAL SYSTEM 360
> COMPUTER THANKS YOU FOR REFERRING
> THIS INTERESTING PATIENT FOR
> THERAPY.

Gerhard smiled. In the next room, Benson was still talking quietly with Ross. Neither of them seemed to have noticed anything different at all.

3

Janet Ross finished the stimulation series profoundly depressed. She stood in the corridor watching as Benson was wheeled away. She had a last glimpse of the white bandages around his neck as the nurse turned the corner; then he was gone.

She walked down the hallway in the other direction, through the multicolored NPS doors. For some reason, she found herself thinking about Arthur's yellow Ferrari. It was so marvelous and elegant and irrelevant to anything. The perfect toy. She wished she were in Monte Carlo, stepping out of Arthur's Ferrari wearing her Balenciaga gown, going up the stairs to the casino to gamble with nothing more important than money.

She looked at her watch. Christ, it was only 12:15. She had half the day ahead of her. What was it like to be a pediatrician? Probably fun. Tickling babies and giving shots and advising mothers on toilet training. Not a bad way to live.

She thought again of the bandages on Benson's shoulder, and went into Telecomp. She had hoped to speak to Gerhard alone, but instead everyone was in the room—McPherson, Morris, Ellis, everyone. They were all jubilant, toasting each other with coffee in Styrofoam cups.

Someone thrust a cup into her hands, and McPherson put his arm around her in a fatherly way. "I gather we turned Benson on to you today."

"Yes, you did," she said, managing to smile.

"Well, I guess you're used to that."

"Not exactly," she said.

The room got quieter, the festive feeling slid away. She felt bad about that, but not really. There was nothing amusing about shocking a person into sexual arousal. It was physiologically interesting, was frightening and pathetic, but not funny. Why did they all find it so goddamned funny?

Ellis produced a hip flask and poured clear liquid into her coffee. "Makes it Irish," he said, with a wink. "Much better."

She nodded, and glanced across the room at Gerhard.

"Drink up, drink up," Ellis said.

Gerhard was talking to Morris about something. It seemed a very intent conversation; then she heard Morris say, ". . . you please pass the pussy?" Gerhard laughed; Morris laughed. It was some kind of joke.

"Not bad, considering," Ellis said. "What do you think?"

"Very good," she said, taking a small sip. She managed to get away from Ellis and McPherson and went over to Gerhard. He was momentarily alone; Morris had gone off to refill his cup.

"Listen," she said, "can I talk to you for a second?"

"Sure," Gerhard said. He bent his head closer to hers. "What is it?"

"I want to know something. Is it possible for you to monitor Benson here, on the main computer?"

"You mean monitor the implanted unit?"

"Yes."

Gerhard shrugged. "I guess so, but why bother? We know the implanted unit is working—"

"I know," she said. "I know. But will you do it anyway, as a precaution?"

Gerhard said nothing. His eyes said: Precaution against what?

"Please?"

"Okay," he said. "I'll punch in a monitoring subroutine as soon as they leave." He nodded to the group. "I'll have the computer check on him twice an hour."

She frowned.

"Four times an hour?"

"How about every ten minutes?" she said.

"Okay," he said. "Every ten minutes."

"Thanks," she said. Then she drained her coffee, feeling the warmth hit her stomach, and she left the room.

4

Ellis sat in a corner of Room 710 and watched the half-dozen technicians maneuvering around the bed. There were two people from the rad lab doing a radiation check; there was one girl drawing blood for the chem lab, to check steroid levels; there was an EEG technician re-setting the monitors; and there were Gerhard and Richards, taking a final look at the interface wiring.

Throughout it all, Benson lay motionless, breathing easily, staring up at the ceiling. He did not seem to notice the people touching him, moving an arm here, shifting a sheet there. He stared straight up at the ceiling.

One of the rad-lab men had hairy hands protruding from the cuffs of his white lab coat. For a moment, the man rested his hairy dark hand on Benson's bandages. Ellis thought about the monkeys he had operated on. There was nothing to that except technical expertise, because you always knew—no matter how hard you pretended —that it was a monkey and not a human being, and if you slipped and cut the monkey from ear to ear, it didn't matter at all. There would be no questions, no relatives, no lawyers, no press, no nothing—not even a nasty note from Requisitions asking what was happening to all those eighty-dollar monkeys. Nobody gave a damn. And neither did he. He wasn't interested in helping monkeys. He was interested in helping human beings.

Benson stirred. "I'm tired," he said. He glanced over at Ellis.

Ellis said, "About ready to wrap it up, boys?"

One by one, the technicians stepped back from the bed, nodding, collected their instruments and their data, and left the room. Gerhard and Richards were the last to go. Finally Ellis was alone with Benson.

"You feel like sleeping?" Ellis said.

"I feel like a goddamned machine. I feel like an automobile in a complicated service station. I feel like I'm being *repaired*."

Benson was getting angry. Ellis could feel his own tension building. He was tempted to call for nurses and orderlies to restrain Benson when the attack came. But he remained seated.

"That's a lot of crap," Ellis said.

Benson glared at him, breathing deeply.

Ellis looked at the monitors over the bed. The brain waves were going irregular, moving into an attack configuration.

Benson wrinkled his nose and sniffed. "What's that smell?" he said. "That awful—"

Above the bed, a red monitor light blinked STIMULATION. The brain waves spun in a distorted tangle of white lines for five seconds. Simultaneously, Benson's pupils dilated. Then the lines were smooth again; the pupils returned to normal size.

Benson turned away, staring out the window at the afternoon sun. "You know," he said, "it's really a very nice day, isn't it?"

5

For no particular reason, Janet Ross came back to the hospital at 11 p.m. She had gone to see a movie with a pathology resident who had been asking her for weeks; finally she had relented. They had seen a murder mystery, which the resident claimed was the only kind of movie he attended. This one featured five murders before she stopped counting them. In the darkness, she had glanced at the resident, and he was smiling. His reaction was so stereotyped—the pathologist drawn to violence and death—that she found herself thinking of the other stereotypes in medicine: the sadistic surgeons and the childish pediatricians and the woman-hating gynecologists. And the crazy psychiatrists.

Afterward, he had driven her back to the hospital because she had left her car in the hospital parking lot. But instead of driving home she had gone up to the NPS. For no particular reason.

The NPS was deserted, but she expected to find Gerhard and Richards at work, and they were, poring over computer print-outs in Telecomp.

They hardly noticed when she came into the room and got herself some coffee. "Trouble?" she said.

Gerhard scratched his head. "Now it's Martha," he said. "First George refuses to be a saint. Now Martha is becoming nice. Everything's screwed up."

Richards smiled. "You have your patients, Jan," he said, "and we have ours."

"Speaking of my patient . . ."

"Of course," Gerhard said, getting up and walking over to the computer console. "I was wondering why you came in." He smiled. "Or was it just a bad date?"

"Just a bad movie," she said.

Gerhard punched buttons on the console. Letters and numbers began to print out. "Here's all the checks since I started it at one-twelve this afternoon."

01:12	NORMAL EEG		04:02	NORMAL EEG
01:22	NORMAL EEG		04:12	NORMAL EEG
01:32	SLEEP EEG		04:22	NORMAL EEG
01:42	SLEEP EEG		04:32	SLEEP EEG
01:52	NORMAL EEG		04:42	NORMAL EEG
02:02	NORMAL EEG		04:52	NORMAL EEG
02:12	NORMAL EEG		05:02	SLEEP EEG
02:22	NORMAL EEG		05:12	NORMAL EEG
02:32	SLEEP EEG		05:22	NORMAL EEG
02:42	NORMAL EEG		05:32	SLEEP EEG
02:52	NORMAL EEG		05:42	NORMAL EEG
03:02	NORMAL EEG		05:52	NORMAL EEG
03:12	SLEEP EEG		06:02	NORMAL EEG
03:22	SLEEP EEG		06:12	NORMAL EEG
03:32	STIMULATION		06:22	NORMAL EEG
03:42	NORMAL EEG		06:32	NORMAL EEG
03:52	SLEEP EEG		06:42	NORMAL EEG

06:52	STIMULATION	09:02	STIMULATION
07:02	NORMAL EEG	09:12	SLEEP EEG
07:12	NORMAL EEG	09:22	NORMAL EEG
07:22	SLEEP EEG	09:32	NORMAL EEG
07:32	SLEEP EEG	09:42	NORMAL EEG
07:42	SLEEP EEG	09:52	NORMAL EEG
07:52	NORMAL EEG	10:02	NORMAL EEG
08:02	NORMAL EEG	10:12	NORMAL EEG
08:12	NORMAL EEG	10:22	NORMAL EEG
08:22	SLEEP EEG	10:32	STIMULATION
08:32	NORMAL EEG	10:42	SLEEP EEG
08:42	NORMAL EEG	10:52	NORMAL EEG
08:52	NORMAL EEG	11:02	NORMAL EEG

"I can't make anything out of this," Ross said, frowning. "It looks like he's dozing on and off, and he's gotten a couple of stimulations, but . . ." She shook her head. "Isn't there another display mode?"

As she spoke, the computer produced another report, adding it to the column of numbers:

11:12   NORMAL EEG

"People," Gerhard said, in mock irritation. "They just can't handle machine data." It was true. Machines could handle column after column of numbers. People needed to see patterns. On the other hand, machines were very poor at recognizing patterns. The classic problem was trying to get a machine to differentiate between the letter "B" and the letter "D." A child could do it; it was almost impossible for a machine to look at the two patterns and discern the difference.

"I'll give you a graphic display," Gerhard said. He punched buttons, wiping the screen. After a

137

moment, cross-hatching for a graph appeared, and the points began to blink on:

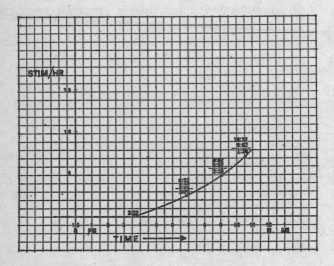

"Damn," she said when she saw the graph.

"What's the matter?" Gerhard said.

"He's getting more frequent stimulations. He had none for a long time, and then he began to have them every couple of hours. Now it looks like one an hour."

"So?" Gerhard said.

"What does that suggest to you?" she said.

"Nothing in particular."

"It should suggest something quite specific,"

she said. "We know that Benson's brain will be interacting with the computer, right?"

"Yes . . ."

"And that interaction will be a learning pattern of some kind. It's just like a kid with a cookie jar. If you slap the kid's hand every time he reaches for the cookies, pretty soon he won't reach so often. Look." She drew a quick sketch.

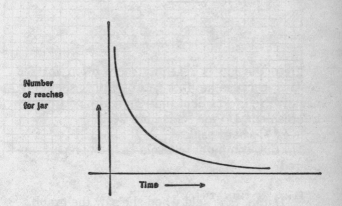

"Now," she said, "that's negative reinforcement. The kid reaches, but he gets hurt. So he stops reaching. Eventually he'll quit altogether. Okay?"

"Sure," Gerhard said, "but—"

"Let me finish. If the kid is normal, it works that way. But if the kid is a masochist, it will be very different." She drew another curve.

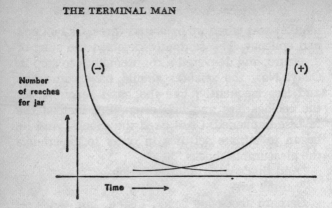

"Here the kid is reaching more often for the cookies, because he likes getting hit. It should be negative reinforcement, but it's really positive reinforcement. Do you remember Cecil?"

"No," Gerhard said.

On the computer console, a new report appeared:

11:22 STIMULATION

"Oh shit," she said. "It's happening."

"What's happening?"

"Benson is going into a positive progression cycle."

"I don't understand."

"It's just like Cecil. Cecil was the first monkey to be wired with electrodes to a computer. That was back in '65. The computer wasn't miniaturized then; it was a big clunky computer, and the

140

monkey was wired up by actual wires. Okay. Cecil had epilepsy. The computer detected the start of a seizure, and delivered a counter-shock to stop it. Okay. Now the seizures should have come less and less frequently, like the hand reaching for the cookies less and less often. But instead the reverse happened. Cecil *liked* the shocks. And he began to initiate seizures in order to experience the pleasurable shocks."

"And that's what Benson is doing?"

"I think so."

Gerhard shook his head. "Listen, Jan, that's all interesting. But a person can't start and stop epileptic seizures at will. They can't control it. The seizures are—"

"Involuntary," she said. "That's right. You have no more control over them than you do over heart rate and blood pressure and sweating and all the other involuntary acts."

There was a long pause. Gerhard said, "You're going to tell me I'm wrong."

On the screen, the computer blinked:

11:32 - - - - - - -

"I'm going to tell you," she said, "that you've cut too many conferences. You know about autonomic learning?"

After a guilty pause: "No."

"It was a big mystery for a long time. Classically, it was believed that you could learn to control only voluntary acts. You could learn to drive a car, but you couldn't learn to lower your blood

141

pressure. Of course, there were those yogis who supposedly could reduce oxygen requirements of their body and slow their heartbeats to near death. They could reverse intestinal peristalsis and drink liquids through the anus. But that was all unproven—and theoretically impossible."

Gerhard nodded cautiously.

"Well, it turns out to be perfectly possible. You can teach a rat to blush in only one ear. Right ear or left ear, take your pick. You can teach it to lower or raise blood pressure or heartbeat. And you can do the same thing with people. It's not impossible. It can be done."

"How?" He asked the question with unabashed curiosity. Whatever embarrassment he had felt before was gone.

"Well, with people who have high blood pressure, for instance, all you do is put them in a room with a blood-pressure cuff on their arm. Whenever the blood pressure goes down, a bell rings. You tell the person to try to make the bell ring as often as possible. They work for that reward—a bell ringing. At first it happens by accident. Then pretty soon they learn how to make it happen more often. The bell rings more frequently. After a few hours, it's ringing a lot."

Gerhard scratched his head. "And you think Benson is producing more seizures to be rewarded with shocks?"

"Yes."

"Well, what's the difference? He still can't have any seizures. The computer always prevents them from happening."

"Not true," she said. "A couple of years ago, a Norwegian schizophrenic was wired up and allowed to stimulate a pleasure terminal as often as he wanted. He pushed himself into a convulsion by overstimulating himself."

Gerhard winced.

Richards, who had been watching the computer console, suddenly said, "Something's wrong."

"What is it?"

"We're not getting readings any more."

On the screen, they saw:

```
11:32  ———————
11:42  ———————
```

Ross looked and sighed. "See if you can get a computer extrapolation of that curve," she said. "See if he's really going into a learning cycle, and how fast." She started for the door. "I'm going to see what's happened to Benson."

The door slammed shut. Gerhard turned back to the computer.

FRIDAY,
MARCH 12, 1971:
BREAKDOWN

1

The seventh (Special Surgical) floor was quiet; there were two nurses at the station. One was making progress notes in a patient's chart; the other was eating a candy bar and reading a movie magazine. Neither paid much attention to Ross as she went to the chart shelf, opened Benson's record, and checked it.

She wanted to be certain that Benson had received all his medications, and to her astonishment she found that he had not. "Why hasn't Benson gotten his thorazine?" she demanded.

The nurses looked up in surprise. "Benson?"

"The patient in seven-ten." She glanced at her watch; it was after midnight. "He was supposed to be started on thorazine at noon. Twelve hours ago."

"I'm sorry . . . may I?" One of the nurses reached for the chart. Ross handed it to her and watched while she turned to the page of nursing orders. McPherson's order for thorazine was circled in red by a nurse, with the cryptic notation "Call."

Ross was thinking that without heavy doses of thorazine Benson's psychotic thinking would be unchecked, and could be dangerous.

"Oh, yes," the nurse said. "I remember now. Dr. Morris told us that only medication orders from him or from Dr. Ross were to be followed. We don't know this Dr. McPhee, so we waited to call him to confirm the therapy. It—"

"Dr. Mc*Pherson*," Ross said heavily, "is the chief of the NPS."

The nurse frowned at the signature. "Well, how are we supposed to know that? You can't read the name. Here." She handed back the chart. "We thought it looked like McPhee, and the only McPhee in the hospital directory is a gynecologist and that didn't seem logical, but sometimes doctors will put a note in the wrong chart by mistake, so we—"

"All right," Ross said, waving her hand. "All right. Just get him his thorazine now, will you?"

"Right away, Doctor," the nurse said. She gave her a dirty look and went to the medicine locker. Ross went down the hall to Room 710.

The cop sat outside Benson's room with his chair tipped back against the wall. He was reading *Secret Romances* with more interest than Janet would have thought likely. She knew without asking where he had gotten the magazine; he had been bored, one of the nurses had given it to him. He was also smoking a cigarette, flicking the ashes in the general direction of an ashtray on the floor.

He looked up as she came down the hall. "Good evening, Doctor."

"Good evening." She stifled an impulse to lecture him on his sloppy demeanor. But the cops weren't under her jurisdiction, and besides, she was just irritated with the nurses. "Everything quiet?" she asked.

"Pretty quiet."

Inside 710 she could hear television, a talk show with laughter. Someone said, "And what did you do then?" There was more laughter. She opened the door.

The room lights were off; the only light came from the glow of the television. Benson had apparently fallen asleep; his body was turned away from the door, and the sheets were pulled up over his shoulder. She clicked the television off and crossed the room to the bed. Gently, she touched his leg.

"Harry," she said softly. "Harry—"

She stopped.

The leg beneath her hand was soft and formless. She pressed down; the "leg" bulged oddly. She reached for the bedside lamp and turned it on, flooding the room with light. Then she pulled back the sheets.

Benson was gone. In his place were three plastic bags of the kind the hospital used to line wastebaskets. Each had been inflated and then knotted shut tightly. Benson's head was represented by a wadded towel; his arm by another.

"Officer," she said, in a low voice, "you'd better get your ass in her."

The cop came bounding into the room, his

149

hand reaching for his gun. Ross gestured to the bed.

"Holy shit," the cop said. "What happened?"

"I was going to ask you."

The cop didn't reply. He went immediately to the bathroom and checked there; it was empty. He looked in the closet. "His clothes are still here—"

"When was the last time you looked into this room?"

"—but his shoes are gone," the cop said, still looking in the closet. "His shoes are missing." He turned and looked at Ross with a kind of desperation. "Where is he?"

"When was the last time you looked into this room?" Ross repeated. She pressed the bedside buzzer to call the night nurse.

"About twenty minutes ago."

Ross walked to the window and looked out. The window was open, but there was a sheer drop of seven stories to the parking lot below. "How long were you away from the door?"

"Look, Doc, it was only a few minutes—"

"How long?"

"I ran out of cigarettes. The hospital doesn't have any machines. I had to go to that coffee shop across the street. I was gone about three minutes. That was around eleven-thirty. The nurses said they'd keep an eye on things."

"Great," Ross said. She checked the bedside table and saw that Benson's shaving equipment was there, his wallet, his car keys . . . all there.

The nurse stuck her head in the door, answering the call. "What is it now?"

"We seem to be missing a patient," Ross said.

"I beg your pardon?"

Ross gestured to the plastic bags in the bed. The nurse reacted slowly, and then turned quite pale.

"Call Dr. Ellis," Ross said, "and Dr. McPherson and Dr. Morris. They'll be at home; have the switchboard put you through. Say it's an emergency. Tell them Benson is gone. Then call hospital security. Is that clear?"

"Yes, Doctor," the nurse said, and hurried from the room.

Ross sat down on the edge of Benson's bed and turned her attention to the cop.

"Where did he get those bags?" the cop said.

She had already figured that out. "One from the bedside wastebasket," she said. "One from the wastebasket by the door. One from the bathroom wastebasket. Two towels from the bathroom."

"Clever," the cop said. He pointed to the closet. "But he can't get far. He left his clothes."

"Took his shoes."

"A man with bandages and a bathrobe can't get far, even if he has shoes." He shook his head. "I better call this in."

"Did Benson make any calls?"

"Tonight?"

"No, last month."

"Look, lady, I don't need any of your lip right now."

She saw then that he was really quite young, in his early twenties, and she saw that he was afraid. He had screwed up, and he didn't know what would happen. "I'm sorry," she said. "Yes, tonight."

"He made one call," the cop said. "About eleven."

"Did you listen to it?"

"No." He shrugged. "I never thought . . ." His voice trailed off. "You know."

"So he made one call at eleven, and left at eleven-thirty." She walked outside to the hallway and looked down the corridor to the nurses' station. There was always somebody on duty there, and he would have to pass the nurses' station to reach the elevator. He'd never make it.

What else could he have done? She looked toward the other end of the hall. There was a stairway at the far end. He could walk down. But seven flights of stairs? Benson was too weak for that. And when he got to the ground-floor lobby, there he'd be, in his bathrobe with his head bandaged. The reception desk would stop him.

"I don't get it," the cop said, coming out into the hallway. "Where could he go?"

"He's a very bright man," Ross said. It was a fact that they all tended to forget. To the cops, Benson was a criminal charged with assault, one of the hundreds of querulous types they saw each day. To the hospital staff, he was a diseased man, unhappy, dangerous, borderline psychotic. Everyone tended to forget that Benson was also brilliant. His computer work was outstanding in a field where many intelligent men worked. On the initial psychological testing at the NPS, his abbreviated WAIS I.Q. test had scored 144. He was fully capable of planning to leave, then listening at the door, hearing the cop and the nurse discuss going for cigarettes—and then making his escape in a matter of minutes. But how?

Benson must have known that he could never get out of the hospital in his bathrobe. He had left his street clothes in his room—he probably couldn't get out wearing those, either. Not at midnight. The lobby desk would have stopped him. Visiting hours had ended three hours before.

What the hell would he do?

The cop went up to the nurses' station to phone in a report. Ross followed along behind him, looking at the doors. Room 709 was a burns patient; she opened the door and looked inside, making sure only the patient was there. Room 708 was empty; a kidney-transplant patient had been discharged that afternoon. She checked that room, too.

The next door was marked SUPPLIES. It was a standard room on surgical floors. Bandages, suture kits, and linen supplies were stored there. She opened the door and went inside. She passed row after row of bottled intravenous solutions; then trays of different kits. Then sterile masks, smocks, spare uniforms for nurses and orderlies—

She stopped. She was staring at a blue bathrobe, hastily wadded into a corner on a shelf. The rest of the shelf contained neatly folded piles of white trousers, shirts, and jackets worn by hospital orderlies.

She called for the nurse.

"It's impossible," Ellis said, pacing up and down in the nurses' station. "Absolutely impossible. He's two days—a day and a half—post-op. He couldn't possibly leave."

"He did," Janet Ross said. "And he did it the only way he could, by changing into an orderly's uniform. Then he probably walked downstairs to the sixth floor and took an elevator to the lobby. Nobody would have noticed him; orderlies come and go at all hours."

Ellis wore a dinner jacket and a white frilly shirt; his bow tie was loosened and he was smoking a cigarette. She had never seen him smoke before. "I still don't buy it," he said. "He was tranked out of his skull with thorazine, and—"

"Never got it," Ross said.

"Never got it?"

"What's thorazine?" the cop said, taking notes.

"The nurses had a question on the order and didn't administer it. He had no sedatives and no tranquilizers since midnight last night."

"Christ," Ellis said. He looked at the nurses as if he could kill them. Then he paused. "But what about his head? It was covered with bandages. Someone would notice that."

Morris, who had been sitting silently in a corner, said, "He had a wig."

"You're kidding."

"I saw it," Morris said.

"What was the color of the wig in question?" the cop said.

"Black," Morris said.

"Oh Christ," Ellis said.

Ross said, "How did he get this wig?"

"A friend brought it to him. The day of admission."

"Listen," Ellis said, "even with a wig, he can't have gotten anywhere. He left his wallet and his money. There are no taxis at this hour."

She looked at Ellis, marveling at his ability to deny reality. He just didn't want to believe that Benson had left; he was fighting the evidence, fighting hard.

"He called a friend," Ross said, "about eleven." She looked at Morris. "You remember who brought the wig?"

"A pretty girl," Morris said.

"Do you remember her name?" Ross said, with a sarcastic edge.

"Angela Black," Morris said promptly.

"See if you can find her in the phone book," Ross said. Morris began to check; the phone rang, and Ellis answered it. He listened, then without comment handed the phone to Ross.

"Yes," Ross said.

"I've done the computer projection." Gerhard said. "It just came through. You were right. Benson is on a learning cycle with his implanted computer. His stimulation points conform to the projected curve exactly."

"That's wonderful," Ross said. As she listened, she glanced at Ellis, Morris, and the cop. They watched her expectantly.

"It's exactly what you said," Gerhard said. "Benson apparently likes the shocks. He's starting seizures more and more often. The curve is going up sharply.

"When will he tip over?"

"Not long," Gerhard said. "Assuming that he doesn't break the cycle—and I doubt that he will —then he'll be getting almost continuous stimulations at six-four a.m."

"You have a confirmed projection on that?" she asked, frowning. She glanced at her watch. It was already 12:30.

"That's right," Gerhard said. "Continuous stimulations starting at six-four this morning."

"Okay," Ross said, and hung up. She looked at the others. "Benson has gone into a learning progression with his computer. He's projected for tip-over at six a.m. today."

"Christ," Ellis said, looking at the wall clock. "Less than six hours from now."

Across the room, Morris had put aside the phone books and was talking to Information. "Then try West Los Angeles," he said, and after a pause, "What about new listings?"

The cop stopped taking notes, and looked confused. "Is something going to happen at six o'clock?"

"We think so," Ross said.

Ellis puffed on his cigarette. "Two years," he

said, "and I'm back on them." He stubbed it out carefully. "Has McPherson been notified?"

"He's been called."

"Check unlisted numbers," Morris said. He listened for a moment. "This is Dr. Morris at University Hospital," he said, "and it's an emergency. We have to locate Angela Black. Now, if—" Angrily, he slammed down the phone. "Bitch," he said.

"Any luck?"

He shook his head.

"We don't even know if Benson called this girl," Ellis said. "He could have called someone else."

"Whoever he called may be in a lot of trouble in a few hours," Ross said. She flipped open Benson's chart. "It looks like a long night. We'd better get busy."

2

The freeway was crowded. The freeway was always crowded, even at 1 a.m. on a Friday morning. She stared ahead at the pattern of red tail-lights, stretching ahead like an angry snake for miles. So many people. Where were they going at this hour?

Janet Ross usually took pleasure in the freeways. There had been times when she had driven

157

home from the hospital at night, with the big green signs flashing past overhead, and the intricate web of overpasses and underpasses, and the exhilarating anonymous speed, and she had felt wonderful, expansive, free. She had been raised in California, and as a child she remembered the first of the freeways. The system had grown up as she had grown, and she did not see it as a menace or an evil. It was part of the landscape; it was fast; it was fun.

The automobile was important to Los Angeles, a city more technology-dependent than any in the world. Los Angeles could not survive without the automobile, as it could not survive without water piped in from hundreds of miles away, and as it could not survive without certain building technologies. This was a fact of the city's existence, and had been true since early in the century.

But in recent years Ross had begun to recognize the subtle psychological effects of living your life inside an automobile. Los Angeles had no sidewalk cafés, because no one walked; the sidewalk café, where you could stare at passing people, was not stationary but mobile. It changed with each traffic light, where people stopped, stared briefly at each other, then drove on. But there was something inhuman about living inside a cocoon of tinted glass and stainless steel, air-conditioned, carpeted, stereophonic tape-decked, power-optioned, isolated. It thwarted some deep human need to congregate, to be together, to see and be seen.

Local psychiatrists recognized an indigenous depersonalization syndrome. Los Angeles was a town of recent emigrants and therefore strangers; cars kept them strangers, and there were few institutions that served to bring them together. Practically no one went to church, and work groups were not entirely satisfactory. People became lonely; they complained of being cut off, without friends, far from families and old homes. Often they became suicidal—and a common method of suicide was the automobile. The police referred to it euphemistically as "single unit fatalities." You picked your overpass, and hit it at eighty or ninety, foot flat to the floor. Sometimes it took hours to cut the body out of the wreckage. . . .

Moving at sixty-five miles an hour, she shifted across five lanes of traffic and pulled off the freeway at Sunset, heading up into the Hollywood Hills, through an area known locally as the Swish Alps because of the many homosexuals who lived there. People with problems seemed drawn to Los Angeles. The city offered freedom; its price was lack of supports.

She came to Laurel Canyon and took the curves fast, tires squealing, headlamps swinging through the darkness. There was little traffic here; she would reach Benson's house in a few minutes.

In theory, she and the rest of the NPS staff had a simple problem: get Benson back before six o'clock. If they could get him back into the hospital, they could uncouple his implanted computer and stop the progression series. Then they could sedate him and wait a few days before relinking him to a new set of terminals. They'd obviously chosen the wrong electrodes the first time around; that was a risk they accepted in advance. It was an acceptable risk because they expected to have a chance to correct any error. But that opportunity was no longer there.

They had to get him back. A simple problem, with a relatively simple solution—check Benson's known haunts. After reviewing his chart, they'd all set out to different places. Ross was going to his house on Laurel. Ellis was going to a strip joint called the Jackrabbit Club, where Benson often went. Morris was going to Autotronics, Inc., in Santa Monica, where Benson was employed; Morris had called the president of the firm, who was coming to the offices to open them up for him.

They would check back in an hour or so to compare notes and progress. A simple plan, and one she thought unlikely to work. But there wasn't much else to do.

She parked her car in front of Benson's house and walked up the slate path to the front door. It was ajar; from inside she could hear the sound of laughter and giggles. She knocked and pushed it open.

"Hello?"

No one seemed to hear. The giggles came from somewhere at the back of the house. She stepped into the front hallway. She had never seen Benson's house, and she wondered what it was like.

Looking around, she realized she should have known.

From the outside, the house was an ordinary wood-frame structure, a ranch-style house as unobtrusive in its appearance as Benson himself. But the inside looked like the drawing rooms of Louis XVI—graceful antique chairs and couches, tapestries on the walls, bare hardwood floors.

"Anybody home?" she called. Her voice echoed through the house. There was no answer, but the laughter continued. She followed the sound toward the rear. She came into the kitchen—antique gas stove, no oven, no dishwasher, no electric blender, no toaster. No machines, she thought. Benson had built himself a world without any sort of modern machine in it.

The kitchen window looked out onto the back of the house. There was a small patch of lawn and a swimming pool, all perfectly ordinary and modern, Benson's ordinary exterior again. The back yard was bathed in greenish light from the underwater pool lights. In the pool, two girls were laughing and splashing. She went outside.

The girls were oblivious to her arrival. They continued to splash and shriek happily; they wrestled with each other in the water. She stood on the pool deck and said, "Anybody home?"

They noticed her then, and moved apart from each other. "Looking for Harry?" one of them said.

"Yes."

"You a cop?"

"I'm a doctor."

One of the girls got out of the pool lithely and began toweling off. She wore a brief red bikini. "You just missed him," the girl said. "But we weren't supposed to tell the cops. That's what he said." She put one leg on a chair to dry it with the towel. Ross realized the move was calculated, seductive, and demonstrative. These girls liked girls, she realized.

"When did he leave?"

"Just a few minutes ago."

"How long have you been here?"

"About a week," the girl in the pool said. "Harry invited us to stay. He thought we were cute."

The other girl wrapped the towel around her shoulders and said, "We met him at the Jackrabbit. He comes there a lot."

Ross nodded.

"He's a lot of fun," the girl said. "A lot of laughs. You know what he was wearing tonight?"

"What?"

"A hospital uniform. All white." She shook her head. "What a riot."

"Did you talk to him?"

"Sure."

"What did he say?"

The girl in the red bikini started back inside the house. Ross followed her. "He said not to tell the cops. He said to have a good time."

"Why did he come here?"

"He had to pick up some stuff."

"What stuff?"

"Some stuff from his study."

162

"Where is the study?"

"I'll show you."

She led her back into the house, through the living room. Her wet feet left small pools on the bare hardwood floor. "Isn't this place wild? Harry's really crazy. You ever heard him talk about things?"

"Yes."

"Then you know. He's really nutty." She gestured around the room. "All this old stuff. Why do you want to see him?"

"He's sick," Ross said.

"He must be," the girl said. "I saw those bandages. What was he, in an accident?"

"He had an operation."

"No kidding. In a hospital?"

"Yes."

"No kidding."

They went through the living room and down a corridor toward the bedrooms. The girl turned right into one room, which was a study—antique desk, antique lamps, overstuffed couches. "He came in here and got some stuff."

"Did you see what he got?"

"We didn't really pay much attention. But he took some big rolls of paper." She gestured with her hands. "Real big. They looked like blueprints or something."

"Blueprints?"

"Well, they were blue on the inside of the roll, and white on the outside, and they were big." She shrugged.

"Did he take anything else?"

"Yeah. A metal box."

"What kind of a metal box?" Ross was thinking of a lunchbox, or a small suitcase.

"It looked like a tool kit, maybe. I saw it open for a moment, before he closed it. It seemed to have tools and stuff inside."

"Did you notice anything in particular?"

The girl was silent then. She bit her lip. "Well, I didn't really see, but . . ."

"Yes?"

"It looked like he had a gun in there."

"Did he say where he was going?"

"No."

"Did he give any clue?"

"No."

"Did he say he was coming back?"

"Well, that was funny," the girl said. "He kissed me, and he kissed Suzie, and he said to have a good time, and he said not to tell the cops. And he said he didn't think he'd be seeing us again." She shook her head. "It was funny. But you know how Harry is."

"Yes," Ross said. "I know how Harry is." She looked at her watch. it was 1:47. There were only four hours left.

3

The first thing that Ellis noticed was the smell: hot, damp, fetid—a dark warm animal smell. He wrinkled his nose in distaste. How could Benson tolerate a place like this?

He watched as the spotlight swung through the darkness and came to rest on a pair of long tapering thighs. There was an expectant rustling in the audience. It reminded Ellis of his days in the Navy, stationed in Baltimore. That was the last time he had been in a place like this, hot and sticky with fantasies and frustrations. That had been a long time ago. It was a shock to think how fast the time had passed.

"Yes, ladies and gentlemen, the incredible, the lovely, *Cynthia Sin*-cere. A big hand for the lovely *Cynthia!*"

The spotlight widened onstage, to show a rather ugly but spectacularly constructed girl. The band began to play. When the spotlight was wide enough to hit Cynthia's eyes, she squinted and began an awkward dance. She paid no attention to the music, but nobody seemed to mind. Ellis looked at the audience. There were a lot of men here—and a lot of very tough-looking girls with short hair.

"Harry Benson?" the manager said, at his elbow. "Yeah, he comes in a lot."

"Have you seen him lately?"

"I don't know about lately," the manager said. He coughed. Ellis smelled sweet alcoholic breath. "But I tell you," the manager said, "I wish he wouldn't hang around, you know? I think he's a little nuts. And always bothering the girls. You know how hard it is to keep the girls? Fucking murder, that's what it is."

Ellis nodded, and scanned the audience. Benson had probably changed clothes; certainly he wouldn't be wearing an orderly's uniform any more. Ellis looked at the backs of the heads, at the area between hairline and shirt collar. He looked for a white bandage. He saw none.

"But you haven't seen him lately?"

"No," the manager said, shaking his head. "Not for a week or so." A waitress went by wearing a rabbitlike white fur bikini. "Sal, you seen Harry lately?"

"He's usually around," she said vaguely, and wandered off with a tray of drinks.

"I wish he wouldn't hang around, bothering the girls," the manager said, and coughed again, sweetly.

Ellis moved deeper into the club. The spotlight swung through smoky air over his head, following the movements of the girl on stage. She was having trouble unhooking her bra. She did a sort of two-step shuffle, hands behind her back, eyes looking vacantly out at the audience. Ellis understood, watching her, why Benson thought of strippers as machines. They were mechanical, no question about it. And artificial—when the bra came off, he could see the U-shaped surgical incision beneath each breast, where the plastic had been inserted.

Jaglon would love this, he thought. It would fit right into his theories about machine sex. Jaglon was one of the Development boys and he was preoccupied with the idea of artificial intelligence merging with human intelligence. He argued that, on the one hand, cosmetic surgery and implanted machinery were making man more mechanical, while on the other hand robot developments were making machines more human. It was only a matter of time before people began having sex with humanoid robots.

Perhaps it's already happening, Ellis thought, looking at the stripper. He looked back at the audience, satisfying himself that Benson was not there. Then he checked a phone booth in the back, and the men's room.

The men's room was small and reeked of vomit. He grimaced again, and stared at himself in the cracked mirror over the washbasin. Whatever else was true about the Jackrabbit Club, it produced an olfactory assault. He wondered if that mattered to Benson.

He went back into the club itself and made his way toward the door. "Find him?" the manager asked.

Ellis shook his head and left. Once outside, he breathed the cool night air, and got into his car. The notion of smells intrigued him. It was a problem he had considered before, but never really resolved in his own mind.

His operation on Benson was directed toward a specific part of the brain, the limbic system. It was a very old part of the brain, in terms of evolution. Its original purpose had been the control of smell. In fact, the old term for it was *rhinencephalon*—the "smelling brain."

The rhinencephalon had developed 150 million years ago, when reptiles ruled the earth. It controlled the most primitive behavior—anger and fear, lust and hunger, attack and withdrawal. Reptiles like crocodiles had little else to direct their behavior. Man, on the other hand, had a cerebral cortex.

But the cerebral cortex was a recent addition. Its modern development had begun only two million years ago; in its present state, the cerebral cortex of man was only 100,000 years old. In terms of evolutionary time scales, that was nothing. The cortex had grown up around the limbic brain, which remained unchanged, embedded deep inside the new cortex. That cortex, which could feel love, and worry about ethical conduct, and write poetry, had to make an uneasy peace with the crocodile brain at its core. Sometimes, as in the case of Benson, the peace broke down, and the crocodile brain took over intermittently.

What was the relationship of smell to all this? Ellis was not sure. Of course, attacks often began with the sensation of strange smells. But was there anything else? Any other effect?

He didn't know, and as he drove he reflected

that it didn't much matter. The only problem was to find Benson before his crocodile brain took over. Ellis had seen that happen once, in the NPS. Ellis had watched it through the one-way glass. Benson had been quite normal—and suddenly he had lashed out against the wall, striking it viciously, picking up his chair, smashing it against the wall. The attack had begun without warning, and had been carried out with utter, total, unthinking viciousness.

Six a.m., he thought. There wasn't much time.

4

"What is it, some kind of emergency?" Farley asked, unlocking the door to Autotronics.

"You could say so," Morris said, standing outside, shivering. It was a cold night, and he had been waiting half an hour. Waiting for Farley to show up.

Farley was a tall, slender man with a slow manner. Or perhaps he was just sleepy. He seemed to take forever to unlock the offices and let Morris inside. He turned on the lights in a rather plain lobby-reception area. Then he went back toward the rear of the building.

The rear of Autotronics was a single cavernous room. Desks were scattered here and there around several pieces of enormous, glittering machinery. Morris frowned slightly.

"I know what you're thinking," Farley said. "You're thinking it's a mess."

"No, I—"

"Well, it is. But we get the job done, I can tell you that." He pointed across the room. "That's Harry's desk, next to Hap."

"Hap?"

Farley gestured to a large, spidery metal construction across the room. "Hap," he said, "is short for Hopelessly Automatic Ping-pong Player." He grinned. "Not really," he said. "But we have our little jokes here."

Morris walked over to the machine, circled around it, staring. "It plays ping-pong?"

"Not well," Farley admitted. "But we're working on that. It's a DOD—Department of Defense— grant, and the terms of the grant were to devise a ping-pong-playing robot. I know what you're thinking. You're thinking it isn't an important project."

Morris shrugged. He didn't like being told what he was thinking all the time.

Farley smiled. "God knows what they want it for," he said. "Of course, the capability would be striking. Imagine—a computer that could recognize a sphere moving rapidly through three-dimensional space, with the ability to contact the sphere and knock it back according to certain rules. Must land between the white lines, not off the table, and so on. I doubt," he said, "that they'll use it for ping-pong tournaments."

170

He went to the back of the room and opened a refrigerator which had a big orange RADIATION sign on it, and beneath, AUTHORIZED PERSONNEL ONLY. He removed two jars. "Want some coffee?"

Morris was staring at the signs.

"That's just to discourage the secretaries," Farley said, and laughed again. His jovial mood bothered Morris. He watched as Farley made instant coffee.

Morris went over to Benson's desk and began checking the drawers.

"What is it about Harry, anyway?"

"How do you mean?" Morris asked. The top drawer contained supplies—paper, pencils, slide rule, scribbled notes and calculations. The second drawer was a file drawer; it seemed to hold mostly letters.

"Well, he was in the hospital, wasn't he?"

"Yes. He had an operation, and left. We're trying to find him now."

"He's certainly gotten strange," Farley said.

"Uh-huh," Morris said. He was thumbing through the files. Business letters, business letters, requisition forms . . .

"I remember when it began," Farley said. "It was during Watershed Week."

Morris looked up from the letters. "During what?"

"Watershed Week," Farley said. "How do you take your coffee?"

"Black."

Farley gave him a cup, stirred artificial cream into his own. "Watershed Week," he said, "was a

171

week in July of 1969. You've probably never heard of it."

Morris shook his head.

"That wasn't an official title," Farley said, "but that was what we called it. Everybody in our business knew it was coming, you see."

"What was coming?"

"The Watershed. Computer scientists all over the world knew it was coming, and they watched for it. It happened in July of 1969. The information-handling capacity of all the computers in the world exceeded the information-handling capacity of all the human brains in the world. Computers could receive and store more information than the 3.5 billion human brains in the world."

"That's the Watershed?"

"You bet it is," Farley said.

Morris sipped the coffee. It burned his tongue, but he woke up a little. "Is that a joke?"

"Hell, no," Farley said. "It's true. The Watershed was passed in 1969, and computers have been steadily pulling ahead since then. By 1975, they'll lead human beings by fifty to one in terms of capacity." He paused. "Harry was awfully upset about that."

"I can imagine," Morris said.

"And that was when it began for him. He got very strange, very secretive."

Morris looked around the room, at the large pieces of computer equipment standing in different areas. It was an odd sensation: the first time he could recall being in a room littered with computers. He realized that he had made some mistakes about Benson. He had assumed that Benson was pretty much like everyone else—but no one who worked in a place such as this was like everyone else. The experience must change you. He remembered that Ross had once said that it was a liberal myth that everybody was fundamentally the same. Lots of people weren't. They weren't like everybody else.

Farley was different, too, he thought. In another situation, he would have dismissed Farley as a jovial clown. But he was obviously bright as hell. Where did that grinning, comic manner come from?

"You know how fast this is moving?" Farley said. "Damned fast. We've gone from milliseconds to nanoseconds in just a few years. When the computer ILLIAC I was built in 1952, it could do eleven thousand arithmetical operations a second. Pretty fast, right? Well, they're almost finished with ILLIAC IV now. It will do two hundred *million* operations a second. It's the fourth generation. Of course, it couldn't have been built without the help of other computers. They used two other computers full time for two years, designing the new ILLIAC."

Morris drank his coffee. Perhaps it was his fatigue, perhaps the spookiness of the room, but he was beginning to feel some kinship with Benson. Computers to design computers—maybe they were taking over, after all. What would Ross say about that? A shared delusion?

"Find anything interesting in his desk?"

"No," Morris said. He sat down in the chair behind the desk and looked around the room. He was trying to act like Benson, to think like Benson, to *be* Benson.

"How did he spend his time?"

"I don't know," Farley said, sitting on another desk across the room. "He got pretty distant and withdrawn the last few months. I know he had some trouble with the law. And I knew he was going into the hospital. I knew that. He didn't like your hospital much."

"How is that?" Morris asked, not very interested. It wasn't surprising that Benson was hostile to the hospital.

Farley didn't answer. Instead, he went over to a bulletin board, where clippings and photos had been tacked up. He removed one yellowing newspaper item and gave it to Morris.

It was from the Los Angeles *Times*, dated July 17, 1969. The headline read: UNIVERSITY HOSPITAL GETS NEW COMPUTER. The story outlined the acquisition of the IBM System 360 computer which was being installed in the hospital basement, and would be used for research, assistance in operations, and a variety of other functions.

"You notice the date?" Farley said. "Watershed Week."

Morris stared at it and frowned.

5

"I am trying to be logical, Dr. Ross."

"I understand, Harry."

"I think it's important to be logical and rational when we discuss these things, don't you?"

"Yes, I do."

She sat in the room and watched the reels of the tape recorder spin. Across from her, Ellis sat back in a chair, eyes closed, cigarette burning in his fingers. Morris drank another cup of coffee as he listened. She was making a list of what they knew, trying to decide what their next step should be.

The tape spun on.

"I classify things according to what I call trends to be opposed," Benson said. "There are four important trends to be opposed. Do you want to hear them?"

"Yes, of course."

"Do you really?"

"Yes, really."

"Well, trend number one is the generality of the computer. The computer is a machine but it's not like any machine in human history. Other machines have a specific function—like cars, or refrigerators, or dishwashers. We expect machines

175

to have specific functions. But computers don't. They can do all sorts of things."

"Surely computers are—"

"Please let me finish. Trend number two is the autonomy of the computer. In the old days, computers weren't autonomous. They were like adding machines; you had to be there all the time, punching buttons, to make them work. Like cars: cars won't drive without drivers. But now things are different. Computers are becoming autonomous. You can build in all sorts of instructions about what to do next—and you can walk away and let the computer handle things."

"Harry, I—"

"Please don't interrupt me. This is very serious. Trend number three is miniaturization. You know all about that. A computer that took up a whole room in 1950 is now about the size of a carton of cigarettes. Pretty soon it'll be smaller than that."

There was a pause on the tape.

"Trend number four—" Benson began, and she clicked the tape off. She looked at Ellis and Morris. "This isn't getting us anywhere," she said.

They didn't reply, just stared with a kind of blank fatigue. She looked at her list of information.

> Benson home at 12:30. Picked up ? blueprints, ? gun, and tool kit.
> Benson not seen in Jackrabbit Club recently.
> Benson upset by UH computer, installed 7/69.

"Suggest anything to you?" Ellis asked.

"No," Ross said. "But I think one of us should

176

talk to McPherson." She looked at Ellis, who nodded without energy. Morris shrugged slightly. "All right," she said. "I'll do it."

It was 4:30 a.m.

"The fact is," Ross said, "we've exhausted all our options. Time is running out."

McPherson stared at her across his desk. His eyes were dark and tired. "What do you expect me to do?" he said.

"Notify the police."

"The police are already notified. They've been notified from the beginning by one of their own people. I understand the seventh floor is swarming with cops now."

"The police don't know about the operation."

"For Christ's sake, the police brought him here for the operation. Of course they know about it."

"But they don't really know what it involves."

"They haven't asked."

"And they don't know about the computer projection for 6 a.m."

"What about it?" he said.

She was becoming angry with him. He was so damned stubborn. He knew perfectly well what she was saying.

"I think their attitude might be different if they knew that Benson was going to have a seizure at six a.m."

"I think you're right," McPherson said. He shifted his weight heavily in his chair. "I think they might stop thinking about him as an escaped man wanted on a charge of assault. And they would begin thinking of him as a crazy murderer with wires in his brain." He sighed. "Right now, their objective is to apprehend him. If we tell them more, they'll try to kill him."

"But innocent lives may be involved. If the projection—"

"The projection," McPherson said, "is just that. A computer projection. It is only as good as its input and that input consists of three timed stimulations. You can draw a lot of curves through three graph points. You can extrapolate it a lot of ways. We have no positive reason to believe he'll tip over at six a.m. In actual fact, he may not tip over at all."

She glanced around the room, at the charts on his walls. McPherson plotted the future of the NPS in this room, and he kept a record of it on his walls, in the form of elaborate, multicolored charts. She knew what those charts meant to him; she knew what the NPS meant to him; she knew what Benson meant to him. But even so, his position was unreasonable and irresponsible.

Now how was she going to say that?

"Look, Jan," McPherson said, "you began by saying that we've exhausted all our options. I disagree. I think we have the option of waiting. I think there is a possibility he will return to the hospital, return to our care. And as long as that is possible, I prefer to wait."

"You're not going to tell the police?"

"No."

"If he doesn't come back," she said, "and if he

attacks someone during a scizure, do you really want that on your head?"

"It's already on my head," McPherson said, and smiled sadly.

It was 5 a.m.

6

They were all tired, but none of them could sleep. They stayed in Telecomp, watching the computer projections as they inched up the plotted line toward a seizure state. The time was 5:30, and then 5:45.

Ellis smoked an entire pack of cigarettes, and then left to get another. Morris stared at a journal in his lap but never turned the page; from time to time, he glanced up at the wall clock.

Ross paced, and looked at the sunrise, the sky turning pink over the thin brown haze of smog to the east.

Ellis came back with more cigarettes.

Gerhard stopped working with the computers to make fresh coffee. Morris got up and stood watching Gerhard make it; not speaking, not helping, just watching.

Ross became aware of the ticking of the wall clock. It was strange that she had never noticed it before, because in fact it ticked quite loudly.

And once a minute there was a mechanical click as the minute hand moved another notch. The sound disturbed her. She began to fix on it, waiting for that single click on top of the quieter ticking. Mildly obsessive, she thought. And then she thought of all the other psychological derangements she had experienced in the past. *Déjà vu*, the feeling that she had been somewhere before; depersonalization, the feeling that she was watching herself from across the room at some social gathering; clang associations, delusions, phobias. There was no sharp line between health and disease, sanity and insanity. It was a spectrum, and everybody fitted somewhere on the spectrum. Wherever you were on that spectrum, other people looked strange to you. Benson was strange to them; without question, they were strange to Benson.

At 6 a.m., they all stood and stretched, glancing up at the clock. Nothing happened.

"Maybe it's six-four exactly," Gerhard said.

They waited.

The clock showed 6:04. Still nothing happened. No telephones rang, no messengers arrived. Nothing.

Ellis slipped the cellophane wrapper off his cigarettes and crumpled it. The sound made Ross want to scream. He began to play with the cellophane, crumpling it, smoothing it out, crumpling it again. She gritted her teeth.

The clock showed 6:10, then 6:15. McPherson came into the room. "So far, so good," he said, smiled bleakly, and left. The others stared at each other.

Five more minutes passed.

"I don't know," Gerhard said, staring at the computer console. "Maybe the projection was wrong after all. We only had three plotting points. Maybe we should run another curve through."

He sat down at the console and punched buttons. The screen glowed with alternative curves, streaking white across the green background. Finally, he stopped. "No," he said. "The computer sticks with the original curve. That should be the one."

"Well, obviously the computer is wrong," Morris said. "It's almost six-thirty. The cafeteria will be opening. Anybody want to have breakfast?"

"Sounds good to me," Ellis said. He got out of his chair. "Jan?"

She shook her head. "I'll wait here awhile."

"I don't think it's going to happen," Morris said. "You better get some breakfast."

"*I'll wait here.*" The words came out almost before she realized it.

"Okay, okay," Morris said, raising his hands. He shot a glance at Ellis, and the two men left. She remained in the room with Gerhard.

"Do you have confidence limits on that curve?" she said.

"I did," Gerhard said. "But I don't know any more. We've passed the confidence limits already. They were about plus or minus two minutes for ninety-nine percent."

"You mean the seizure would have occurred between six-two and six-six?"

"Yeah, roughly." He shrugged. "But it obviously didn't happen."

"It might take time before it was discovered."

"It might," Gerhard nodded. He didn't seem convinced.

She returned to the window. The sun was up now, shining with a pale reddish light. Why did sunrises always seem weaker, less brilliant, than sunsets? They should be the same.

Behind her she heard a single electronic *beep*.

"Oh-oh," Gerhard said.

She turned. "What is it?"

He pointed across the room to a small mechanical box on a shelf in the corner. The box was attached to a telephone. A green light glowed on the box.

"What is it?" she repeated.

"That's the special line," he said. "The twenty-four-hour recording for the dog tag."

She went over and picked up the telephone from its cradle. She listened and heard a measured, resonant voice saying, ". . . should be advised that the body must not be cremated or damaged in any way until the implanted atomic material has been removed. Failure to remove the material presents a risk of radioactive contamination. For detailed information—"

She turned to Gerhard. "How do you turn it off?"

He pressed a button on the box. The recording stopped.

"Hello?" she said.

There was a pause. Then a male voice said, "Whom am I speaking to?"

"This is Dr. Ross."

"Are you affiliated with the"—a short pause—"the Neuropsychiatric Research Unit?"

"Yes, I am."

"Get a pencil and paper. I want you to take an address down. This is Captain Anders of the Los Angeles police."

She gestured to Gerhard for something to write with. "What's the problem, Captain?"

"We have a murder here," Anders said, "and we've got some questions for your people."

7

Three patrol cars were pulled up in front of the apartment building off Sunset. The flashing red lights had already drawn a crowd, despite the early hour and the morning chill. She parked her car down the street and walked back to the lobby. A young patrolman stopped her.

"You a tenant?"

"I'm Dr. Ross. Captain Anders called me."

He nodded toward the elevator. "Third floor, turn left," he said, and let her through. The crowd watched curiously as she crossed the lobby and waited for the elevator. They were standing outside, looking in, peering over each other's shoulders, whispering among themselves. She wondered what they thought of her. The flashing lights from the patrol cars bathed the lobby intermittently with a red glow. Then the elevator came, and the doors closed.

The interior of the elevator was tacky: plastic paneling made to look like wood, worn green carpeting stained by innumerable pets. She waited impatiently for it to creak up to the third floor. She knew what these buildings were like—full of hookers, full of fags, full of drugs and transients. You could rent an apartment without a long lease, just month to month. It was that kind of place.

She stepped off at the third floor and walked down to a cluster of cops outside an apartment. Another policeman blocked her way; she repeated that she was here to see Captain Anders, and he let her through with the admonition not to touch anything.

It was a one-bedroom apartment furnished in pseudo-Spanish style. Or at least she thought it was. Twenty men were crowded inside, dusting, photographing, measuring, collecting. It was impossible to visualize how it had looked before the onslaught of police personnel.

Anders came over to her. He was young, in his middle thirties, wearing a conservative dark suit. His hair was long enough to hang over the back of his collar and he wore horn-rimmed glasses. The effect was almost professorial, and quite unexpected. It was strange how you built up prejudices. When he spoke, his voice was soft: "Are you Dr. Ross?"

"Yes."

"Captain Anders." He shook hands quickly and firmly. "Thank you for coming. The body is in the bedroom. The coroner's man is in there, too."

He led the way into the bedroom. The deceased was a girl in her twenties, sprawled nude across the bed. Her head was crushed and she had been stabbed repeatedly. The bed was soaked with blood, and the room had the sickly sweet odor of blood.

The rest of the room was in disarray—a chair by the dressing table knocked over, cosmetics and lotions smeared on the rug, a bedside lamp broken. Six men were working in the room, one of them a doctor from the medical examiner's office. He was filling out the death report.

"This is Dr. Ross," Anders said. "Tell her about it."

The doctor shrugged toward the body. "Brutal methodology, as you can see. Strong blow to the left temporal region, producing cranial depression and immediate unconsciousness. The weapon was that lamp over there. Blood of her type and some of her hair are affixed to it."

Ross glanced over at the lamp, then back to the body. "The stab wounds?"

"They're later, almost certainly post-mortem. She was killed by the blow to the head."

Ross looked at the head. It was squashed in on one side, like a deflated football, distorting the features of what had once been a conventionally pretty face.

"You'll notice," the doctor said, moving closer to the girl, "that she's put on half her make-up. As we reconstruct it, she's sitting at the dressing table, over there, making up. The blow comes from above and from the side, knocking her over in the chair, spilling the lotions and crap. Then she's lifted up"—the doctor raised his arms and frowned in mock effort, lifting an invisible body—"from the chair and placed on the bed."

"Somebody pretty strong?"

"Oh, yes. A man for sure."

"How do you know that?"

"Pubic hair in the shower drain. We've found two varieties. One matches hers, the other is male. Male pubic hair as you know is more circular, less elliptical in cross section than female hair."

"No," Ross said. "I didn't know that."

"I can give you a reference on it, if you want," the doctor said. "It's also clear that her killer had intercourse with her before the murder. We've got a blood type on the seminal fluid and it's AO. The man apparently takes a shower after intercourse, and then comes out and kills her."

Ross nodded.

"Following delivery of the blow to the head, she's lifted up and placed on the bed. At this time, she's not bleeding much. No blood to speak of on the dressing table or rug. But now her killer picks up some instrument and stabs her in the stomach several times. You'll notice that the deepest wounds are all in the lower abdomen, which may have some sexual connotations for the killer. But that's just guessing on our part."

Ross nodded but said nothing. She had decided the coroner's man was a creep; she wasn't going to tell him more than she had to. She moved closer to the body to examine the stab wounds. They were all small, puncture-like in appearance, with a good deal of skin tearing around the wounds.

"You find a weapon?"

"No," the doctor said.

"What do you think it was?"

"I'm not sure. Nothing very sharp, but something strong—it took a lot of force to penetrate this way with a relatively blunt instrument."

"Another argument that it's a man," Anders said.

"Yes. I'd guess it was something metal, like a blunt letter opener, or a metal ruler, or a screwdriver. Something like that. But what's really interesting," the doctor went on, "is this phenomenon here." He pointed to the girl's left arm, which was outstretched on the bed and mutilated badly by stab wounds. "You see, he stabbed her in the stomach, and then stabbed her arm, moving out in a regular way, a succession of stabbings. Now, notice: when he's past the arm, he continues to stab. You can see the tears in the sheet and blanket. They continue out in a straight line."

He pointed to the tears.

"Now," the doctor said, "in my book that's perseveration. Automatic continuation of pointless movement. Like he was some kind of machine that just kept going and going. . . ."

"That's correct," Ross said.

"We assume," the doctor said, "that it represents some kind of trance state. But we don't know if it was organic or functional, natural or artificially induced. Since the girl let him into the apartment freely, this trance-like state developed only later."

Ross realized that the coroner's man was showing off, and it irritated her. This was the wrong time to be playing Sherlock Holmes.

Anders handed her the metal dog tag. "We were proceeding routinely with the investigation," he said, "when we found this."

Ross turned the tag over in her hand.

I HAVE AN IMPLANTED ATOMIC PACEMAKER. DIRECT PHYSICAL INJURY OR FIRE MAY RUPTURE THE CAPSULE AND RELEASE TOXIC MATERIALS. IN THE EVENT OF INJURY OR DEATH CALL NPS, (213) 652–1134.

"That was when we called you," Anders said. He watched her carefully. "We've leveled with you," he said. "Now it's your turn."

"His name is Harry Benson," she said. "He's thirty-four and he has psychomotor epilepsy."

The doctor snapped his fingers. "I'll be damned."

"What's psychomotor epilepsy?" Anders said.

At that moment, a plainclothesman came in from the living room. "We got a trace on the prints," he said. "They're listed in the Defense data banks, of all places. This guy had classified clearance from 1968 to the present. His name's Harry Benson, lives in L.A."

"Clearance for what?" Anders said.

"Computer work, probably," Ross said.

"That's right," the plainclothesman said. "Last three years, classified computer research."

Anders was making notes. "They have a blood type on him?"

"Yeah. Type AO is what's listed."

Ross turned to the doctor. "What do you have on the girl?"

"Name's Doris Blankfurt, stage name Angela Black. Twenty-six years old, been in the building six weeks."

"What does she do?"

"Dancer."

Ross nodded.

Anders said, "Does that have some special meaning?"

"He has a thing about dancers."

"He's attracted to them?"

"Attracted and repelled," she said. "It's rather complicated."

He looked at her curiously. Did he think she was putting him on?

"And he has some kind of epilepsy?"

"Yes. Psychomotor epilepsy."

Anders made notes. "I'm going to need some explanations," he said.

"Of course."

"And a description, pictures—"

"I can get you all that."

"—as soon as possible."

She nodded. All her earlier impulses to resist the police, to refuse to cooperate with them, had vanished. She kept staring at the girl's caved-in head. She could imagine the suddenness, the viciousness of the attack.

She glanced at her watch. "It's seven-thirty now," she said. "I'm going back to the hospital, but I'm stopping at home to clean up and change. You can meet me there or at the hospital."

"I'll meet you there," Anders said. "I'll be finished here in about twenty minutes."

"Okay," she said, and gave him the address.

8

The shower felt good, the hot water like stinging needles against her bare skin. She relaxed, breathed the steam, and closed her eyes. She had always liked showers, even though she knew it was the masculine pattern. Men took showers, women took baths. Dr. Ramos had mentioned that once. She thought it was bullshit. Patterns were made to be broken. She was an individual.

Then she'd discovered that showers were used to treat schizophrenics. They were sometimes calmed by alternating hot and cold spray.

"So now you think you're schizophrenic?" Dr.

Ramos had said, and laughed heartily. He didn't often laugh. Sometimes she tried to make him laugh, usually without success.

She turned off the shower and climbed out, pulling a towel around her. She wiped the steam off the bathroom mirror and stared at her reflection. "You look like hell," she said, and nodded. Her reflection nodded back. The shower had washed away her eye make-up, the only make-up she wore. Her eyes seemed small now, and weak with fatigue. What time was her hour with Dr. Ramos today? Was it today?

What day was it, anyway? It took her a moment to remember that it was Friday. She hadn't slept for at least twenty-four hours, and she was having all the sleepless symptoms she'd remembered as an intern. An acid gnawing in her stomach. A dull ache in her body. A kind of slow confusion of the mind. It was a terrible way to feel.

She knew how it would progress. In another four or five hours, she would begin to daydream about sleeping. She would imagine a bed, and the softness of the mattress as she lay on it. She would begin to dwell on the wonderful sensations that would accompany falling asleep.

She hoped they found Benson before long. The mirror had steamed over again. She opened the bathroom door to let cool air in, and wiped a clean space with her hand again. She was starting to apply fresh make-up when she heard the doorbell.

That would be Anders. She had left the front door unlocked. "It's open," she shouted, and then returned to her make-up. She did one eye, then paused before the second. "If you want coffee, just boil water in the kitchen," she said.

She did her other eye, pulled the towel tighter around her, and leaned out toward the hallway. "Find everything you need?" she called.

Harry Benson was standing in the hallway. "Good morning, Dr. Ross," he said. His voice was pleasant. "I hope I haven't come at an inconvenient time."

It was odd how frightened she felt. He held out his hand and she shook it, hardly conscious of the action. She was preoccupied with her own fear. Why was she afraid? She knew this man well; she had been alone with him many times before, and had never been afraid.

The surprise was part of it, the shock of finding him here. And the unprofessional setting: she was acutely aware of the towel, her still-damp bare legs.

"Excuse me a minute," she said, "and I'll get some clothes on."

He nodded politely and went back to the living room. She closed the bedroom door and sat down on the bed. She was breathing hard, as if she had run a great distance. Anxiety, she thought, but the label didn't really help. She remembered a patient who had finally shouted at her in frustration, "Don't tell me I'm depressed. I feel *terrible!*"

She went to the closet and pulled on a dress, hardly noticing which one it was. Then she went back into the bathroom to check her appearance. Stalling, she thought. This is not the time to stall.

She took a deep breath and went outside to talk with him.

He was standing in the middle of the living room, looking uncomfortable and confused. She saw the room freshly, through his eyes: a modern, sterile, hostile apartment. Modern furniture, black leather and chrome, hard lines; modern paintings on the walls; modern, glistening, machinelike, efficient, a totally hostile environment.

"I never would have thought this of you," he said.

"We're not threatened by the same things, Harry." She kept her voice light. "Do you want some coffee?"

"No, thanks."

He was neatly dressed, in a jacket and tie, but his wig, the black wig, threw her off. Also his eyes: they were tired, distant—the eyes of a man near the breaking point of fatigue. She remembered how the rats had collapsed from excessive pleasurable stimulation. Eventually they lay spread-eagled on the floor of the cage, panting, too weak to crawl forward and press the shock lever one more time.

"Are you alone here?" he said.

"Yes, I am."

There was a small bruise on his left cheek, just below the eye. She looked at his bandages. They just barely showed, a bit of white between the bottom of his wig and the top of his collar.

"Is something wrong?" he asked.

"No, nothing."

"You seem tense." His voice sounded genuinely concerned. Probably he'd just had a stimulation. She remembered how he had become sexually interested in her after the test stimulations, just before he was interfaced.

"No . . . I'm not tense." She smiled.

"You have a very nice smile," he said.

She glanced at his clothes, looking for blood. The girl had been soaked; Benson must have been covered with blood, yet there was none on his clothes. Perhaps he'd dressed after taking a second shower. After killing her.

"Well," she said, "I'm going to have some coffee." She went into the kitchen with a kind of relief. It was somehow easier to breathe in the kitchen, away from him. She put the kettle on the burner, turned on the gas, and stayed there a moment. She had to get control of herself. She had to get control of the situation.

The odd thing was that while she had been shocked to see him suddenly in her apartment, she was not really surprised that he had come. Some psychomotor epileptics feared their own violence.

But why hadn't he returned to the hospital?

She went out to the living room. Benson was standing by the large windows, looking out over the city, which stretched away for miles in every direction.

"Are you angry with me?" he said.

"Angry? Why?"

"Because I ran away."

"Why did you run away, Harry?" As she spoke, she felt her strength coming back, her control. She could handle this man. It was her job. She'd been alone with men more dangerous than this. She remembered a six-month period at Cameron State Hospital, where she had worked with psychopaths and multiple murderers—charming, engaging, chilling men.

"Why? Because." He smiled, and sat down in a chair. He wriggled around in it, then stood up, sitting down again on the sofa. "All your furniture is so uncomfortable. How can you live in such an uncomfortable place?"

"I like it."

"But it's uncomfortable." He stared at her, a faint challenge in the look. She wished again that they were not meeting here. This environment was too threatening, and Benson reacted to threats with attack.

"How did you find me, Harry?"

"You're surprised I knew where you lived?"

"Yes, a little."

"I was careful," he said. "Before I went into the hospital, I found out where you lived, where Ellis lived, where McPherson lived. I found out where everybody lived."

"Why?"

"Just in case."

"What were you expecting?"

He didn't reply. Instead, he got up and walked

to the windows, looked out over the city. "They're searching for me out there," he said. "Aren't they?"

"Yes."

"But they'll never find me. The city is too big."

From the kitchen, her kettle began to whistle. She excused herself and went in to make coffee. Her eyes scanned the counter, searching for something heavy. Perhaps she could hit him over the head. Ellis would never forgive her, but—

"You have a picture on your wall," Benson called. "A lot of numbers. Who did that?"

"A man named Johns."

"Why would a man draw numbers? Numbers are for machines."

She stirred the instant coffee, poured in milk, went back out and sat down.

"Harry . . ."

"No, I mean it. And look at this. What is this supposed to mean?" He tapped another picture with his knuckles.

"Harry, come and sit down."

He stared at her for a moment, then came over and sat on the couch opposite her. He seemed tense, but a moment later smiled in a relaxed way. For an instant, his pupils dilated. Another stimulation, she thought.

What the hell was she going to do?

"Harry," she said, "what happened?"

"I don't know," he said, still relaxed.

"You left the hospital . . ."

"Yes, I left the hospital wearing one of those white suits. I figured it all out. Angela picked me up."

"And then?"

"And then we went to my house. I was quite tense."

"Why were you tense?"

"Well, you see, I know how this is all going to end."

She wasn't sure what he was referring to. "How is it going to end?"

"And after we left my house, we went to her apartment, and we had some drinks, and we made love, and then I told her how it was going to end. That was when she got scared. She wanted to call the hospital, to tell them where I was. . . ." He stared off into space, momentarily confused. She didn't want to press the point. He had had a seizure and he would not remember killing the girl. His amnesia would be total and genuine.

But she wanted to keep him talking. "Why did you leave the hospital, Harry?"

"It was in the afternoon," he said, turning to look at her. "I was lying in bed in the afternoon, and I suddenly realized that everybody was taking care of me, *taking care*, servicing me, like a machine. I was afraid of that all along."

In some distant, detached, and academic corner of her mind, she felt that a suspicion was confirmed. Benson's paranoia about machines was, at bottom, a fear of dependency, of losing self-reliance. He was quite literally telling the truth when he said he was afraid of being taken care of. And people usually hated what they feared.

But then Benson was dependent on her. And how would he react to that?

"You people lied to me," he said suddenly.

"Nobody lied to you, Harry."

He began to get angry. "Yes, you did, you—" He broke off and smiled again. The pupils were briefly larger: another stimulation. They were very close now. He'd tip over again soon.

"You know something? That's the most wonderful feeling in the world," he said.

"What feeling?"

"That buzz."

"Is that how it feels?"

"As soon as things start to get black—buzz!— and I'm happy again," Benson said. "Beautifully warm and happy."

"The stimulations," she said.

She resisted the impulse to look at her watch. What did it matter? Anders had said he would be coming in twenty minutes, but anything could delay him. And even if he came, she wondered if he could handle Benson. A psychomotor epileptic out of control was an awesome thing. Anders would probably end up shooting Benson, or trying to. And she didn't want that.

"But you know what else?" Benson said. "The buzz is only nice occasionally. When it gets too heavy, it's . . . suffocating."

"Is it getting heavy now?"

"Yes," he said. And he smiled.

In that moment when he smiled, she was stunned into the full realization of her own helplessness. Everything she had been taught about controlling patients, everything about directing the flow of thought, about watching the speech patterns, was useless here. Verbal maneuvers would not work, would not help her—any more than they would help control a rabies victim, or a person with a brain tumor. Benson had a physical problem. He was in the grip of a machine that was inexorably, flawlessly pushing him toward a seizure. Talk couldn't turn off the implanted computer.

There was only one thing she could do, and that was get him to the hospital. How? She tried an appeal to his intellectual functions. "Do you understand what's happening, Harry? The stimulations are overloading you, pushing you into seizures."

"The feeling is nice."

"But you said yourself it's not always nice."

"No, not always."

"Well, don't you want to have that corrected?"

He paused a moment. "Corrected?"

"Fixed. Changed so that you don't have seizures any more." She had to choose her words carefully.

"You think I need to be fixed?" His words reminded her of Ellis: the surgeon's pet phrase.

"Harry, we can make you feel better."

"I feel fine, Dr. Ross."

"But, Harry, when you went to Angela's—"

"I don't remember anything about that."

"You went there after you left the hospital."

"I don't remember anything. Memory tapes are all erased. Nothing but static. You can put it on audio if you want, and listen to it yourself." He opened his mouth, and made a hissing sound. "See? Just static."

"You're not a machine, Harry," she said softly. "Not yet."

Her stomach churned. She was physically sick with tension. Again that detached part of her mind noted the interesting physical manifestation of an emotional state. She was grateful for the detachment, even for a few instants of it.

But she was also angry at the thought of Ellis and McPherson, and all those conferences when she had argued that implanting machinery into Benson would exaggerate his pre-existing delusional state. They hadn't paid any attention.

She wished they were here now.

"You're trying to make me into a machine," he said. "You all are. I'm fighting you."

"Harry—"

"*Let me finish.*" His face was taut; abruptly, it loosened into a smile.

Another stimulation. They were coming only minutes apart now. Where was Anders? Where was anybody? Should she run out into the hall screaming? Should she try to call the hospital? The police?

"It feels so good," Benson said, still smiling. "That feeling, it feels so good. Nothing feels as good as that. I could just swim in that feeling forever and ever."

"Harry. I want you to try and relax."

"I'm relaxed. But that's not what you really want, is it?"

"What do I want?"

"You want me to be a good machine. You want

200

me to obey my masters, to follow instructions. Isn't that what you want?"

"You're not a machine, Harry."

"And I never will be." His smile faded. "Never. Ever."

She took a deep breath. "Harry," she said, "I want you to come back to the hospital."

"No."

"We can make you feel better."

"No."

"We care about you, Harry."

"You care about me." He laughed, a nasty hard sound. "You don't care about *me*. You care about your experimental preparation. You care about your scientific protocol. You care about your follow-up. You don't care about *me*."

He was becoming excited and angry. "It won't look so good in the medical journals if you have to report so many patients observed for so many years, and one died because he went nuts and the cops killed him. That will reflect badly."

"Harry—"

"I *know*," Benson said. He held out his hands. "I was sick an hour ago. Then, when I woke up, I saw blood under my fingernails. Blood. I know." He stared at his hands, curling them to look at the nails. Then he touched his bandages. "The operation was supposed to work," he said. "But it isn't working."

And then, quite abruptly, he began to cry. His face was bland, but the tears rolled down his cheeks. "It isn't working," he said. "I don't understand, it isn't working. . . ."

Equally abruptly, he smiled. Another stimulation. This one had come less than a minute after the one previously. She knew that he'd tip over in the next few seconds.

"I don't want to hurt anyone," he said, smiling cheerfully.

She felt sympathy for him, and sadness for what had happened. "I understand," she said. "Let's go back to the hospital."

"No, no . . ."

"I'll go with you. I'll stay with you all the time. It will be all right."

"*Don't argue with me!*" He snapped to his feet, fists clenched, and glared down at her. "I will not listen—" He broke off, but did not smile.

Instead, he began to sniff the air.

"What is that smell?" he said. "I hate that smell. What is it? I hate it, do you hear me, I *hate* it!"

He moved toward her, sniffing. He reached his hands out toward her.

"Harry . . ."

"I hate this feeling," he said.

She got up off the couch, moving away. He followed her clumsily, his hands still outstretched. "I don't want this feeling, I don't want it," he said. He was no longer sniffing. He was fully in a trance state, coming toward her.

"Harry . . ."

His face was blank, an automaton mask. His arms were still extended toward her. He almost seemed to be sleep-walking as he advanced on her. His movements were slow and she was able to back away from him, maintaining distance.

Then, suddenly, he picked up a heavy glass ashtray and flung it at her. She dodged; it struck one of the large windows, shattering the glass.

He leaped for her and threw his arms around her, holding her in a clumsy bear hug. He squeezed her with incredible strength. "Harry," she gasped, "Harry." She looked up at his face and saw it was still blank.

She kneed him in the groin.

He grunted and released her, bending at the waist, coughing. She moved away from him and picked up the phone. She dialed the operator. Benson was still bent over, still coughing.

"Operator."

"Operator, give me the police."

"Do you want the Beverly Hills police, or the Los Angeles police?"

"I don't care!"

"Well, which do you—"

She dropped the phone. Benson was stalking her again. She heard the tiny voice of the operator saying, "Hello, hello . . ."

Benson tore the phone away and flung it behind him across the room. He picked up a floor lamp and held it base outward. He began to swing it in large hissing arcs. She ducked it once and felt the gush of air in the wake of the heavy metal base. If it hit her, it would kill her. It would kill her. The realization pushed her to action.

She ran to the kitchen. Benson dropped the lamp and followed her. She tore open drawers, looking for a knife. She found only a small paring knife. Where the hell were her big knives?

Benson was in the kitchen. She threw a pot at him blindly. It clattered against his knees. He moved forward.

The detached and academic part of her mind was still operating, telling her that she was making a big mistake, that there was something in the kitchen she could use. But what?

Benson's hands closed around her neck. The grip was terrifying. She grabbed his wrists and tried to pull them away. She kicked up with her leg, but he twisted his body away from her, then pressed her back against the counter, pinning her down.

She could not move, she could not breathe. She began to see blue spots dancing before her eyes. Her lungs burned for air.

Her fingers scratched along the counter, feeling for something, anything, to strike him with. She touched nothing.

The kitchen . . .

She flung her hands around wildly. She felt the handle of the dishwasher, the handle to the oven, the machines in her kitchen.

Her vision was greenish. The blue spots were larger. They swam sickeningly before her. She was going to die in the kitchen.

The kitchen, the kitchen, *dangers of the kitchen*. It came to her in a flash, just as she was losing consciousness.

Microwaves.

She no longer had any vision; the world was dull gray, but she could still feel. Her fingers touched the metal of the oven, the glass of the oven door, then up . . . up to the controls . . . she twisted the dial. . . .

Benson screamed.

The pressure around her neck was gone. She slumped to the floor. Benson was screaming, horrible agonized sounds. Her vision came back to her slowly and she saw him, standing over her, clutching his head in his hands. Screaming.

He paid no attention to her as she lay on the floor, gasping for breath. He twisted and writhed, holding his head and howling like a wounded animal. Then he rushed from the room, still screaming.

And she slid smoothly and easily into unconsciousness.

9

The bruises were already forming—long, purplish welts on both sides of her neck. She touched them gently as she looked into the mirror.

"When did he leave?" Anders said. He stood in the doorway to the bathroom, watching her.

"I don't know. Around the time I passed out."

He looked back toward the living room. "Quite a mess out there."

"I imagine so."

"Why did he attack you?"

"He had a seizure."

"But you're his doctor—"

"That doesn't matter," she said. "When he has a seizure, he's out of control. Totally. He'd kill his own child during a seizure. People have been known to do that."

Anders frowned uncertainly. She could imagine the trouble he was having with the idea. Unless you had seen a psychomotor seizure, you could not comprehend the unreasonable, brutal violence of an attack. It was completely beyond any normal life experience. Nothing else was like it, analogous to it, similar to it.

"Umm," Anders said finally. "But he didn't kill you."

Not quite, she thought, still touching the bruises. The bruises would get much worse in the next few hours. What could she do about it? Make-up? She didn't have any. A high-necked sweater?

"No," she said, "he didn't kill me. But he would have."

"What happened?"

"I turned on the oven."

Anders looked puzzled. "Is that a cure for epilepsy?"

"Hardly. But it affected Benson's electronic machinery. I have a microwave oven. Microwave radiation screws up pacemaking machinery. It's a big problem for cardiac pacemakers now. Dangers of the kitchen. There have been a lot of recent articles."

"Oh," Anders said.

He left the room to make some calls, while she dressed. She chose a black turtleneck sweater and a gray skirt, and stepped back to look at herself in the mirror. The bruises were hidden. Then she noticed the colors, black and gray. That wasn't like her. Too somber, too dead and cold. She considered changing, but didn't.

She heard Anders talking on the phone in the living room. She went out to the kitchen to make herself a drink—no more coffee; she wanted Scotch on the rocks—and as she poured it, she saw the long scratches in the wooden counter that her fingernails had left. She looked at her fingernails. Three of them were broken; she hadn't noticed before.

She made the drink and went out to sit in the living room.

"Yes," Anders was saying into the phone. "Yes, I understand. No . . . no idea. Well, we're trying." There was a long pause.

She went to the broken window and looked out at the city. The sun was up, lighting a dark band of brown air that hung above the buildings. It was really a lethal place to live, she thought. She should move to the beach where the air was better.

"Well, listen," Anders said angrily, "none of this would have happened if you'd kept that fucking guard at his door in the hospital. I think you better keep that in mind."

She heard the phone slam down, and turned.

"Shit," he said. "Politics."

"Even in the police department?"

"Especially in the police department," he said. "Anything goes wrong, and suddenly there's a scramble to see who can get stuck with it."

"They're trying to stick you?"

"They're trying me on for size."

She nodded, and wondered what was happening back at the hospital. Probably the same thing. The hospital had to maintain its image in the community; the chiefs of service would be in a sweat; the director would be worrying about fundraising. Somebody at the hospital would get stuck. McPherson was too big; she and Morris were too small. It would probably be Ellis—he was an assistant professor. If you fired an assistant professor it had connotations of firing a temporary appointment who had proven himself too aggressive, too reckless, too ambitious. Much better than firing a full professor, which was very messy and reflected badly on the earlier decision that had given him tenure.

It would probably be Ellis. She wondered if he knew. He had just recently bought a new house in Brentwood. He was very proud of it; he had invited everyone in the NPS to a housewarming party next week. She stared out the window, through the shattered glass.

Anders said, "Listen, what does epilepsy have to do with cardiac pacemakers?"

"Nothing," she said, "except that Benson has a brain pacemaker, very similar to a cardiac pacemaker."

Anders flipped open his notebook. "You better start from the beginning," he said, "and go slowly."

"All right." She set down her drink. "Let me make one call first."

Anders nodded, sat back, and waited while she called McPherson. Then, as calmly as she could, she explained everything she knew to the policeman.

10

McPherson hung up the telephone and stared out his office window at the morning sun. It was no longer pale and cold; there was the full warmth of morning. "That was Ross," he said.

Morris nodded from the corner. "And?"

"Benson came to her apartment. She lost him." Morris sighed.

"It doesn't seem to be our day," McPherson said. He shook his head, not taking his eyes off the sun. "I don't believe in luck," he said. He turned to Morris. "Do you?"

Morris was tired; he hadn't really been listening. "Do I what?"

"Believe in luck."

"Sure. All surgeons believe in luck."

"I don't believe in luck," McPherson repeated. "Never did. I always believed in planning." He gestured to the charts on his wall, then lapsed, staring at them.

The charts were large things, four feet across, and intricately done in many colors. They were really glorified flow charts with timetables for technical advances. He had always been proud of them. For instance, in 1967 he had examined the state of three areas—diagnostic conceptualization, surgical technology, and microelectronics—and concluded that they would all come together to allow an operation for psychomotor epilepsy in July of 1971. They had beaten his estimate by four months, but it was still damned accurate.

"Damned accurate," he said.

"What?" Morris said.

McPherson shook his head. "Are you tired?"

"Yes."

"I guess we're all tired. Where's Ellis?"

"Making coffee."

McPherson nodded. Coffee would be good. He rubbed his eyes, wondering when he would be able to sleep. Not for a while—not until they had Benson back. And that could take many hours more, perhaps another day.

He looked again at the charts. Everything had been going so well. Electrode implantation four months ahead of schedule. Computer simulation of behavior almost nine months ahead—but that, too, was having problems. George and Martha programs were behaving erratically. And Form Q?

He shook his head. Form Q might never get off the ground now, although it was his favorite project, and had always been. Form Q on the flow chart for 1979, with human application beginning in 1986. In 1986 he would be seventy-five years old—if he was still alive—but he didn't worry about that. It was the idea, the simple idea, that intrigued him.

Form Q was the logical outgrowth of all the work at the NPS. It began as a project called Form Quixoticus, because it seemed so impossible. But McPherson felt certain that it would happen because it was so necessary. For one thing, it was a question of size; for another, a question of expense.

A modern electronic computer—say, a third-generation IBM digital computer—would cost several million dollars. It drew an enormous amount of power. It consumed space voraciously. Yet the largest computer still had the same number of circuits as the brain of an ant. To make a computer with the capacity of a human brain would require a huge skyscraper. Its energy demands would be the equivalent of a city of half a million.

Obviously, nobody would ever try to build such a computer using current technology. New methods would have to be found—and there wasn't much doubt in McPherson's mind what the methods would be.

Living tissues.

The theory was simple enough. A computer, like a human brain, was composed of functioning units—little flip-flop cells of one kind or another. The size of those units had shrunk considerably over the years. They would continue to shrink as large-scale integration and other microelectronic techniques improved. Power requirements would also decrease.

211

But the individual units would never become as small as a nerve cell, a neuron. You could pack a billion nerve cells into one cubic inch. No human miniaturization method would ever achieve that economy of space. Nor would any human method ever produce a unit that operated on so little power as a nerve cell.

Therefore, make your computers from living nerve cells. It was already possible to grow isolated nerve cells in tissue culture. It was possible to alter them artificially in different ways. In the future, it would be possible to grow them to specification, to make them link up in specified ways.

Once you could do that, you could make a computer that was, say, six cubic feet in volume, but contained thousands of billions of nerve cells. Its energy requirements would not be excessive; its heat production and waste products would be manageable. Yet it would be the most intelligent entity on the planet, by far.

Form Q.

Preliminary work was already being done in a number of laboratories and government research units around the country. Advances were being made.

But for McPherson the most exciting prospect was not a superintelligent organic computer. That was just a side product. What was really interesting was the idea of an organic prosthesis for the human brain.

Because once you developed an organic computer—a computer composed of living cells, and deriving energy from oxygenated, nutrified blood

—then you could transplant it into a human being. And you would have a man with two brains.

What would that be like? McPherson could hardly imagine it. There were endless problems, of course. Problems of interconnection, problems of location, speculative problems about competition between the old brain and the new transplant. But there was plenty of time to solve that before 1986. After all, in 1950 most people still laughed at the idea of going to the moon.

Form Q. It was only a vision now, but with funding it would happen. And he had been convinced that it would happen, until Benson left the hospital. That changed everything.

Ellis stuck his head in the office door. "Anybody want coffee?"

"Yes," McPherson said. He looked over at Morris.

"No," Morris said. He got up out of his chair. "I think I'll replay some of Benson's interview tapes."

"Good idea," McPherson said, though he did not really think so. He realized that Morris had to keep busy—had to do something, anything, just to remain active.

Morris left, Ellis left, and McPherson was alone with his multicolored charts, and his thoughts.

11

It was noon when Ross finished with Anders, and she was tired. The Scotch had calmed her, but it had intensified her fatigue. Toward the end she had found herself stumbling over words, losing track of her thoughts, making statements and then amending them because they were not exactly what she had intended to say. She had never felt so tired, so drugged with fatigue, in her life.

Anders, on the other hand, was maddeningly alert. He said, "Where do you suppose Benson is now? Where would he be likely to go?"

She shook her head. "It's impossible to know. He's in a post-seizure state—post-ictal, we call it —and that's not predictable."

"You're his psychiatrist," Anders said. "You must know a lot about him. Isn't there any way to predict how he'll act?"

"No," she said. God, she was tired. Why couldn't he understand? "Benson is in an abnormal state. He's nearly psychotic, he's confused, he's receiving stimulations frequently, he's having seizures frequently. He could do anything."

"If he's confused . . ." Anders let his voice trail off. "What would he do if he was confused? How would he behave?"

"Look," she said, "it's no good. It's no damned good, working that way. He could do *anything*."

"Okay," Anders said. He glanced at her briefly, and sipped his coffee.

Why couldn't he just let it go, for Christ's sake? His desire to psych out Benson and track him down was ludicrously unrealistic. Besides, everybody knew how this was going to turn out. Somebody would spot Benson and shoot him, and that would be the end of it. Even Benson had said—

She paused, frowning. What had he said? Something about how it would all end. What were his exact words? She tried to remember, but couldn't. She had been too frightened to pay close attention.

"These are the impossible ones," Anders said, getting up and walking to the window. "In another city, you might have a chance, but not in Los Angeles. Not in five hundred square miles of city. It's bigger than New York, Chicago, San Francisco, and Philadelphia put together. Did you know that?"

"No," she said, hardly listening.

"Too many places to hide," he said. "Too many ways to escape—too many roads, too many airports, too many marinas. If he's smart, he's left already. Gone to Mexico or to Canada."

"He won't do that," she said.

"What will he do?"

"He'll come back to the hospital."

There was a pause. "I thought you couldn't predict his behavior," Anders said.

215

LOS ANGELES POLICE DEPARTMENT
MISCELLANEOUS CRIME REPORT
☐ Shots Find ☐ Attempt

DR 705 90 14 - A

Page 1 of 1		

PREMISES

14	Business
01	BANK/SAV. LOAN
09	HOSPITAL
12	MEDICAL OFF
15	PUBLIC DEPOT
16	RESTAURANT
11	LAUNDROMAT
20	OTHER:

10	Store
08	LIQUOR
12	OTHER:

13	Residence
09	SUSPECTS
00	VICTIMS
03	APT./PROJECT
04	HOTEL
05	MOTEL
07	SINGLE FAMILY
08	OTHER:

11	Vehicle
01	SUSPECTS
02	VICTIM'S
03	TAXI
10	OTHER:

15	Miscellaneous
01	ALLEY
02	CARPORT
06	GARAGE
07	PARK
08	PKG. LOT
14	SCHOOL
15	STREET
16	PED. TUNNEL
17	PED. OVER YARD
18	YARD
19	OTHER

VICTIM'S NAME (Last, first, middle – Firm name, if business)
BLACK, ANGELA —

TYPE OF CRIME
HOH

R.D. 04

LOCATION OF OCCURRENCE

	MO.	DAY	YEAR	DAY WK.	TIME		REPORTED:	MO.	DAY	YEAR	TIME
OCCURRED: ON OR BTWN	3	12	71	F	6:05AM		3	12	71	6:55 AM
AND	3	12	71	F	6:10AM					

V/S SEX, DESCENT, AGE
F - CAUC - 26

VICTIM'S CONDITION (Normal, Hospitalized, etc.)
DEAD

☐ VEH. SEEN: NO. SEX   DESCENT
☐ SUSP. SEEN:

ADV. VICTS, BIRTHPLACE – CITY/STATE/(& D O B

INVESTIGATIVE DIVISION(S) & PERSON NOTIFIED
LAPD - HOM - ANDERS / STAFF

CONNECTED REPORT(S) – TYPE & DR. NO.
DEATH REPORT (711 398) + PRELIMINARY FINDINGS REPORT

PHONES RES.   BUS.

Day Phone-X

CODE:	V–Victim R–Person Reporting W–Witness					
V	Name & Phones Listed Above	RES.		ADDRESS	CITY	PHONE
		BUS.				
R	Jos. R. ALLPORT	RES.			LOS ANGELES	
		BUS.				
		RES.				
		BUS.				

VEHICLE

LIC. NO.	STATE	MAKE/MODEL		MFG.	YEAR	TYPE	

	Interior		Exterior	Modified	Body (CIRCLE IF APPL.)		Wheels	Windows (CIRCLE IF APPL.)
4	STEREO TAPE	4 PAINTED INSCR.	4 FRONT	4 DAMAGE	4 RIGHT	4 MAGS	4 DAMAGE	4 RIGHT 4 TINTED
2	MIRROR ORNAM	2 STICKER/DECAL	2 REAR	2 SIDE	2 REAR	2 CHROME RIMS	2 SIDE	2 REAR 2 COVERED
1	FLOOR SHIFT	1 RUST/PRIMER	1 OTHER	1 LEFT	1 FRONT	1 UNIQUE SIZE	1 LEFT	1 FRONT 1 DECAL/PLAQUE

FURTHER VEHICLE DESCRIPTION (INCLUDE UNIQUE COLORS)

(CIRCLE IF APPL.)	
4	UPHOLSTERY
2	BUCKET SEATS
1	HEADLINER

(CIRCLE IF APPL.)	
4	CUSTOM
2	TORN
1	COVERED/TORN

(CIRCLE IF APPL.)	
4	EQUIP. ADDED
2	EQUIP. MISSING
1	UNIQUE ITEM

TOP • COLORS • BOTTOM

MISCELLANEOUS CRIME REPORT

NAME & ADDRESS IF KNOWN, NAME, BKG. NO. & CHARGE IF ARRESTED, — 7734 LAUREL CANYON

	SEX	DESCENT	HAIR	EYES	HEIGHT	WEIGHT	AGE	CLOTHING
1	N	CAUC	BL	BR	5:8	146	34	—
2								
3								

SUSPECT

PERSONAL ODDITIES

SUSP. NO. 1 2 3

300 — Amputee
1 — LEG
2 — ARM
3 — FOOT
4 — HAND
5 — EAR
6 — FINGERS

301 — Deformed
1 — LEG
2 — ARM
3 — LIMP
4 — HAND
5 — FINGERS
6 — BOWLEGGED

302 — Tattoo
1 — ARM
2 — HAND
3 — FINGERS
4 — CHEST/NECK

303
1 — PICTURES
2 — DESIGNS

303 — Tattoo (cont.)
3 — NAMES
4 — WORDS
5 — INITIALS
6 — PACHUCO

304 — Facial Scars
1 — CHEEK
2 — CHIN
3 — FOREHEAD
4 — LIP
5 — NOSE
6 — EAR
7 — EYEBROW

305 — Facial Oddity
0 — BIRTHMARKS
1 — POCKMARKS
2 — MOLES
3 — FRECKLES
4 — PIMPLES
5 — LIPS - THICK
6 — LIPS - THIN
7 — CHIN - PROTRUDED
8 — CHIN - RECEDES
9 — HOLLOW CHEEK

307 — Teeth
1 — MISSING
2 — GOLD
3 — BROKEN
4 — FALSE
5 — STAINED/DECAY
6 — PROTRUDING
7 — IRREGULAR

308 — Body Scars
1 — ARM
2 — HAND
3 — WRIST
4 — NECK
5 — BURN
6 — CHEST

309 — Speech
0 — IMPEDIMENT
1 — ACCENT (U.S.)
2 — ACCENT (OTHER)
3 — LISPS
4 — STUTTERS
5 — HARE LIP
6 — MUMBLES
7 — RAPID
8 — SOFT/LOW
9 — REFINED

311 — Eyes
1 — MISSING
2 — CROSSED
3 — SUNGLASSES
4 — GLASSES (PLAIN)
5 — BULGING
6 — SQUINT/BLINK
7 — SLANTED

312 — Hair Type
1 — DYED
2 — PROCESSED
3 — WIG/TOUPEE
4 — CREW CUT
5 — BALD
6 — AFRO
7 — THIN/RECEDED
8 — STRAIGHT

313
1 — WAVY
2 — BUSHY
3 — CURLY

314 — Facial Hair
1 — MUST. - CHINESE
2 — GOATEE
3 — BEARD - FULL
4 — MUST - HEAVY
5 — MUST - THIN
6 — MUST - MEDIUM
7 — BROWS - HEAVY
8 — UNSHAVEN

315 — Ears
1 — CAULIFLOWER
2 — PIERCED
3 — PROTRUDING
4 — CLOSE TO HEAD
5 — LARGE
6 — SMALL
7 — THIN

316 — Nose
1 — CROOKED
2 — HOOKED
3 — UPTURNED
4 — LONG
5 — BROAD
6 — FLAT
7 — SMALL
8 — THIN

317 — Face
1 — NEGRO W/CAUC. FEATURES
2 — HI CHEEK BONE
3 — LONG
4 — BROAD
5 — THIN
6 — ROUND

318 — Complexion
1 — DARK
2 — SALLOW
3 — RUGGY
4 — LIGHT/FAIR
5 — MEDIUM

319 — Other:

WEAPON

40 — GUN - CALIBER
10 — REVOLVER
11 — AUTOMATIC
12 — 2 INCH
13 — 4 INCH
14 — 6 INCH OR MORE
16 — BLUE STEEL
17 — NICKEL PLATED
18 — UNUSUAL GRIPS
21 — RIFLE
23 — SHOTGUN
24 — SAWED OFF
19 — RUSTY/DEFECTIVE
24 — MACHINE GUN
20 — RARE TYPE GUN
26 — TOY GUN
25 — OTHER GUN
30 — KNIFE
31 — SWITCH BLADE
33 — BLADE OVER 6 INCH
32 — BODILY FORCE (ONLY)
42 — CAUSTIC CHEM/POISON
45 — FIRECRACKERS

40
41 — LIQUOR/DRUGS
47 — FIXED OBJ. (WALL ETC.)
40 — BLACKJACK/CLUB
44 — EXPLOSIVES
48 — RAZOR
49 — SCALDING LIQUID
50 — MISSILE, ROCK
51 — BELT, CORD, WIRE

40
52 — BOTTLE, BRICK, GLASS
53 — VEHICLE
55 — ASPHYXIATION, SUFFOCATION
56 — DROWNING
55 — NARCOTICS
57 — AXE, CLEAVER
58 — ICE PICK
59 — SCISSORS, FORK
60 — GAS, CARBON MONOXIDE
61 — PAINT, TAR, CRAYON
63 — BB GUN, AIR RIFLE, PELLET GUN, SLINGSHOT
62 — FLOODING
FIRE
80 — OTHER/UNKNOWN:

CHECKED

0A100 (4/71)

MISCELLANEOUS CRIME REPORT   Page 2 of 2   DR

TRADEMARKS

(22) Abnormal Acts
- 66 URINATION
- 65 DEFECATION
- 55 PHOTOGRAPHED VICT.
- 56 SET FIRE
- 57 PUT OBJ. IN VAGINA
- 61 SADISM (PLEASURE FROM INFLICTING PAIN)
- 62 SODOMY
- 54 FETISHISM (EXCITED BY OBJ.—FOOT, HAIR, ETC.)
- 60 OTHER UNUSUAL ACT

Suspect's Actions
- 23 DAMAGED BUILDING
- 33 DAMAGED PUBLIC PROP.
- 37 COMMITTED SEX ACTS IN PRESENCE OF VICTIM
- 39 HARBORED A RUNAWAY
- 43 OTHER:

(22) Pretended To Be
- 31 POLICE
- 40 OTHER:

(22) Victim Was
- 61 POLICEMAN
- 57 FIREMAN
- 58 LANDLORD

(21) Type
- 27 HOMOSEXUAL
- 28 RIOT
- 21 CULT RITUAL
- 34 ORGANIZED GANG
- 22 DISRUPTIVE PRESENCE—SCHOOL
- 13 CAUSED HOSTILE CROWD TO GATHER
- 42 TRAIN WRECK—TAMPER
- 31 MAIL—MAILBOX TAMPER
- 17 CHILD STEALING
- 14 CHILD BEATING
- 16 WIFE BEATING
- OTHER: *epileptic*

(26) Quarrel
- 50 REVENGE
- 60 TRAFFIC (T/A)
- 56 JUV. PARTY
- 51 BUSINESS
- 53 DRUNKEN
- 54 GAMBLING
- 55 JEALOUS
- 58 FAMILY
- 57 LANDLORD/NEIGHBOR
- 52 COMMON—LAW
- OTHER: *Unknown*

(24) Suspect Wore
- 03 CLOTHES OF OPPOSITE SEX
- 10 MASK—FACE—COVER
- 04 UNUSUAL CLOTHES

(24) Lingerie Involved
- 41 CUT OR TORN
- 44 OTHER:

(25) Bombings
- 81 PRIOR WARNING
- 82 FAILED TO EXPLODE
- 83 EXPLODED
- 84 CAUSED FIRE

(24) Telephone
- 80 TONE FROM WALL
- 81 CONNECT WIRES
- CONTACTED BY
- 90 OTHER:

(24) Solicited/Offered
- 36 RIDE
- 25 ASSISTANCE
- 34 MONEY
- 39 OTHER:

(22) Shots Fired
- 93 AT VICTIM
- 96 AT INHABITED DWELL.
- 98 AT MOVING VEH.
- OTHER:

(22) Initial Contact
- 17 SUSPECT IN VEHICLE
- 15 VICTIM IN VEHICLE
- 20 SUSPECT A PED.
- 07 VICTIM A PED.
- 08 BAR
- 06 INVITATION
- 11 PLACE OF ENTERTAINMENT
- RESIDENCE
- SUSP. A RELATIVE
- 19 VICTIM KNOWS SUSP.

(23) Reason
- 84 SEX
- 83 ROBBERY
- 81 BURGLARY
- 82 RACIAL HOSTILITY
- 85 STRIKE/LABOR TROUBLE
- SUSPECT INSANE
- 88 OTHER:

(25) Force
- 54 HANDCUFFED
- 48 COVERED VICT'S. FACE
- 49 TIED VICT. TO OBJECT
- 47 BURNED VICTIM
- 53 GAGGED
- 45 BIT
- 45 BOUND
- 51 CUT/STABBED
- 41 BRUTAL ASSAULT
- 48 CHOKED
- 44 BORE THREATS, SCARES, NO BOND FOUND
- 70 OTHER

(22) Vehicle Involved
- 71 CAUSED DAMAGE TO VEHICLE
- 76 FORCED WAY INTO VICTIM'S VEHICLE
- 83 OTHER:

(1) IDENTIFY ADDITIONAL SUSPECTS ON A SECOND FACE SHEET. IDENTIFY ADDITIONAL WITNESSES. (2) RECONSTRUCT THE CRIME. (3) DESCRIBE PHYSICAL EVIDENCE—STATE LOCATION FOUND AND BY WHOM. GIVE DISPOSITION. (4) SUMMARIZE OTHER DETAILS RELATING TO CRIME. (5) INDICATE TIME AND LOCATION WHERE VICTIM AND WITNESS CAN BE LOCATED BY DAY. INVESTIGATOR. NO AVAILABLE PHONE. (6) LIST STOLEN ITEMS—EXCEPT IF CASH IS THE ONLY ITEM TAKEN—ON A PROPERTY SUPPLEMENTAL REPORT, FORM 03.05.0.

(2) Victim noted suspect to act generally friendly. Relations occurred and sexual intercourse obtained. Following this, victim and suspect took showers. Then victim was afflicting making up when suspect struck her on head with lamp. This assault caused death of

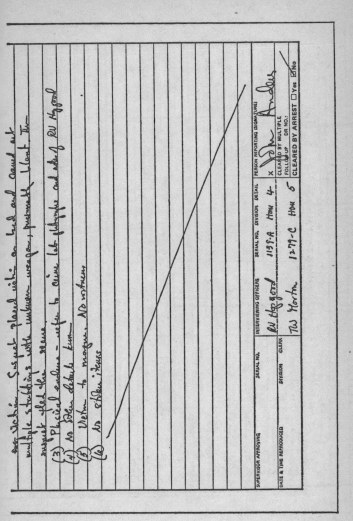

See Victim. Suspect placed victim on bed and caused cut multiple stabbings with unknown weapon, presumably blunt. Then suspect fled the scene.

(3) Physical evidence - note to crime lab photographs and note of PW Haggard

(4) No other details known

(5) Victim to morgue. No autopsy.

(6) No other witness

SUPERVISOR APPROVING	SERIAL NO.	INTERVIEWING OFFICERS	SERIAL NO.	DIVISION DETAIL	PERSON REPORTING (SIGNATURE)
		PW Haggard	113F-A	HOM 4	x John Anders
DATE & TIME REPRODUCED	DIVISION	CLERK			CLEARED BY MULTIPLE FOLLOW UP OR NO.:
		TW Hortin	1-77-C	HOM 5	CLEARED BY ARREST ☐ Yes ☒ No

Los Angeles Police Department
DEATH REPORT

NAME OF DECEASED (LAST, FIRST, MIDDLE)
BLACK, ANGELA —

DR. 711398

| DESCRIPTION of DECEASED | SEX F | DESCENT CAUC | HAIR BLOND | EYES BL |
| HEIGHT 5'4" | WEIGHT 110 | AGE 26 | BUILD MED | COMPLEXION FAIR |

RPT. DIST. 04   TYPE (Ind., Acc., Nat.) HOM
RPT. DIST. 09   TYPE ORIG. RPT. HOM

IDENTIFYING MARKS AND CHARACTERISTICS

LOCATION OF OCCURRENCE
SAME

DATE/TIME ORIGINAL ILL./INJ.
6:10 AM 4/12/71

OCCUPATION OF DECEASED
DANCER

DATE/TIME RPTD. TO P.D.
4/12/71 6:52 AM

CLOTHING AND JEWELRY WORN
NUDE BODY

LOCATION OF ORIGINAL ILLNESS OR INJURY
SAME

DATE/TIME DECEASED DISCOVERED
7:04 AM 4/12/71

DATE/TIME DEATH OCCURRED
6:10 AM 4/12/71

RELATIVES NOTIFIED BY
COR

REMOVED TO (Address)
MORGUE - LA COUNTY

REMOVED BY (name & unit)
COR

DECEASED'S RESIDENCE ADDRESS
AT LOCATION OF OCCURRENCE

PROBABLE CAUSE OF DEATH

REASON (Quarrel—Illness—Revenge, etc.)

DECEASED'S BUSINESS ADDRESS
NONE KNOWN

INVESTIGATIVE DIVISION(S) OR UNIT(S) NOTIFIED AND PERSONS CONTACTED

CODE: R—Person reporting death   D—Person discovering deceased   I—Person identifying deceased   W—Witness

CODE	NEAREST RELATIVE UNKNOWN	RELATIONSHIP	NOTIFIED YES ☐ NO ☐	ADDRESS	CITY	PHONE	X
D/I	Joe R. Allport Sgt MSc			RES. ☐ BUS. ☐ SAME	LA Bgh.		X
				RES. ☐ BUS. ☐			
				RES. ☐ BUS. ☐			

NAME

BUSINESS ADDRESS

PHONE

DOCTOR IN ATTENDANCE

SOURCE OF CALL (HOW NOTIFIED AND BY WHOM)
CARLSON - CORONER'S OFF
71 → LAPD (HOM)

CORONER'S CASE NUMBER: 554/71/AB   ASSIGNED BY: ALAMI

| DISPOSITION OF PROPERTY | ☒ RELEASED TO CORONER | RECEIPT ☒ YES ☐ NO | RECEIPT NUMBER 2034526 |
| | ☐ RELEASED TO RELATIVE | NAME | ADDRESS |

(1) RECONSTRUCT THE CIRCUMSTANCES SURROUNDING THE DEATH, (2) DESCRIBE PHYSICAL EVIDENCE, LOCATION FOUND AND GIVE DISPOSITION.
See Misc Inves. rept DR. 70526114-A

Friday, March 12, 1971: Breakdown

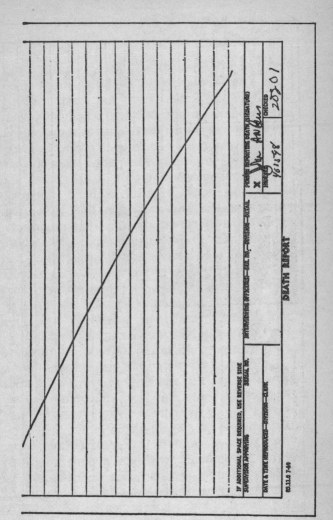

"It's just a feeling," she said, "that's all."

"We'd better go to the hospital," he said.

The NPS looked like the planning room for a war. All patient visits had been canceled until Monday; no one but staff and police were admitted to the fourth floor. But for some reason, all the Development people were there, and they were running around with horrified looks on their faces, obviously worried that their grants and their jobs were in jeopardy. Phones rang constantly; reporters were calling in; McPherson was locked in his office with hospital administrators; Ellis was swearing at anyone who came within ten yards of him; Morris was off somewhere and couldn't be found; Gerhard and Richards were trying to free some telephone lines so they could run a projection program using another computer, but all the lines were in use.

Physically, the NPS was a shambles—ashtrays heaped with cigarette butts, coffee cups crumpled on the floor, half-eaten hamburgers and tacos everywhere, jackets and uniforms thrown across the backs of chairs. And the telephones never stopped ringing: as soon as anyone hung up on a call, the phone rang again instantly.

Ross sat with Anders in her office and went over the Miscellaneous Crime Report, checking the description of Benson. The description was computerized, but it read out fairly accurately: *male Caucasian black hair brown eyes 5'8" 140# 34 years old.* Personal oddities: *312/3 wig,* and

319/1 bandages on neck. Thought to be armed with: *40/11 revolver.* Trademarks: *23/60 abnormal act (other)—perseveration.*

Reason for crime: *23/86 suspect insane.*

Ross sighed. "He doesn't really fit your computer categories."

"Nobody does," Anders said. "All we can hope is that it's accurate enough to allow somebody to identify him. We're also circulating his picture. Several hundred photos are being run off now, and distributed around the city. That'll help."

"What happens now?" Ross said.

"We wait," he said. "Unless you can think of a hiding place he'd use."

She shook her head.

"Then we wait," he said.

12

It was a broad, low-ceilinged, white-tiled room, lit brightly by overhead fluorescent lights. Six stainless-steel tables were set out in a row, each emptying into a sink at one end of the room. Five of the tables were empty; the body of Angela Black lay on the sixth. Two police pathologists and Morris were bent over the body as the autopsy proceeded.

Morris had seen a lot of autopsies in his day,

but the autopsies he attended as a surgeon were usually different. In this one, the pathologists spent nearly half an hour examining the exterior appearance of the body and taking photographs before they made the initial incision. They paid a lot of attention to the external appearance of the stab wounds, and what they called a "stretch laceration" appearance to the wounds.

One of the pathologists explained that this means the wounds were caused by a blunt object. It didn't cut the skin; it pulled it and caused a split in the taut portion. Then the instrument went in, but the initial split was always slightly ahead of the deeper penetration track. They also pointed out that skin hair had been forced down into the wounds in several places—further evidence of a blunt object producing the cuts.

"What kind of blunt object?" Morris had asked.

They shook their heads. "No way to know yet. We'll have to take a look at the penetration."

Penetration meant the depth that the weapon had entered the body. Determining penetration was difficult; skin was elastic and tended to snap back into shape; underlying tissues moved around before and after death. It was a slow business. Morris was tired. His eyes hurt. After a time, he left the autopsy room and went next door to the police lab, where the girl's purse contents were spread out on a large table.

Three men went through it: one identifying the objects, one recording them, and the third tagging them. Morris watched in silence. Most of the objects seemed commonplace: lipstick, compact, car keys, wallet, Kleenex, chewing gum, birth control pills, address book, ball-point pen, eye shadow, hair clip. And two packs of matches.

"Two packs of matches," one of the cops intoned. "Both marked Airport Marina Hotel."

Morris sighed. They were going through this so slowly, so patiently. It was no better than the autopsy. Did they really think they'd find anything this way? He found the plodding routine intolerable. Janet Ross called that the surgeon's disease, this urge to take decisive action, the inability to wait patiently. Once in an early NPS conference where they were considering a stage-three candidate—a woman named Worley—Morris had argued strongly for taking her as a surgical candidate, even though she had several other problems. Ross had laughed; "poor impulse control," she had said. In that moment, he could cheerfully have killed her, and his murderous feelings were not relieved when Ellis then said, in a clinical, quiet tone, that he agreed that Mrs. Worley was an inappropriate surgical candidate. Morris felt let down in the worst way, even though McPherson said that he thought the candidate had some worth, and probably should be listed as a "possible" and held for a while.

Poor impulse control, he thought. The hell with her.

"Airport Marina, huh?" one of the cops said. "Isn't that where all the stewardesses stay?"

"I dunno," the other cop said.

Morris hardly listened. He rubbed his eyes and decided to get more coffee. He'd been awake for thirty-six hours straight, and he wasn't going to last much longer.

He left the room and went upstairs looking for a coffee machine. There must be coffee someplace in the building. Even cops drank coffee; everybody drank coffee. And then he stopped, shivering.

He knew something about the Airport Marina.

The Airport Marina was where Benson had first been arrested, on suspicion of beating up a mechanic. There was a bar in the hotel; it had happened there. Morris was sure of it.

He glanced at his watch and then went out to the parking lot. If he hurried, he'd beat rush-hour traffic to the airport.

A jet screamed overhead and descended toward the runway as Morris took the airport off-ramp from the freeway and drove down Airport Boulevard. He passed bars and motels and car-rental offices. On the radio, he heard the announcer drone: "And on the San Diego Freeway, there is an accident involving a truck blocking three northbound lanes. Computer projection of flow is twelve miles an hour. On the San Bernadino Freeway, a stalled car in the left lane south of the Exeter off-ramp. Computer projection of traffic flow is thirty-one miles an hour . . ."

Morris thought of Benson again. Perhaps computers really were taking over. He remembered a funny little Englishman who had lectured at the hospital and told the surgeons that soon operations would be done with the surgeon on another continent—he would work using robot hands, the signals being transmitted via satellite. The idea had seemed crazy, but his surgical colleagues had squirmed at the thought.

"On the Ventura Freeway west of Haskell, a two-car collision has slowed traffic. Computer projection is eighteen miles an hour."

He found himself listening to the traffic report intently. Computers or not, the traffic report was vital to anyone who lived in Los Angeles. You learned to pay attention to any traffic report automatically, the way people in other parts of the country automatically paid attention to weather reports.

Morris had come to California from Michigan. For the first few weeks after his arrival, he had asked people what the weather was going to be like later in the day, or on the following day. It seemed to him a natural question for a newcomer to ask, and a natural ice breaker. But he got very strange, puzzled looks from people. Later he realized that he had come to one of the few places in the world where the weather was of no interest to anyone—it was always more or less the same, and rarely discussed.

But automobiles! Now there was a subject of almost compulsive fascination. People were always interested in what kind of car you drove, how you liked it, whether it was reliable, what troubles you had had with it. In the same vein, driving experiences, bad traffic, short-cuts you had found, accidents you had experienced, were always welcome conversation topics. In Los Angeles, anything relating to cars was a serious matter, worthy of as much time and attention as you could devote to it.

He remembered, as a kind of final proof of the idiocy of it all, that an astronomer had once said that if Martians looked at Los Angeles, they would probably conclude that the automobile was the dominant life form of the area. And, in a sense, they would be right.

He parked in the lot of the Airport Marina Hotel and entered the lobby. The building was as incongruous as its name, with that California quality of bizarre mixtures—in this case, a sort of plastic-and-neon Japanese inn. He went directly to the bar, which was dark and nearly deserted at 5 p.m. There were two stewardesses in a far corner, talking over drinks; one or two businessmen seated at the bar; and the bartender himself, staring off vacantly into space.

Morris sat at the bar. When the bartender came over, he pushed Benson's picture across the counter. "You ever seen this man?"

"What'll it be?" the bartender said.

Morris tapped the picture.

"This is a bar. We serve liquor."

Morris was beginning to feel strange. It was the kind of feeling he sometimes had when he began an operation and felt like a surgeon in a movie. Something very theatrical. Now he was a private eye.

"His name is Benson," Morris said. "I'm his doctor. He's very ill."

"What's he got?"

Morris sighed. "Have you seen him before?"

"Sure, lots of times. Harry, right?"

"That's right. Harry Benson. When was the last time you saw him?"

"An hour ago." The man shrugged. "What's he got?"

"Epilepsy. It's important to find him. Do you know where he went?"

"Epilepsy? No shit." The bartender picked up the picture and examined it closely in the light of a glowing Schlitz sign behind the bar. "That's him, all right. But he dyed his hair black."

"Do you know where he went?"

"He didn't look sick to me. Are you sure you're—"

"Do you know where he went?"

There was a long silence. The bartender looked grim. Morris instantly regretted his tone. "You're no fucking doctor," the bartender said. "Now beat it."

"I need your help," Morris said. "Time is very important." As he spoke, he opened his wallet, took out his identification cards, credit cards, everything with an M.D. on it. He spread them across the counter.

The bartender didn't even glance at them.

"He is also wanted by the police," Morris said.

"I knew it," the bartender said. "I knew it."

"And I can get some policeman down here to help question you. You may be an accessory to murder." Morris thought that sounded good. At least it sounded dramatic.

The bartender picked up one of the cards, peered at it, dropped it. "I don't know nothing," he said. "He comes in sometimes, that's all."

"Where did he go today?"

"I don't know. He left with Joe."

"Who's Joe?"

"Mechanic. Works the late shift at United."

"United Air Lines?"

"That's right," the bartender said. "Listen, what about this—"

But Morris was already gone.

In the hotel lobby, he called the NPS and got through the switchboard to Captain Anders.

"Anders here."

"Listen, this is Morris. I'm at the airport. I have a lead on Benson. About an hour ago, he was seen in the bar of the Airport Marina Hotel. He left with a mechanic named Joe who works for United. Works the evening shift."

There was a moment of silence. Morris heard the scribbling sound of a pencil. "Got it," Anders said. "Anything else?"

"No."

"We'll get some cars out right away. You think he went to the United hangars?"

"Probably."

"We'll get some cars out right away."

"What about—"

Morris stopped, and stared at the receiver. It

was dead in his hand. He took a deep breath and tried to decide what to do next. From now on, it was police business. Benson was dangerous. He should let the police handle it.

On the other hand, how long would it take them to get here? Where was the nearest police station? Inglewood? Culver City? In rush hour traffic, even with their sirens it might take twenty minutes. It might take half an hour.

That was too much time. Benson might leave in half an hour. Meanwhile, he ought to keep track of him. Just locate Benson, and keep track of him.

Not interfere. But not let him get away, either.

The large sign said UNITED AIR LINES—MAINTENANCE PERSONNEL ONLY. There was a guardhouse beneath the sign. Morris pulled up, leaned out of his car.

"I'm Dr. Morris. I'm looking for Joe."

Morris was prepared for a lengthy explanation. But the guard didn't seem to care. "Joe came on about ten minutes ago. Signed in to hangar seven."

Ahead of him, Morris saw three very large airplane hangars, with parking lots behind. "Which one is seven?"

"Far left," the guard said. "Don't know why he went there, except maybe the guest."

"What guest?"

"He signed in a guest. . . ." The guard consulted his clipboard. "A Mr. Benson. Took him to seven."

"What's in seven?"

"A DC-10 that's in for major overhaul. Nothing doing there—they're waiting for a new engine. It'll be another week in there. Guess he wanted to show it to him."

"Thanks," Morris said. He drove past the gates, onto the parking lot, and parked close to hangar seven. He got out of the car, then paused. The fact was, he really didn't know whether Benson was in the hangar or not. He ought to check that. Otherwise, when the police arrived he might appear a fool. He might sit here in this parking lot while Benson escaped.

He thought he'd better check. He was not afraid. He was young and in good physical condition. He was also fully aware that Benson was dangerous. That foreknowledge would protect him. Benson was most dangerous to those who didn't recognize the lethal nature of his illness.

He decided to take a quick look inside the hangar to make sure Benson was inside. The hangar was an enormous structure but didn't seem to have any doors, except for the giant doors to admit the airplane. They were now closed. How did you get in?

He scanned the exterior of the building, which was mostly corrugated steel. Then he saw a normal-sized door to the far left. He got back in his car and drove up to it, parked, and entered the hangar.

It was pitch black inside. And totally silent. He stood by the door for a moment, then heard a low groan. He ran his hands along the walls, feeling for a light switch. He touched a steel box, felt it carefully. There were several large heavy-duty switches.

He threw them.

One by one, the overhead lights came on, very bright and very high. He saw in the center of the hangar a giant plane, glinting with reflections from the overhead bulbs. It was odd how much more enormous it seemed inside a building. He walked toward it, away from the door.

He heard another groan.

At first he could not determine where it was coming from. There was no one in sight; the floor was bare. But there was a ladder near the far wing. He walked beneath the high sleek tail assembly toward the ladder. The hangar smelled of gasoline and grease, sharp smells. It was warm.

Another groan.

He walked faster, his footsteps echoing in the cavernous hangar space. The groan seemed to be coming from somewhere inside the airplane. How did you get inside? It was an odd thought: he'd made dozens of airplane trips. You always got on by a ramp near the cockpit. But here, in the hangar . . . the plane was so damned enormous, how could you possibly get inside?

He passed the two jet engines of the near wing. They were giant cylinders, black turbine blades inside. Funny the engines had never seemed so big before. Probably never noticed.

There was still another groan.

He reached the ladder and climbed up. Six feet in the air, he came to the wing, a gleaming expanse of flat silver, nubbled with rivets. A sign said STEP HERE. There were drops of blood by the sign. He looked across the wing and saw a man covered with blood lying on his back. Morris moved closer and saw that the man's face was horribly mangled, and his arm was twisted back at a grotesquely unnatural angle.

He heard a noise behind him. He spun.

And then, suddenly, all the lights in the hangar went out.

Morris froze. He had a sense of total disorientation, of being suspended in air in vast and limitless blackness. He did not move. He held his breath. He waited.

The injured man groaned again. There was no other sound. Morris knelt down, not really knowing why. Somehow he felt safer being close to the metal surface of the wing. He was not conscious of being afraid, just badly confused.

Then he heard a soft laugh. And he began to be afraid.

"Benson?"

There was no reply.

"Benson, are you there?"

No reply. But footsteps, moving across the concrete floor. Steady, quietly echoing footsteps.

"Harry, it's Dr. Morris."

Morris blinked his eyes, trying to adjust to the darkness. It was no good. He couldn't see anything. He couldn't see the edges of the wing; he couldn't see the outline of the fuselage. He couldn't see a fucking thing.

The footsteps came closer.

"Harry, I want to help you." His voice cracked as he spoke. That certainly conveyed his fear to Benson. He decided to shut up. His heart was pounding, and he was breathing hard, gasping for breath.

"Harry . . ."

No reply. But the footsteps stopped. Perhaps Benson was giving up. Perhaps he had had a stimulation. Perhaps he was changing his mind.

A new sound: a metallic creak. Quite close.

Another creak.

He was climbing the ladder.

Morris was drenched with cold sweat. He still could see nothing, nothing at all. He was so disoriented he no longer remembered where he was on the wing. Was the ladder in front of him or behind?

Another creak.

He tried to fix the sound. It was coming somewhere in front of him. That meant he was facing the tail, the rear of the wing. Facing the ladder.

Another creak.

How many steps were there? Roughly six feet, six steps. Benson would be standing on the wing soon. What could he use for a weapon? Morris patted his pockets. His clothes were soaked and clinging with sweat. He had a momentary thought that this was all ridiculous, that Benson was the patient and he was the doctor. Benson would listen to reason. Benson would do as he was told.

Another creak.

A shoe! Quickly, he slipped off his shoe, and cursed the fact that it had a rubber sole. But it was better than nothing. He gripped the shoe tightly, held it above his head, ready to swing. He had a mental image of the beaten mechanic, the disfigured, bloody face. And he suddenly realized that he was going to have to hit Benson very hard, with all the strength he had.

He was going to have to try to kill Benson.

There were no more creaking sounds, but he could hear breathing. And then, distant at first but growing rapidly louder, he heard sirens. The police were coming. Benson would hear them, too, and would give up.

Another creak.

Benson was going back down the ladder. Morris breathed a sigh of relief.

Then he heard a peculiar scratching sound and felt the wing beneath his feet shake. Benson had not climbed down. He had continued to climb up, and was now standing on the wing.

"Dr. Morris?"

Morris almost answered, but didn't. He knew then that Benson couldn't really see, either. Benson needed a voice fix. Morris said nothing.

"Dr. Morris? I want you to help me."

The sirens were louder each moment. Morris had a momentary elation at the thought that Benson was going to be caught. This whole nightmare would soon be over.

"Please help me, Dr. Morris."

Perhaps he was sincere, Morris thought. Perhaps he really meant it. If that were so, then as his doctor he had a duty to help him.

"Please?"

Morris stood. "I'm over here, Harry," he said. "Now, just take it easy and—"

Something hissed in the air. He felt it coming before it hit. Then he felt agonizing pain in his mouth and jaw, and he was knocked backward, rolling across the wing. The pain was awful, worse than anything he had ever felt.

And then he fell into blackness. It was not far to fall from the wing to the ground. But it seemed to be taking a long time. It seemed to take forever.

13

Janet Ross stood outside the treatment room in the emergency ward, watching through the small glass window. There were six people in there taking care of Morris, all clustered around him. She couldn't see much. All she could really see were his feet. He had one shoe on; the other was off. There was a lot of blood; most of the EW people were spattered with it.

Standing outside with her, Anders said, "I don't have to tell you what I think of this."

"No," she said.

"The man is terribly dangerous. Dr. Morris should have waited for the police."

"But the police didn't catch him," she said, suddenly angry. Anders didn't understand anything. He didn't understand how you could feel responsible for a patient, how you could want to take care of somebody.

"Morris didn't catch him, either," Anders said.

"And why didn't the police get him?"

"Benson was gone when they got to the hangar. There are several exits from the hangar, and they couldn't all be covered. They found Morris under the wing and the mechanic on top of the wing, and they were both pretty badly hurt."

The treatment-room door opened. Ellis came out, looking haggard, unshaven, defeated.

"How is he?" Ross said.

"He's okay," Ellis said. "He won't have much to say for a few weeks, but he's okay. They're taking him to surgery now, to wire up his jaw and get all the teeth out." He turned to Anders. "Did they find the weapon?"

Anders nodded. "Two-foot section of lead pipe."

"He must have got it right in the mouth," Ellis said. "But at least he didn't inhale any of the loose teeth. The bronchi are clean on lung films." He put his arm around Janet. "They'll fix him up."

"What about the other one?"

"The mechanic?" Ellis shook his head. "I wouldn't place bets. His nose was shattered and the nasal bones were driven up into the substance of the brain. He's leaking CSF through the nostrils. Lot of bleeding and a big problem with encephalitis."

Anders said, "How do you assess his chances?"

"He's on the critical list."

"All right," Anders said. He walked off.

Ross walked with Ellis out of the emergency ward toward the cafeteria. Ellis kept his arm around her shoulders. "This has turned into a horrible mess," he said.

"Will he really be all right?"

"Sure."

"He was kind of good-looking. . . ."

"They'll get his jaw back together. He'll be fine." She shuddered.

"Cold?"

"Cold," she said, "and tired. Very tired."

She had coffee with Ellis in the cafeteria. It was 6:30, and there were a lot of staff people eating. Ellis ate slowly, his movements showing fatigue. "It's funny," he said.

"What?"

"I had a call this afternoon from Minnesota. They have a professorship in neurosurgery to fill. Asked me if I was interested."

She didn't say anything.

"Isn't that funny?"

"No," she said.

"I told them I wasn't considering anything until I was fired here," he said.

"Are you sure that'll happen?"

"Aren't you?" he said. He stared across the cafeteria at all the nurses and interns and residents in white. "I wouldn't like Minnesota," he said. "It's too cold."

"But it's a good school."

"Oh, yes. A good school." He sighed. "A fine school."

She felt sorry for him, and then suppressed the emotion. He had brought it on himself, and against her advice. For the last twenty-four hours, she had not allowed herself to say "I told you so" to anyone; she had not allowed herself to think it. For one thing, it wasn't necessary to say it. For another, it would not be useful in helping Benson, which was her chief concern.

But she didn't have much sympathy now for the brave surgeon. Brave surgeons risked other people's lives, not their own. The most a surgeon could lose was his reputation.

"Well," he said, "I better get back to the NPS. See how things are going. You know what?"

"What?"

"I hope they kill him," Ellis said. And he walked away toward the elevators.

The operation began at 7 p.m. She watched from the overhead glass viewing booth as Morris was wheeled into the OR, and the surgeons draped him. Bendixon and Curtiss were doing the procedure; they were both good plastic surgeons; they would fix him up as well as anybody possibly could.

But it was still a shock to watch as the sterile gauze packs were taken away from Morris's face and the flesh exposed. The upper part of his face was normal, though pale. The lower part was a red mash, like butcher's meat. It was impossible to find the mouth in all the redness.

Ellis had seen that in the emergency ward. It was shocking to her now, even at a distance. She could imagine the effect much closer.

She stayed to watch as the drapes were placed over the body, and around the head. The surgeons were gowned and gloved; the instrument tables set in position; the scrub nurses stood ready. The whole ritual of preparing for surgery was carried out smoothly and efficiently. It was a wonderful ritual, she thought, so rigid and so perfect that nobody would ever know—and the surgeons themselves probably didn't consider—that they were operating on a colleague. The ritual, the fixed procedure, was anaesthetic for the surgeon just as gas was anaesthetic for the patient.

She stayed a few moments longer, and then left the room.

14

As she approached the NPS, she saw that a cluster of reporters had cornered Ellis outside the building. He was answering their questions in clear bad humor; she heard the words "mind control" repeated several times.

Feeling slightly guilty, she cut around to the far entrance and took the elevator to the fourth floor. Mind control, she thought. The Sunday supplements were going to have a field day with mind control. And then there would be solemn editorials in the daily papers, and even more solemn editorials in the medical journals, about the hazards of uncontrolled and irresponsible research. She could see it coming.

Mind control. Christ.

The truth was that everybody's mind was controlled, and everybody was glad for it. The most powerful mind controllers in the world were parents, and they did the most damage. Theorists usually forgot that nobody was born prejudiced, neurotic, or hung-up; those traits required a helping hand. Of course, parents didn't intentionally damage their children. They merely inculcated attitudes that they felt would be important and useful to their children.

Newborn children were little computers waiting to be programmed. And they would learn whatever they were taught, from bad grammar to bad attitudes. Like computers, they were undiscriminating; they had no way to differentiate between good ideas and bad ones. The analogy was quite exact: many people had remarked on the childishness and the literalness of computers. For example, if you could instruct a computer to "Put on your shoes and socks," the computer would certainly reply that socks could not be fitted over shoes.

All the important programming was finished by the age of seven. Racial attitudes, sexual attitudes, ethical attitudes, religious attitudes, national attitudes. The gyroscope was set, and the children let loose to spin off on their predetermined courses.

Mind control.

What about something as simple as social conventions? What about shaking hands when you meet someone? Facing forward in elevators? Passing on the left? Having your wineglass on the right? Hundreds of little conventions that people needed in order to stereotype social interaction— take away any of them, and you produce unbearable anxiety.

People needed mind control. They were glad to have it. They were hopelessly lost without it.

But let a group of people try to solve the greatest problem in the world today—uncontrolled violence—and suddenly there are shouts from all sides: mind control, mind control!

Which was better, control or uncontrol?

She got off at the fourth floor, brushed past several policemen in the hallway, and went into her office. Anders was there, hanging up the telephone. And frowning.

"We just got our first break," he said.

"Oh?" Her irritation dissipated in a wave of expectancy.

"Yes," Anders said, "but I'll be damned if I know what it means."

"What happened?"

"Benson's description and his pictures are being circulated downtown, and somebody recognized him."

"Who?"

"A clerk in Building and Planning, in City Hall. He said Benson came in ten days ago. Building and Planning files specifications on all public structures erected within city limits, and they administer certain building codes."

Ross nodded.

"Well, Benson came in to check specs on a building. He wanted to review electrical blueprints. Said he was an electrical engineer, produced some identification."

Ross said, "The girls at his house said he'd come back for some blueprints."

"Well, apparently he got them from Building and Planning."

"What are they for?"

"University Hospital," Anders said. "He has the complete wiring system for the entire hospital. Now what do you make of that?"

They stared at each other.

By eight o'clock, she was almost asleep standing up. Her neck was hurting badly, and she had a headache. She realized that she didn't have a choice any more—either she got some sleep, or she'd pass out. "I'll be on the floor if you need me," she told Anders, and left. She walked down the corridor of the NPS, past several uniformed cops. She no longer noticed them; it seemed as if there had always been cops in the hallways for as long as she could remember.

She looked into McPherson's office. He was sitting behind his desk, head on his shoulder, sleeping. His breath came in short, ragged gasps. It sounded as if he were having nightmares. She closed the door quietly.

An orderly walked past her, carrying filled ashtrays and empty coffee cups. It was strange to see an orderly doing cleaning duties. The sight triggered a thought in her mind—something unusual, some question she couldn't quite formulate.

It nagged at her mind, but she finally gave up on it. She was tired; she couldn't think clearly. She came to one of the treatment rooms and saw that it was empty. She went in, closed the door, and lay down on the examination couch.

She was almost instantly asleep.

15

In the lounge, Ellis watched himself on the 11-o'clock news. It was partly vanity and partly morbid curiosity that made him do it. Gerhard was also there, and Richards, and the cop Anders.

On the screen, Ellis squinted slightly into the camera as he answered the questions of a group of reporters. Microphones were jammed up toward his face, but he seemed to himself calm. That pleased him. And he found his answers reasonable.

The reporters asked him about the operation, and he explained it briefly but clearly. Then one asked, "Why was this operation done?"

"The patient," Ellis answered, "suffers from intermittent attacks of violent behavior. He has organic brain disease—his brain is damaged. We are trying to fix that. We are trying to prevent violence."

No one could argue with that, he thought. Even McPherson would be pleased with it as a polite answer.

"Is that common, brain damage associated with violence?"

"We don't know how common it is," Ellis said. "We don't even know how common brain damage alone is. But our best estimates are that ten million Americans have obvious brain damage, and five million more have subtle brain damage."

"Fifteen million?" one reporter said. "That's one person in thirteen."

Pretty quick, Ellis thought. He'd figured it out later as one in fourteen.

"Something like that," he replied on the screen. "There are two and a half million people with cerebral palsy. There are two million with convulsive disorders, including epilepsy. There are six million with mental retardation. There are probably two and a half million with hyperkinetic behavior disorders."

"And all of these people are violent?"

"No, certainly not. But an unusually high proportion of violent people, if you check them, have brain damage. *Physical* brain damage. Now, that shoots down a lot of theories about poverty and discrimination and social injustice and social disorganization. Those factors contribute to violence, of course. But physical brain damage is also a major factor. And you can't correct physical brain damage with social remedies."

There was a pause in the reporters' questions. Ellis remembered the pause, and remembered being elated by it. He was winning; he was running the show.

"When you say violence—"

"I mean," Ellis said, "attacks of unprovoked violence initiated by single individuals. It's the biggest problem in the world today, violence. And it's a huge problem in this country. In 1969, more Americans were killed or attacked in this country than have been killed or wounded in all the years of the Vietnam war. Specifically—"

The reporters were in awe.

"—we had 14,500 murders, 36,500 rapes, and 306,500 cases of aggravated assault. All together a third of a million cases of violence. That doesn't include automobile deaths, and a lot of violence is carried out with cars. We had 56,000 deaths in autos, and three million injuries."

"You always were good with figures," Gerhard droned, watching.

"It's working, isn't it?" Ellis said.

"Yeah. Flashy." Gerhard sighed. "But you have a squinty, untrustworthy look."

"That's my normal look."

Gerhard laughed.

On the screen, a reporter was saying, "And you think these figures reflect physical brain disease?"

"In large part," Ellis said. "In large part. One of the clues pointing to physical brain disease in a single individual is a history of repeated violence. There are some famous examples. Charles Whitman, who killed seventeen people in Texas, had a malignant brain tumor and told his psychiatrist for weeks before that he was having thoughts about climbing the tower and shooting people. Richard Speck engaged in several episodes of brutal violence before he killed eight nurses. Lee Harvey Oswald repeatedly attacked people, including his wife on many occasions. Those were famous cases. There are a third of a million cases every year that are not famous. We're trying to correct that violent behavior with surgery. I don't think that's a despicable thing. I think it's a noble goal and an important goal."

"But isn't that mind control?"

Ellis said, "What do you call compulsory education through high school?"

"Education," the reporter said.

And that ended the interview. Ellis got up angrily. "That makes me look like a fool," he said.

"No, it doesn't," Anders, the cop, said.

SATURDAY, MARCH 13, 1971: TERMINATION

1

She was being pounded, beaten senseless by brutal, jarring blows. She rolled away and moaned.

"Come on," Gerhard said, shaking her. "Wake up, Jan."

She opened her eyes. The room was dark. Someone was leaning over her.

"Come on, come on, wake up."

She yawned. The movement sent streaks of pain down through her neck. "What is it?"

"Telephone for you. It's Benson."

That jolted her awake faster than she would have thought possible. Gerhard helped her sit up, and she shook her head to clear it. Her neck was a column of pain, and the rest of her body was stiff and aching, but she ignored that.

"Where?"

"Telecomp."

She went outside into the hallway, blinking in the bright light. The cops were still there, but they were tired now, eyes dulled, jaws slack. She followed Gerhard into Telecomp.

Richards held out the phone to her, saying, "Here she is."

She took the receiver. "Hello? Harry?"

251

Across the room, Anders was listening on an extension.

"I don't feel good," Harry Benson said. "I want it to stop, Dr. Ross."

"What's the matter, Harry?" She could hear the fatigue in his voice, the slow and slightly childlike quality. What would one of those rats say after twenty-four hours of stimulation?

"Things aren't working very well. I'm tired."

"We can help you," she said.

"It's the feelings," Benson said. "They're making me tired now. That's all. Just tired. I want them to stop."

"You'll have to let us help you, Harry."

"I don't believe you will."

"You have to trust us, Harry."

There was a long pause. Anders looked across the room at Ross. She shrugged. "Harry?" she said.

"I wish you never did this to me," Benson said. Anders checked his watch.

"Did what?"

"The operation."

"We can fix it for you, Harry."

"I wanted to fix it myself," he said. His voice was very childlike, almost petulant. "I wanted to pull out the wires."

Ross frowned. "Did you try?"

"No. I tried to pull off the bandages, but it hurt too much. I don't like it when it hurts."

He was really being quite childlike. She wondered if the regression was a specific phenomenon, or the result of fear and fatigue.

"I'm glad you didn't pull—"

"But I have to do *something*," Benson said. "I have to stop this feeling. I'm going to fix the computer."

"Harry, you can't do that. We have to do that for you."

"No. I'm going to fix it."

"Harry," she said, in a low, soothing, maternal voice. "Harry, please trust us."

There was no reply. Breathing on the other end of the line. She looked around the room at the tense, expectant faces.

"Harry, please trust us. Just this once. Then everything will be all right."

"The police are looking for me."

"There are no police here." she said. "They've all gone. You can come here. Everything will be all right."

"You lied to me before," he said. His voice was petulant again.

"No, Harry, it was all a mistake. If you come here now, everything will be all right."

There was a very long silence, and then a sigh. "I'm sorry," Benson said. "I know how it's going to end. I have to fix the computer myself."

"Harry—"

There was a click, and then the buzz of a disconnection. Ross hung up. Anders immediately dialed the phone company and asked whether they had been able to trace the call. So that was why he had been looking at his watch, she thought.

"Hell," Anders said, and slammed the phone

down. "They couldn't get a trace. They couldn't even find the incoming call. Idiots." He sat down across the room from Ross.

"He was just like a child," she said, shaking her head.

"What did he mean about fixing the computer?"

"I suppose he meant tearing out the wires from his shoulder."

"But he said he tried that."

"Maybe he did, maybe he didn't," she said. "He's confused now, under the influence of all the stimulations and all the seizures."

"Is it physically possible to pull out the wires, and the computer?"

"Yes," she said. "At least, animals do it. Monkeys . . ." She rubbed her eyes. "Is there any coffee?"

Gerhard poured her a cup.

"Poor Harry," she said. "He must be terrified out there."

Across the room, Anders said, "How confused do you suppose he is, really?"

"Very." She sipped the coffee. "Is there any sugar left?"

"Confused enough to mix up computers?"

"We're out of sugar," Gerhard said. "Ran out a couple of hours ago."

"I don't understand," she said.

"He had wiring plans for the hospital," Anders said. "The main computer, the computer that assisted in his operation, is in the hospital basement."

She set down her coffee cup and stared at him.

She frowned, rubbed her eyes again, picked the coffee up, then set it down once more. "I don't know," she said finally.

"The pathologists called while you were asleep," Anders said. "They determined that Benson stabbed the dancer with a screwdriver. He attacked the mechanic, and he attacked Morris. Machines and people connected with machines. Morris was connected with his own mechanization."

She smiled slightly. "*I'm* the psychiatrist around here."

"I'm just asking. Is it possible?"

"Sure, of course it's possible . . ."

The telephone rang again. Ross answered it. "NPS."

"Pacific Telephone liaison here," a male voice said. "We've rechecked that trace for Captain Anders. Is he there?"

"Just a minute." She nodded to Anders, who picked up the phone.

"Anders speaking." There was a long pause. Then he said, "Would you repeat that?" He nodded as he listened. "And what was the time period you checked? I see. Thank you."

He hung up, and immediately began dialing again. "You better tell me about that atomic power pack," he said as he dialed.

"What about it?"

"I want to know what happens if it's ruptured," Anders said, then turned away as his call was put through. "Bomb squad. This is Anders, homicide." He turned back to Ross.

Ross said, "He's carrying around thirty-seven

grams of radioactive plutonium, Pu-239. If it breaks open, you'll expose everyone in the area to serious radiation."

"What particles are emitted?"

She looked at him in surprise.

"I've been to college," he said, "and I can even read and write, when I have to."

"Alpha particles," she said.

Anders spoke into the phone. "Anders, homicide," he said. "I want a van at University Hospital right away. We've got a possible radiation hazard pending. Man and immediate environment may be contaminated with an alpha emitter, Pu-239." He listened, then looked at Ross. "Any possibility of explosion?"

"No," she said.

"No explosive," Anders said. He listened. "All right. I understand. Get them here as quickly as you can."

He hung up. Ross said, "Do you mind telling me what's going on?"

"The phone company rechecked that trace," Anders said. "They've determined that there were no calls into the hospital from the outside at the time Benson called. None at all."

Ross blinked.

"That's right," Anders said. "He must have called from somewhere inside the hospital."

Ross stared out the fourth-floor window at the parking lot, and watched as Anders gave instructions to at least twenty cops. Half of them went into the main hospital building; the rest remained outside, in little groups, talking together quietly, smoking. Then a white bomb-squad van rumbled up, and three men in gray metallic-looking suits lumbered out. Anders talked to them briefly, then nodded and stayed with the van, unpacking some very peculiar equipment.

Anders walked back toward the NPS.

Alongside her, Gerhard watched the preparations. "Benson won't make it," he said.

"I know," she said. "I keep wondering if there is any way to disarm him, or immobilize him. Could we make a portable microwave transmitter?"

"I thought of that," Gerhard said. "But it's unsafe. You can't really predict the effect on Benson's equipment. And you know it'll raise hell with all the cardiac pacemakers in other patients in the hospital."

"Isn't there anything we can do?"

Gerhard shook his head.

"There must be *something*," she said.

He continued to shake his head. "Besides," he said, "pretty soon the incorporated environment takes over."

"Theoretically."

Gerhard shrugged.

The incorporated environment was one of the notions from the Development group of the NPS. It was a simple idea with profound implications. It began with something that everybody knew: that the brain was affected by the environment. The environment produced experiences that became memories, attitudes, and habits—things that got translated into neural pathways among brain cells. And these pathways were fixed in some chemical or electrical fashion. Just as a common laborer's body altered according to the work he did, so a person's brain altered according to past experience. But the change, like the calluses on a worker's body, persisted after the experience ended.

In that sense, the brain incorporated past environments. Our brains were the sum total of past experiences—long after the experiences themselves were gone. That meant that cause and cure weren't the same thing. The cause of behavior disorders might lie in childhood experiences, but you couldn't cure the disorder by eliminating the cause, because the cause had disappeared by adulthood. The cure had to come from some other direction. As the Development people said, "A match may start a fire, but once the fire is burning, putting out the match won't stop it. The problem is no longer the match. It's the fire."

As for Benson, he had had more than twenty-four hours of intense stimulation by his implanted computer. That stimulation had affected his brain by providing new experiences and new expectations. A new environment was being incorporated. Pretty soon, it would be impossible to predict how the brain would react. Because it wasn't Benson's old brain any more—it was a new brain, the product of new experiences.

Anders came into the room. "We're ready," he said.

"I can see."

"We've got two men for every basement access, two for the front door, two for the emergency ward, and two for each of the three elevators. I've kept men away from the patient-care floors. We don't want to start trouble in those areas."

Considerate of you, she thought, but said nothing.

Anders glanced at his watch. "Twelve-forty," he said. "I think somebody should show me the main computer."

"It's in the basement," she said, nodding toward the main building. "Over there."

"Will you show me?"

"Sure," she said. She didn't really care. She no longer maintained any illusions about her ability to affect the outcome of events. She realized that she was in the grip of an inexorable process involving many people and many past decisions. What would happen would happen.

She walked down the corridor with Anders, and found herself thinking about Mrs. Crail. It was odd; she hadn't thought of Mrs. Crail in years. Emily Crail had been her first patient as a psychiatric resident, years ago. The woman was fifty, her children grown, her husband bored with her. She was suicidally depressed. Janet Ross had taken the case with a sense of personal responsibility; she was young and eager, and she fought Mrs. Crail's impulses like a general fighting a war —marshaling resources, planning strategies, revising and updating battle plans. She nursed Mrs. Crail through two unsuccessful suicide attempts.

259

And then she began to realize that there were limits to her own energy, skills, and knowledge. Mrs. Crail was not improving; her suicidal attempts became more crafty; eventually she succeeded in killing herself. But by that time, Ross had—fortunately—detached herself from the patient.

As she was detached from Benson now.

They had reached the far end of the corridor when behind them, from Telecomp, they heard Gerhard shout, "Janet! Janet, are you still here?"

She returned to Telecomp, with Anders following along curiously. Inside the computer room, the console lights were flickering unsteadily.

"Look at this," Gerhard said, pointing to one print-out console.

CURRENT PROGRAM TERMINATED.
PROGRAM CHANGE
IN 05 04 02 01 00
PROGRAM CHANGE

"The main computer is going to a new program," Gerhard said.

"So what?"

"We didn't instruct that."

"What's the new program?"

"I don't know," Gerhard said. "We didn't instruct any change."

Ross and Anders watched the console.

NEW PROGRAM READS AS

Then there was nothing. No further letters appeared on the screen. Anders said, "What does it mean?"

"I don't know," Gerhard said. "Maybe another time-sharing terminal is overriding us, but that shouldn't be possible. We locked in priority for our terminal for the last twelve hours. Ours should be the only terminal that can initiate program changes."

The console flashed up new letters.

> NEW PROGRAM READS AS MACHINE MAL-FUNCTION ALL PROGRAMMING TERMINATED TERMINATED TERMINATED TERMINATED TERMINATED TERMINATED TERMINATED TERMINATED TERMINATED

"What?" Gerhard said. He started to punch buttons on the console, then quit. "It isn't accepting any new instructions."

"Why not?"

"Something must be wrong with the main computer in the basement."

Ross looked at Anders. "You better show me that computer," he said.

Then, as they watched, one of the consoles went completely dead. All its lights blinked off; the TV screen shrank to a single fading white dot. A second console went off, then a third. The teleprinter stopped printing.

"The computer has shut itself down," Gerhard said.

"It probably had help," Anders said.

He went with Ross to the elevators.

It was a damp evening, and cold as they hurried across the parking lot toward the main building. Anders was checking his gun, turning it sideways to catch the light from the parking-lot lamps.

"I think you should know one thing," she said. "It's no good threatening him with that. He won't respond rationally to it."

Anders smiled. "Because he's a machine?"

"He just won't respond. If he has a seizure, he won't see it, won't recognize it, won't react appropriately to it."

They entered the hospital through the brightly lit main entrance, and walked back to the central elevator banks. Anders said, "Where's the atomic pack located?"

"Beneath the skin of his right shoulder."

"Where, exactly?"

"Here," she said, pointing to her own shoulder, tracing a rectangle.

"That size?"

"Yes. About the size of a pack of cigarettes."

"Okay," Anders said.

They took the elevator to the basement. There were two cops in the elevator car, and they were both tense, fidgety, hands touching their guns.

As they rode down, Anders nodded to his own gun. "You ever fire one of these?"

"No."

"Never at all?"

"No."

He didn't say anything after that. The elevator

doors opened. They felt the coolness of the basement air and looked down the corridor ahead—
bare concrete walls, unpainted; overhead pipes
running along the ceiling, harsh electric lighting.
They stepped out. The doors closed behind them.

They stood for a moment, listening. They heard
nothing except the distant hum of power equipment. Anders whispered, "Anybody usually in the
basement at night?"

She nodded. "Maintenance people. Pathologists,
if they're still going."

"The pathology labs are down here?"

"Yes."

"Where's the computer?"

"This way."

She led him down the corridor. Straight ahead
was the laundry room. It was locked for the night,
but huge carts with bundles of laundry were outside in the corridor. Anders eyed the bundles cautiously before they moved on to the central
kitchens.

The kitchens were shut down, too, but the
lights were on, burning in a vast expanse of
white-tiled rooms, with stainless-steel steam tables
in long rows. "This is a short cut," she said as
they went through the kitchen. Their footsteps
echoed on the tiles. Anders walked loosely, holding his gun slightly ahead, barrel pointed out to
the side.

They passed through the kitchen and back into
another hallway. It was almost identical to the
one they had left. Anders glanced at her question-

ingly. She knew he was lost; she remembered the months it had taken her to learn her way through the basement. "Turn right," she said.

They passed a sign on the wall: EMPLOYEES REPORT ALL ACCIDENTS TO YOUR SUPERVISOR. It showed a man with a small cut on his finger. Further down was another sign: NEED A LOAN? SEE YOUR CREDIT UNION.

They turned right down another corridor, and approached a small section containing vending machines—hot coffee, doughnuts, sandwiches, candy bars. She remembered all the late nights when she had been a resident in the hospital and had come down to the vending machines for a snack. The old days, when being a doctor seemed like a good and hopeful thing to be. Great advances would be made during her lifetime; it would be exciting; she would be a part of it.

Anders peered into the vending area, then paused. He whispered: "Have a look at this."

She looked, astonished. Every machine had been smashed. There were candy bars and sandwiches wrapped in plastic strewn across the floor. Coffee was pouring in short, arterial spurts from the coffee vender onto the floor.

Anders stepped around the puddles of coffee and soda and touched the dents and tears in the metal of the machines. "Looks like an axe," he said. "Where would he get an axe?"

"Fire-extinguisher stations have them."

"I don't see the axe here," he said, looking around the room. Then he glanced at her.

She didn't reply. They left the vending area and

continued down the corridor. They came to a turn in the tunnels.

"Which way now?"

"Left," she said. And she added: "We're very close."

Ahead of them, the hall took another turn. Ross knew that hospital records was around the turn, and just beyond that, the computer. The planners had located the computer near the records room because they eventually hoped to computerize all the hospital records.

Suddenly Anders froze. She stopped and listened with him. They heard footsteps, and humming—somebody humming a tune.

Anders put his finger to his lips, and gestured to Ross to stay where she was. He moved forward, toward the turn in the corridor. The humming was louder. He paused at the turn and looked cautiously around the corner. Ross held her breath.

"Hey!" a male voice shouted, and suddenly Anders's arm flicked around the corner like a snake, and a man sprawled across the floor, skidding down the hall toward Ross. "Hey!" A bucket of water sloshed across the floor. Ross saw that it was an elderly maintenance man. She went over to him.

"What the—"

"Sh-h-h," she said, a finger to her lips. She helped the man back to his feet.

Anders came back. "Don't leave the basement," he said to the man. "Go to the kitchen and wait. *Don't try to leave.*" His voice was an angry hiss.

Ross knew what he was saying. Anyone who tried to leave the basement now was likely to be shot by the waiting cops.

The man was nodding, frightened and confused.

"It's all right," Ross said to him.

"I didn't do nothin'."

"There's a man down here we have to find," Ross said. "Just wait until it's over."

"Stay in the kitchen," Anders said.

The man nodded, brushed himself off, and walked away. He looked back once, shaking his head. She and Anders continued along the corridor, turned a corner, and came to the records section. A large sign sticking out from the wall said: PATIENT RECORDS.

Anders looked at her questioningly. She nodded. They went inside.

Records was a giant space, filled with floor-to-ceiling shelves of patient records. It was like an enormous library. Anders paused in surprise.

"Lot of bookkeeping," she said.

"Is this every patient the hospital ever had?"

"No," she said. "Every patient seen in the last five years. The others are stored in a warehouse."

"Christ."

They moved down the parallel stacks of shelves quietly, Anders leading with his gun. Occasionally he would pause to look through a gap in the shelves to another corridor. They saw no one at all.

"Anybody on duty here?"

"Should be."

She scanned the rows of charts. The record room always impressed her. As a practicing doctor she had an image of medical practice that involved large numbers of patients. She had treated hundreds, seen thousands for a single hour or a few weeks. Yet the hospital records ran into the millions—and that was just one hospital, in one city, in one country. Millions and millions of patients.

"We have a thing like this, too," Anders said. "You lose records often?"

"All the time."

He sighed. "So do we."

At that moment, a young girl no more than fifteen or sixteen came around the corner. She carried a stack of records in her arms. Anders had his gun up in an instant. The girl looked, dropped the records, and started to scream.

"*Quiet*," Anders hissed.

The scream was cut off abruptly, to a kind of gurgle. The girl's eyes were wide.

"I'm a policeman," Anders said. He flicked out his shoulder wallet to show the badge. "Have you seen anyone here?"

"Anyone . . ."

"This man." He showed her the picture.

She looked at it, and shook her head.

"You're sure?"

"Yes . . . I mean, no . . . I mean . . ."

Ross said, "I think we should go on to the computer." In some way, she was embarrassed at frightening the girl. The hospital hired high school and college students part-time to do the clerical work in records; they weren't paid much.

Ross herself remembered when she had been frightened at about the same age. She had been walking in the woods with a boy. They had seen a snake. The boy told her it was a rattlesnake, and she was terrified. Much later she learned he had been teasing her. The snake was harmless. She had resented—

"All right," Anders said. "The computer. Which way?"

Ross led the way out. Anders turned back once to the girl, who was picking up the charts she had dropped. "Listen," he said. "If you do see this man, don't talk to him. Don't do anything except shout your bloody head off. You understand?"

She nodded.

And then Ross realized that the rattlesnake was real, this time. It was all real.

They came out into the corridor again, and continued down it toward the computer section. The computer section was the only refinished part of the basement. The bare concrete floor changed abruptly to blue carpeting; one corridor wall had been knocked out to install large glass windows that looked in, from the corridor, to the room that housed the main banks of the computer. Ross remembered when the computer was being installed; it seemed to her that the windows were an unnecessary expense, and she had mentioned it to McPherson.

"Better let the people see what's coming," McPherson had replied.

"What does that mean?"

"It means that the computer is just a machine. Bigger and more expensive than most, but still just a machine. We want people to get used to it. We don't want them to fear or worship it. We want them to see it as part of the environment."

Yet every time she passed the computer section, she had the opposite feelings: the special treatment, the hallway carpeting, and the expensive surroundings served to make the computer special, unusual, unique. She thought it significant that the only other place in the hospital where the floor was carpeted was outside the small nondenominational chapel on the first floor. She had the same sense here: a shrine to the computer.

Did the computer care if there were carpets on the floor?

In any case, the employees of the hospital had provided their own reaction to the spectacle inside the glass windows. A handwritten sign had been taped to the glass: DO NOT FEED OR MOLEST THE COMPUTER.

She and Anders crouched down below the level of the window. Anders peered over cautiously.

"What do you see?" she said.

"I think I see him."

She looked, too. She was aware that her heart was suddenly pounding; her body was tense and expectant.

Inside the room there were six magnetic tape units, a broad L-shaped console for the central processor, a printer, a card-punch reader, and two disc drive units. The equipment was shiny, sharp-edged, gleaming. It sat quiet under even, fluorescent lighting. She saw no one—just the equipment, isolated, alone. It reminded her of Stonehenge, the vertical stone columns.

Then she saw him: a man moving between two tape units. White orderly's coat, black hair.

"It's him," she said.

"Where's the door?" Anders asked. For no good reason, he was checking his gun again. He snapped the revolver chamber closed with a loud click.

"Down there." She pointed down the corridor to the door, perhaps ten feet away.

"Any other entrances or exits?"

"No."

Her heart was still pounding. She looked from Anders to the gun and back to Anders.

"Okay. You stay down." Anders pressed her down to the floor as he spoke. Then he crawled forward to the door. He paused, got to his knees, and looked back at her once. She was surprised to see that he was frightened. His face was taut, his body hunched tensely. He held the gun stiffly forward by his straight arm.

We're all afraid, she thought.

Then, with a loud slam, Anders knocked the door open and flung himself on his belly into the room. She heard him shout, "Benson!" And then almost immediately there was a gunshot. This was followed by a second shot, and a third. She could not tell who was firing. She saw Anders's feet sticking out of the door as he lay on the carpeting. Gray smoke billowed out through the open door and rose lazily in the corridor.

There were two more shots and a loud scream of pain. She closed her eyes and pressed her cheek to the carpet. Anders shouted: "Benson! Give it up, Benson!"

It won't do any good, she thought. Didn't Anders understand?

Still more shots, in rapid succession. Suddenly, the glass window above her shattered, and large slabs of glass fell over her shoulders, onto her hair. She shook it off. And then to her astonishment Benson landed on the corridor floor beside her. He had thrown himself through the glass window and landed quite close to her. His body was just a few feet from her. She saw that one leg was bloody, red seeping onto the white trouser leg.

"Harry—"

Her voice cracked strangely. She was terrified. She knew she should not be afraid of this man— that was a disservice to him, a betrayal of her profession, and a loss of some important trust—but she was afraid nonetheless.

Benson looked at her, eyes blank and unseeing. He ran off down the basement corridor.

"Harry, wait—"

"Never mind," Anders said, coming out of the computer room, sprinting after Benson, holding his gun stiffly in his hand. The policeman's posture was absurd; she wanted to laugh. She heard Benson's running footsteps echoing faintly down the tunnel. Then Anders turned a corner, continuing after him. The footsteps blended in staccato echoes.

And then she was alone. She got to her feet, dazed, feeling sick. She knew what was going to happen now. Benson, like a trapped animal, would head for one of the emergency exits. As soon as he appeared outside—where it was safe to shoot —the waiting policemen would gun him down. All the exits were covered. There was no possible escape. She didn't want to be there to see it.

Instead, she went into the computer room and looked around. The main computer was demolished. Two magnetic tape banks were knocked over; the main control panel was riddled with fine round punctures, and sparks sputtered and dripped from the panel toward the floor. She ought to control that, she thought. It might start a fire. She looked around for a fire extinguisher and saw Benson's axe lying on the carpet in a corner. And then she saw the gun.

Curious, she picked it up. It was surprisingly heavy, much heavier than she expected. It felt big and greasy and cold in her hand. She knew Anders had his gun; therefore this must be Benson's. Benson's gun. She stared at it oddly, as if it might tell her something about him.

From somewhere in the basement, there were four gunshots in rapid succession. They echoed through the labyrinthine hospital tunnels. She walked to the broken windows and looked out at the tunnels. She saw nothing, heard nothing.

It must be finished, she thought. The sputtering, hissing sound of sparks behind her made her turn. There was also a slapping sound, repetitive and monotonous. She saw that one of the magnetic tape reels had spun out, and the edge of the tape was slapping against the hardware spindle.

She went back to the reel and turned it off. She glanced up at one of the display consoles, which was now printing "ERMINA" over and over. "ERMINA, ERMINA." Then there were two more gunshots, not so distant as the others, and she realized that somehow Benson was still alive, still going. She stood in a corner of the demolished computer room and waited.

Another gunshot, very close now.

She ducked down behind one of the magnetic tape banks as she heard approaching footsteps. She was aware of the irony: Benson had been hiding behind the computers, and now she was hiding, cowering behind the metal columns, as if they could protect her in some way.

She heard someone gasping for breath; the footsteps paused; the door to the computer room opened, then closed with a slam. She was still hidden behind the tape bank, and could not see what was happening.

A second set of running feet went past the computer room and continued down the corridor, fading into echoes. Everything was quiet. Then she heard heavy breathing and a cough.

She stood.

Harry Benson, in his torn white orderly's clothes, his left leg very red, was sprawled on the carpet, his body half-propped up against the wall.

He was sweating; his breath came in ragged gasps; he stared straight ahead, unaware of anyone else in the room.

She still held the gun in her hand, and she felt a moment of elation. Somehow it was all going to work out. She was going to get him back alive. The police hadn't killed him, and by the most unbelievable stroke of luck she had him alone, to herself. It made her wonderfully happy.

"Harry."

He looked over slowly and blinked. He did not seem to recognize her for a moment, and then he smiled. "Hello, Dr. Ross."

It was a nice smile. She had the brief image of McPherson, with his white hair, bending over to congratulate her on saving the project and getting Benson back alive. And then she remembered, quite incongruously, how her own father had gotten sick and had suddenly had to leave her medical-school graduation ceremonies. Why did she think of that now?

"Everything is going to be all right, Harry," she said. Her voice was full of confidence; it pleased her.

She wanted to reassure him, so she did not move, did not approach him. She stayed across the room, behind the computer data bank.

He continued to breathe heavily, and said nothing for a moment. He looked around the room at the demolished computer equipment. "I really did it," he said. "Didn't I?"

"You're going to be fine, Harry," she said. She was drawing up a schedule in her mind. He could undergo emergency surgery on his leg that night, and in the morning they could disconnect his computer, reprogram the electrodes, and everything would be corrected. A disaster would be salvaged. It was the most incredible piece of luck. Ellis would keep his house. McPherson would continue to expand the NPS into new areas. They would be grateful. They would recognize her achievement and appreciate what she—

"Dr. Ross . . ." He started to get up, wincing in pain.

"Don't try to move. Stay where you are, Harry."

"I have to."

"Stay where you are, Harry."

Benson's eyes flashed briefly, and the smile was gone. "Don't call me Harry. My name is Mr. Benson. Call me Mr. Benson."

There was no mistaking the anger in his voice. It surprised her and upset her. She was trying to help him. Didn't he know that she was the only one who still wanted to help him? The others would be just as happy if he died.

He continued to struggle to his feet.

"*Don't move, Harry.*" She showed him the gun then. It was an angry, hostile move. He had angered her. She knew she shouldn't get angry at him, but she had.

He grinned in childish recognition. "That's my gun."

"I have it now," she said.

He still grinned, a fixed expression, partly from pain. He got to his feet and leaned heavily against the wall. There was a dark red stain on the carpet where his leg had rested. He looked down and saw it.

"I'm hurt," he said.

"Don't move. You'll be all right."

"He shot me in the leg . . ." He looked from the blood up to her. His smile remained. "You wouldn't use that, would you?"

"Yes," she said, "if I had to."

"You're my doctor."

"Stay where you are, Harry."

"I don't think you would use it," Benson said. He took a step toward her.

"Don't come closer, Harry."

He smiled. He took another step, unsteady, but he maintained his balance. "I don't think you would."

His words frightened her. She was afraid that she would shoot him, and afraid that she would not. It was the strangest set of circumstances, alone with this man, surrounded by the wreckage of a computer.

"Anders!" she shouted. "*Anders!*" Her voice echoed through the basement.

Benson took another step. His eyes never left her face. He started to fall, and leaned heavily on one of the disc drive consoles. It tore his white jacket at the armpit. He looked at the tear numbly. "It tore. . . ."

"Stay there, Harry. Stay there." It's like talking to an animal, she thought. Do not feed or molest the animals. She felt like a lion tamer in the circus.

He hung there a moment, supporting himself

on the drive console, breathing heavily. "I want the gun," he said. "I need it. Give it to me."

"Harry—"

With a grunt, he pushed away from the console and continued moving toward her.

"*Anders!*"

"It's no good," Benson said. "There's no time left, Dr. Ross." His eyes were on her. She saw the pupils expand briefly as he received a stimulation. "That's beautiful," he said, and smiled.

The stimulation seemed to halt him for a time. He was turned inward, enjoying the sensation. When he spoke again, his voice was calm and distant. "You see," he said, "they are after me. They have turned their little computers against me. The program is hunt. Hunt and kill. The original human program. Hunt and kill. Do you understand?"

He was only a few steps away. She held the gun in her hand stiffly, as she had seen Anders hold it. But her hand was shaking badly. "Please don't come closer, Harry," she said. "Please."

He smiled.

He took another step.

She didn't really know what she was going to do until she found herself squeezing the trigger, and the gun discharged. The noise was painfully loud, and the gun snapped in her hand, flinging her arm up, almost knocking her off her feet. She was thrown back against the far wall of the computer room.

Benson stood blinking in the smoke. Then he smiled again. "It's not as easy as it looks."

She gripped the gun in her hand. It felt warm now. She raised it, but it was shaking worse than before. She steadied it with the other hand.

Benson advanced.

"No closer, Harry. I mean it."

A flood of images overcame her. She saw Benson as she had first met him, a meek man with a terrifying problem. She saw him in a montage of all the hour-long interviews, all the tests, all the drug trials. He was a good person, an honest and frightened person. Nothing that had happened was his fault. It was her fault, and Ellis's fault, and McPherson's fault, and Morris's fault.

Then she thought of Morris, the face mashed into a red pulp, deformed into butcher meat.

"Dr. Ross," Benson said. "You're my doctor. You wouldn't do anything to hurt me."

He was very close now. His hands reached out for the gun. Her whole body was shaking as she watched the hands move closer, within inches of the barrel, reaching for it, reaching for it . . .

She fired at point-blank range.

With remarkable agility, Benson jumped and spun in the air, dodging the bullet. She was pleased. She had managed to drive him back without hurting him. Anders would arrive any minute to help subdue him before they took him to surgery.

Benson's body slammed hard into the printing unit, knocking it over. It began to clatter in a monotonous, mechanical way as the keys printed out some message. Benson rolled onto his back.

Blood spurted in heavy thick gushes from his chest. His white uniform became darkly red.

"Harry?" she said.

He did not move.

"Harry? Harry?"

She didn't remember clearly what happened after that. Anders returned and took the gun from her hand. He moved her to the side of the room as three men in gray suits arrived, carrying a long plastic capsule on a stretcher. They opened the capsule up; the inside was lined in a strange, yellow honeycomb insulation. They lifted Benson's body—she noticed they were careful, trying to keep the blood off their special suits—and placed him inside the capsule. They closed it and locked it with special locks. Two of the men carried it away. A third went around the room with a Geiger counter, which chattered loudly. Somehow the sound reminded her of an angry monkey. The man went over to Ross. She couldn't see his face behind the gray helmet he wore; the glass was fogged.

"You better leave this area," the man said.

Anders put his arm around her shoulders. She began to cry.

Postscript:
A Note on Psychomotor Epilepsy

Since the publication of this book in its hard-cover edition, several neurologists have advised me that the syndrome of psychomotor epilepsy is incorrectly portrayed in significant ways. These professionals emphasize that psychomotor epileptics are no more prone to criminal behavior than other individuals in society. They also agree that a psychomotor epileptic in the midst of a seizure is unlikely to injure anyone, except by accident. They regard complex, purposeful aggressive behavior in the course of a seizure to be either extremely rare, or nonexistent.

When pressed to explain the well-documented incidents of assault by psychomotor epileptics, these neurologists argue that such assaultative behavior, even when repetitive, sudden, and inappropriate, is not actual seizure activity. Some refer to it as "epileptiform" behavior. Others say that epilepsy *per se* is not the issue; they argue that any kind of brain damage—whether it produces epilepsy or not—may lead to episodic loss of inhibitions governing violent behavior.

Whether or not one finds these explanations satisfactory, it seems unarguable that most neurologists who treat psychomotor epileptics as patients have found their patients to be very different from Harry Benson in *THE TERMINAL MAN*. The overwhelming majority of psychomotor epileptics are not violent or sexually disturbed; their seizures are under good control, and they lead rich and rewarding lives, holding good jobs and raising families.

In the face of considerable controversy among clinical neuroscientists, I am persuaded that the understanding of the relationship between organic brain damage and violent behavior is not so clear as I thought at the time I wrote the book. I believe that this is a research area that will prove enormously fruitful in the coming years. But in the meantime, I am concerned that I may have inadvertently hampered the attempts of well-controlled epileptics to function in a society that still retains a lingering prejudice against epilepsy.

Michael Crichton
Los Angeles
December 1972

Annotated Bibliography

GENERAL

1. Wiener, N. *The Human Use of Human Beings: Cybernetics and Society*. Boston: Houghton Mifflin, 1954; Avon paperback, 1967.
    The first and most influential statement on the relationship between man and machine.

2. Wooldridge, D. E. *The Machinery of the Brain*. New York: McGraw-Hill, 1963.
    A remarkably clear explanation of how the brain works, written by a man with a background in the physical sciences.

3. London, P. *Behavior Control*. Harper & Row, 1969; Perennial paperback, 1971.
    A lucid book which places psychosurgery in the context of other forms of behavior control.

4. Wolstenholme, G., ed., *Man and His Future*. London: Churchill, 1963.
    See particularly the chapter by Hoagland for a different perspective on control of behavior.

5. Koestler, A. *The Ghost in the Machine*. New York: Macmillan, 1967.
    See particularly Chapter 16, on the three brains.

6. Delgado, J. M. R. *Physical Control of the Mind: Toward a Psychocivilized Society*. New York: Harper & Row, 1968.

A full statement, in layman's terms, of past research and future directions in psychosurgery by one of the most prominent researchers and advocates of the technique.

7. Mark, V., and Ervin, F. *Violence and the Brain.* New York: Harper & Row, 1970.
   Places psychomotor epilepsy in the context of related violence-producing disorders. A good discussion, with pictures, of psychosurgical techniques.

8. Calder, Nigel. *The Mind of Man,* New York: Viking, 1970.
   An entertaining, well-illustrated survey of brain research. Requires absolutely no scientific background; but the text is frequently a little superficial.

9. Bruner, Jerome. *On Knowing, Essays for the Left Hand.* Cambridge: Harvard University Press, 1962.
   See particularly the essay on control of human behavior. An elegantly written book.

10. Apter, Michael J. *The Computer Simulation of Behavior.* New York: Harper Colophon, 1971.
    Extensive, complicated in places, excellent references.

PSYCHOMOTOR EPILEPSY

1. Delgado, J. M. R., et al. "Intracerebral Radio Stimulation and Recording in Completely Free Patients." *J. Nervous and Mental Disease,* 147(1968):329–340.
   A highly important report on the state of ESB technology some years ago.

2. Fenton, G. W., et al. "Homicide, Temporal Lobe Epilepsy and Depression: A Case Report." *Brit. J. Psychiatry*, 111(1965):304–306.
> One of many such cases in the literature.

3. Kenna, J. C., et al. "Depersonalization in Temporal Lobe Epilepsy and the Organic Psychoses." *Brit J. Psychiatry*, 111 (1965):293–299.

4. Holowach, J., et al. "Psychomotor Seizures in Childhood, a Clinical Study of 120 Cases." *Pediatrics*, 59(1961):339–345.
> A good review of the disease entity, as well as its manifestations in children.

5. Serafetinides, E. A., et al. "Some Observations on Memory Impairment After Temporal Lobectomy for Epilepsy." *J. Neurol. Neurosurg. Psychiat.*, 25(1962): 251–255.
> Showing difficulties in the alternative surgical therapy to stereotactic procedures.

6. Hommes, O. R. "Psychomotor Epilepsy: A Neurological Approach to Hysteria." *Psychiat. Neurol. Neurochir.*, 67(1964):497–519.
> Unusual symptoms in five patients.

7. Serafetinides, E. A. "Aggressiveness in Temporal Lobe Epileptics and Its Relation to Cerebral Dysfunction and Environmental Factors." *Epilepsia*, 6(1965): 33–42.
> Thirty-six of 100 temporal-lobe epileptics in this study showed aggressive behavior. Most had an accompanying character disorder.

8. Greenberg, R., et al. "Sleep Patterns in Temporal Lobe Epilepsy." *Comprehensive Psychiatry*, 9(1968): 194–199.

9. Green, J. R. "Temporal Lobectomy, with Special Reference to Selection of Epileptic Patients." *J. Neurosurg.*, 26(1966):584–593.

In many ways a good, brief review.

10. Falconer, M. A. "Surgical Treatment of Temporal Lobe Epilepsy." *New Zealand Med. J.*, 66(1964): 539–542.

Concentrating on lobectomy.

11. Chase, R. A., et al. "Ictal Speech Automatisms and Swearing: Studies on the Auditory Feedback Control of Speech." *J. Nervous and Mental Disease*, 144(1967):406–420.

12. Ellinwood, E. H., Jr. "Amphetamine Psychosis: Theoretical Implications." *International J. of Neuropsych.*, 4(1968):45–54.

Drawing attention to the similarity between amphetamine psychosis and temporal-lobe epileptic psychoses.

13. Hierons, R., et al. "Impotence in Patients with Temporal Lobe Lesions." *Lancet*, 2(1966):761–763.

14. Weiss, A. A. "Psychodiagnostic Follow-Up of Eight Cases of Temporal Lobectomy." *Israel Ann. Psychiat.*, 3–4(1962):259–266.

15. Falconer, M. A. "Problems in Neurosurgery: 1. Temporal Lobe Epilepsy." *Trans. Med. Soc. London*, 82(1967):111–126.

16. Falconer, M. A., et al. "Temporal Lobe Epilepsy Due to Distant Lesions: Two Cases Relieved by Operation." *Brain*, 85(1961):521–534.

17. Serafetinides, E. A., et al. "The Effects of Temporal Lobectomy in Epileptic Patients with Psychosis." *J. Ment. Sci.*, 108(1962):584–593.

A paper suggesting that confusional states will clear as the epilepsy clears, but that schizophrenic and schizophrenic-like psychoses are often unaffected by treatment.

18. Reiher, J., et al. "Combined Electroencephalography and Sonoencephalography in Temporal Lobe Epilepsy." *Neurology*, 19(1969):157–159.

19. Bishop, M. P., et al. "Intracranial Self-Stimulation in Man." *Science*, 140(1963):394–396.
Use of ESB techniques in non-epileptic patients, nearly a decade ago.

20. Bloch, S. "Aetiological Aspects of the Schizophrenia-Like Psychosis of Temporal Lobe Epilepsy." *Med. J. Australia*, 66(1969):451–453.

21. Anastasopoulos, G., et al. "Transient Bulimia-Anorexia and Hypersexuality Following Pneumoencephalography in a Case of Psychomotor Epilepsy." *J. Neuropsych.*, 4(1963):135–142.

22. Fenyes, I., et al. "Temporal Epilepsies with Deep-seated Eliptogenic Foci: Postoperative Course." *Archives of Neurology* 4(1964):559–571.

23. Adams, John E. "The Future of Stereotaxic Surgery." *J. Am. Med. Assn.* 198(1966):648–652.
A summary of other uses for this surgical method.

24. Rand, R. W., et al. "Chronic Stereotactic Implantation of Depth Electrodes for Psychomotor Epilepsy." *Acta Neurochirurgica*, 11(1968):609–630.
A particularly clear, if technical, statement of stereotactic techniques.

25. Stevens, J. R. "Psychiatric Implications of Psy-

chomotor Epilepsy." *Arch. Gen. Psych.* 14(1966): 461–471.

26. Bennett, A. E. "Mental Disorders Associated with Temporal Lobe Epilepsy." *Dis. of the Nervous System,* 26(1965):275–280.

27. Kolarsky, A., et al. "Male Sexual Deviation: Association with Early Temporal Lobe Damage." *Arch. Gen. Psychiat.,* 17(1967):735–743.

28. Crandall, P. H., et al. "Clinical Applications of Studies on Stereotactically Implanted Electrodes in Temporal-Lobe Epilepsy." *J. Neurosurgery* 20(1964): 827–840.

29. Walker, E. A. "Temporal Lobectomy." *J. Neurosurgery,* 26(1966):642–649.
    A clear description of an alternative procedure.

30. Glaser, G. H. "The Problem of Psychosis in Psychomotor Temporal Lobe Epileptics." *Epilepsia,* 5 (1964):271–278.

31. Hunter, R., et al. "Temporal Lobe Epilepsy Supervening on Longstanding Transvestism and Fetishism: A Case Report." *Epilepsia,* 4(1963):60–65.

32. Duffy, J. C., et al. "Psychic and Somatic Interactions in Psychomotor Epilepsy." *Psychosomatics,* 7(1966):353–356.

33. Strobos, R. J., et al. "Mechanisms in Temporal Lobe Seizures." *Arch. Neurology,* 5(1961):48–57.

34. Stevenson, H. G. "Psychomotor Epilepsy Associated with Criminal Behaviour." *Med. J. Australia,* 60(1963):784–785.

35. Roth, M., et al. "Temporal Lobe Epilepsy and the Phobic Anxiety-Depersonalization Syndrome." *Comprehensive Psychiatry* 3(1963):130–151, 215–226.

36. Aird, R. B., et al. "Antecedents of Temporal Lobe Epilepsy." *Arch. Neurology* 16(1967):67–73.

ELECTRONICS

1. Yatteau, R. F. "Radar-Induced Failure of a Demand Pacemaker." *New Eng. J. Med.*, 283(1971): 1447–1448.

2. Carleton, R. A., et al. "Environmental Influence on Implantable Cardiac Pacemakers." *J. Am. Med. Assn.*, 190(1964):938–940.

3. Pickers, B. A., et al. "Inhibition of a Demand Pacemaker and Interference with Monitoring Equipment by Radio-Frequency Transmissions." *Brit. Med. J.*, 2(1969):504–506.

4. Norman, J. C., et al. "Implantable Nuclear-Powered Cardiac Pacemakers." *New Eng. J. Med.*, 283(1971): 1203–1206.

5. Knapp, D. E., et al. "Nuclear Electrical Power Sources for Biomedical Applications." Proceedings of the Fourth Intersociety Energy Conversion Engineering Conference, Washington, D.C., September 22–26, 1969. New York: American Institute of Chemical Engineers, 1969, pp. 101–106.

6. Slotnick, D. L. "The Fastest Computer." *Sci. Am.*, 224(1971):76–87.

ABOUT THE AUTHOR

Still under thirty years of age, MICHAEL CRICHTON is a man of many trades. Born in Chicago and educated at Harvard College and the Harvard Medical School, he received his MD in 1969. As an author, he made his reputation with *The Andromeda Strain*, which was both a bestseller and a major motion picture. Since then other books have appeared, pseudonymously and otherwise, notably *Five Patients*, a work of medical nonfiction. But a good part of his time is now spent on films. Dr. Crichton has already written the screenplay for the film of *THE TERMINAL MAN*. The original book, written in California while *Andromeda* was shooting, went through seven drafts during a two-year period before it satisfied its author. As for its author—who is in fact not only author, physician and moviemaker but also a Post-Doctoral Fellow on leave of absence from the Salk Institute for Biological Studies in La Jolla, California—he confesses that he has a half dozen other book projects in mind.